His black eyes flashed in warning,

but when he met her gaze, Miranda was overcome by the strange tenderness she saw there. Something moved inside her, warming, unfolding like the bud of a flower. Her lips parted as she struggled to break the silence with words that would not come.

"I know your heart is good, Miranda Howell," Ahkeah said, "but your efforts to help the *Dine* will only make enemies for you—dangerous enemies, on both sides."

"Including you?"

Time froze as he loomed above her, his eyes smoldering with unspoken secrets. His thin lips were sensually curved, his sharp bronze face much too close to her own.

"Including me?" His husky voice echoed her question as his gaze held her captive. "Make no mistake, *bilagaana* woman. You and I have been enemies from the first moment we set eyes on each other."

Acclaim for Elizabeth Lane's recent books

Bride on the Run
"Enjoyable and satisfying all around,
BRIDE ON THE RUN is an excellent
Western romance you won't want to miss!"
—Romance Reviews Today (romrevtoday.com)

Shawnee Bride
"A fascinating, realistic story."
—*Rendezvous*

Apache Fire
"Enemies, lovers, raw passion, taut sexual tension,
murder and revenge—Indian romance fans are in
for a treat with Elizabeth Lane's sizzling tale of
forbidden love that will hook you until the last moment."
—*Romantic Times*

**DON'T MISS THESE OTHER
TITLES AVAILABLE NOW:**

#607 HER DEAREST SIN
Gayle Wilson
#609 BRIDE OF THE ISLE
Margo Maguire
#610 CHASE WHEELER'S WOMAN
Charlene Sands

NAVAJO SUNRISE

ELIZABETH LANE

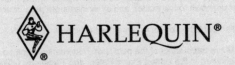

HARLEQUIN®

TORONTO • NEW YORK • LONDON
AMSTERDAM • PARIS • SYDNEY • HAMBURG
STOCKHOLM • ATHENS • TOKYO • MILAN • MADRID
PRAGUE • WARSAW • BUDAPEST • AUCKLAND

ISBN 0-373-29208-2

NAVAJO SUNRISE

Copyright © 2002 by Elizabeth Lane

Visit us at www.eHarlequin.com

Printed in U.S.A.

Please address questions and book requests to:
Harlequin Reader Service
U.S.: 3010 Walden Ave., P.O. Box 1325, Buffalo, NY 14269
Canadian: P.O. Box 609, Fort Erie, Ont. L2A 5X3

Author Note

Navajo culture is so rich and complex that an outsider, trying to describe it in a story, is bound to make mistakes. For any errors contained in this book, I ask the forgiveness of my readers and all those whom my words may have offended.

Navajo Sunrise is set against a background of real historical events, but the story itself is the product of my own imagination. Except for Barboncito, Manuelito, Theodore H. Dodd and General William Tecumseh Sherman, the characters are fictitious and bear no resemblance to actual persons, living or dead.

Elizabeth Lane

Prologue

New Mexico
March, 1864

Ahkeah stood in the cold moonlight, staring down at the grave the *bilagáana* soldiers had forbidden him to dig. His hands were raw and bleeding, the nails worn to stubs from scraping away the half-frozen earth. His eyes and throat stung as if he had just walked through a forest fire.

Even now that the grave was finished, the top piled high with stones, he feared it might not be deep enough to protect his wife's body from the marauding foxes and coyotes that would close in after he was gone. She had died that afternoon, on the fifth day of the long walk from Dinétah to the place the soldiers called Fort Sumner—died in agony, her body swollen with a child that would not have lived even if she'd had the strength to give it birth. The passing soldier who'd fired a bullet into her temple had probably

done her a kindness. Even so, it had taken three of
Ahkeah's friends, gripping him from behind, to keep
him from leaping on the blue-coat and tearing him
apart with his bare hands.

At the time he had wanted the soldier to shoot him
as well. He had wanted nothing more than to lie on
the icy ground beside the body of his sweet young
wife, free from the burdens of grief and shame and
from the hunger that gnawed at his vitals. But even
then reason had whispered that it was his duty to live.
There were people who needed him—his small
daughter, Nizhoni, whose name meant beauty, and his
mother's elder sister, who had watched her entire
family die on the cliffs at Canyon de Chelly, and had
not spoken since. And there were others—so many
others who needed his strength and his voice.

The crescent moon that hung above the mesa cast
ghostly shadows across the desolation of the high
New Mexico desert. Through the darkness, the lonely
wail of a coyote drifted to Ahkeah's ears. The yelping
cry was echoed by another, then another. At one time
Ahkeah would have welcomed the calls of his wild
brothers. Now they only chilled his blood, because he
knew that the sharp-nosed creatures would be gathering around the bodies of the Diné who had fallen
along the trail.

He had begun scraping out the grave as soon as he
knew his wife was dead; but the soldiers, jabbing him
with the points of their bayonets, had forced him to
leave her and move on with the rest of his people.
Only after the dismal procession had made camp for

the night and settled into sleep was he able to slip past the sentries and race back along the trail to where she lay.

Now the grave was finished. The remains of his beloved were as secure as he could make them. But how many others lay unburied along this trail of tears and misery? How many bones would lie scattered on the sand because there was no one to dig the graves?

Turning in the darkness, he faced the direction of the four sacred mountains that marked the boundaries of Dinétah, the homeland of his people. There, the great headman Manuelito and the last of his followers were still holding out against the overwhelming forces of Kit Carson and his regulars. Ahkeah longed to be with them in the mountains, to fight and die as a free man.

But Manuelito himself, his handsome face creased with weariness, had asked him to join the trek to the new reservation at Bosque Redondo, the place the Diné called Hwéeldi—the fort. "Our people will need you, Ahkeah," he had said. "You grew up as a slave among the *bilagáana,* and you speak as they do. Go now, and be the voice of the Diné in this evil time. Go and speak for us all."

Speak for us all.

Swallowing his bitterness, Ahkeah turned away from the sacred mountains and started back the way he had come. What words could he speak that were not hateful and angry? At one time the Diné had been the lords of the earth, their herds, fields and orchards the envy of all the land. He himself had owned more

cattle and horses than a man could count in half a
day, and his beautiful wife had worn robes of soft
wool from her own sheep and necklaces of the finest
silver. Then the *bilagáana* had come, wanting their
land, and everything had changed.

Be the voice of our people, Manuelito had told him.
But the Diné needed more than a voice. They needed
food in their bellies and clothes on their backs. They
needed dignity, hope and pride—things the *bilagáana*
had taken away and flung far beyond their reach.

Perhaps forever.

Ahkeah moved with care as he neared the sleeping
camp, slipping from shadow to shadow in the moonlit
darkness. Even at this hour the sentries would be on
patrol. If they caught him outside the boundary…

His pulse lurched as a flock of wood doves exploded, squawking, from the spidery branches of a
creosote bush. Had the startled birds alerted the sentries? Ahkeah froze where he stood, ears straining,
hearing nothing but the sound of departing wings.

What if the soldiers had already missed him? What
if they were waiting for him in camp, knowing he
would return to his precious daughter? Some of the
blue-coats were just following orders. But there were
vicious brutes among them, men who would relish the
chance to make an example of any Diné who broke
the rules—especially one who spoke to them as a
man, in their own language.

The wind peppered Ahkeah's face with blowing
sand as he crept along the fringe of the camp. The
huddled forms of his people lay scattered on the cold

ground where they had fallen. Here and there, where the soldiers slumbered in their warm blankets, the embers of dying campfires glowed in the night.

He had left Nizhoni with her old aunt in the lee of a sheltering rock, beyond the supply wagon. If he could manage to cross that last small distance without being seen…

But it was already too late. Ahkeah saw four soldiers, armed with clubs, step out from behind the wagon, and he knew they had been waiting for him. Glancing to one side, he saw others appear out of the shadows. Their pale eyes reflected glints of firelight as they encircled him, cutting off all hope of escape.

Cursing and whooping, they fell on him like a pack of hungry wolves.

Chapter One

Bosque Redondo, New Mexico
March, 1868

Miranda Howell hunched wearily on the seat of the U.S. Army buckboard, her slim body bundled into the folds of her thick woolen cape. The cold spring wind stung her cheeks and peppered her face with alkali dust. Two weeks from tomorrow would be Easter Sunday, but nothing about this desolate sweep of country made her feel like celebrating.

"I didn't realize New Mexico would be so cold," she murmured, her eyes scanning the treeless horizon. "It'll be dark soon. How much longer before we reach the fort?"

"Not long. 'Bout an hour, I reckon." The pimple-cheeked young corporal was one of nine soldiers who'd drawn the duty of escorting the major's daughter the 175-mile distance from Santa Fe to Fort Sumner. The other eight rode guard on the wagon, four strung out in front and four bringing up the rear. Their rifles lay across their saddles, loaded and ready. For coyotes, they'd told her, exchanging furtive winks.

In the early hours of the journey, Miranda had made an effort to smile and be pleasant with them. But after four long days of travel she was too tired to be sociable. Her eyes stared across the desert landscape, which glowed like brimstone in the light of the setting sun. A lone crow screeched harshly as it passed overhead, then flapped down behind a clump of rocks, where, judging from the odor, some ill-fated creature lay dead.

What could have possessed any sane group of men to build a fort in such a dreary place? Miranda wondered. For that matter, what was *she* doing here? She could have chosen to spend the holiday with Phillip's parents on Cape Cod. Their seashore estate would be beautiful this time of year, and they had made it clear that, as their future daughter-in-law, she would be more than welcome. Why had she chosen to spend the next two weeks a thousand miles from nowhere, with the rough and taciturn father she scarcely knew?

"We ought to be seein' Navajos afore long," the young driver said. "They got their diggins' all over the flat."

"Diggings? You mean to say they're miners?" Miranda asked, trying to imagine what might lie beneath such barren, lime-encrusted earth.

"Miners? Them Injuns?" The young driver snorted contemptuously. "Shucks, no. They dig themselves holes in the ground to keep out of the weather—lessn' they can find some old hides or sheets of tin to put up for a shack. Why should the lazy buggers mine or farm or even hunt when they can live on handouts from the good old United States Government?''

"You mean, they have no houses? No means of employment?" Miranda asked, horrified.

"Hell—" the young man swore, then broke off and began again. "'Scuse me, miss, but they's Navajos. An' Navajos got their own ways of doin' things. General Carleton, afore he got his butt—'scuse me again, miss—afore he was dismissed from runnin' this place, he got the idea of havin' 'em build big adobe apartment houses like the Pueblos got. Right smart idea, if you ask me. But the Navajos, they wouldn't have none of it. Wanted to live apart in their own kind of houses, little round huts they call hogans. Finally Carleton just threw up his hands and told 'em to go ahead! But did they build any hogans? Did they build anything a'tall? Look around you!''

The corporal worked his tobacco out of his cheek and spat over the edge of the wagon. "Only thing Navajos is any good at is forgin' fake ration tokens so they can steal more supplies! Now that Carleton's gone there's been talk of movin' 'em out, most likely to the Injun Territories in Oklahoma. Good riddance, I'd say. But nobody's holdin' their breath for that, I tell you, 'specially now that the Injun Bureau's took 'em over from the army. Danged government bureaucrats won't do much more'n hand out more flour and blankets.''

"But what a wretched way for people to live!"

Miranda exclaimed in genuine horror. "No work, no homes, no dignity! Surely someone could help them, teach them—"

"Beggin' your pardon, miss, but the Navajos brought their troubles on theirselves. They was raidin' and murderin' over half of Arizona afore Kit Carson and his boys brought 'em to heel an' marched the lot of 'em here to Bosque Redondo."

"Bosque Redondo?" Miranda frowned. "That means round grove in Spanish, doesn't it? I certainly don't see any grove in these parts!"

The corporal snorted with laughter. "Weren't no more than a few trees to begin with, and the Navajos cut those down for firewood the first winter. Now there's no shade in summer and nothin' to burn when it gets cold. Never think past tomorrow, them murderin' redskin fools. If you ask me, Carson shoulda killed 'em all while he had the chance!"

Miranda pulled her cloak tighter about her shoulders, willing herself to ignore the young driver's unsettling talk. It would not do for her to get caught up in this Navajo business, she lectured herself. She had come to New Mexico to spend the holidays with her father, the last time they would be together before her June wedding, perhaps the last time ever. Nothing could be allowed to spoil their time together.

"There. Told you we'd be seein' 'em soon." The corporal's nasal twang cut into her thoughts. Miranda leaned forward on the wagon seat. She shaded her eyes and scanned the horizon, expecting mounted savages to come whooping over the next rise. Only when the corporal nudged her arm and pointed sharply to the left did she realize her first Navajo was little more than a stone's throw away.

Miranda turned, looked—and felt her heart contract with pity.

The old Navajo woman stood in the dust at the roadside, her withered body outlined against the blazing vermilion sunset. The desert wind whipped her faded rags against her bones, and the imploring hands that stretched upward like the thin branches of a winter tree shook with age and cold.

"Stop!" Miranda seized the corporal's arm. The outriders swiveled their heads at the sound of her voice. They slowed their mounts, but did not halt.

"Didn't you hear me?" Miranda tightened her grip, demanding the corporal's attention. "I said stop the wagon! We've got to do something!"

His washed-out eyes stared at her blankly. "Do somethin'? For *her,* you mean? Lawse sake, miss, what for? That ain't nothin' but a dirty old squaw." He spat another stream of tobacco over the side of the still-moving wagon. "Anyhow, we got to get you to the fort afore nightfall, or your pa will be fixin' to throw us all in the stockade!"

He lifted the reins to slap them down on the backs of the plodding mules, but Miranda, anticipating the move, lunged forward, snatched the leather lines from his grip and jerked the team to an abrupt halt.

"What the hell—" the corporal sputtered.

"She's not just a dirty old squaw. She's a human being, and she needs help!" Miranda declared. "As for you and your fellow soldiers, if you don't want to get involved, the least you can do is stand back and allow me to do what I can!''

The outriders had stopped now, and turned their mounts. They watched with varying degrees of amusement as Miranda lifted the skirt of her gray serge traveling suit and clambered down, unassisted, from the buckboard. None of them, it appeared, had the manners to help her or the compassion to aid a fellow being in need.

Over the past four years Miranda had read newspaper articles about the Navajos and how they'd been rounded up and force-marched from their homeland to the bleakness of Fort Sumner. But only now, at her first sight of a real Navajo, did the words she'd read take on life and meaning. In one shriveled face and a pair of twisted, begging hands, she saw the misery of an entire people. It tore at her heart and fueled her sense of outrage to a fever pitch.

The wispy-haired crone was clad in the remnant of a coarse woolen shift, handwoven in a striped pattern that might once have been colorful but was now faded and dirty, showing patches of warp where the weave had worn away. She shrank into herself as Miranda approached, her bare arms folding inward like the legs of a frozen insect. The small mewling noises she made scarcely sounded human.

"It's all right, I won't hurt you," Miranda murmured, edging closer. She could see terror in the raisin-black eyes, and something else—something so disturbing that her heart crept into her throat.

"Give me those leftover biscuits from lunch," she said softly, glancing up at the corporal in the wagon. When he hesitated, her eyes narrowed so sharply that he lunged to do her bidding. As the daughter of his commanding officer, Miss Miranda Howell was not without power.

Seconds later the biscuits were in Miranda's hands. "Here, take them." She held the food at arm's length, standing quietly as the old woman crept toward her like a frightened, starving animal. "It's all right," Miranda urged gently. "No one's going to hurt you."

"I'd back off if I was you, miss." One of the outriders spoke into the windy silence. "I know that old squaw. Crazy Sally, they call her. Hear tell she lit into a soldier one time and bit him on the arm. Tore him open so bad he needed stitches from the medic. No tellin' what she might do to you."

Miranda swallowed a knot of uneasiness as she chose to ignore the man's warning. "It's all right, Sally," she coaxed, even more gently than before. "We don't mean you any harm. Just take the food."

Madness flashed in the ancient eyes as the old woman sidled closer. With a sudden move she snatched the biscuits away with her little clawed hands and scampered to the shelter of a dark sandstone outcrop. There she squatted on her haunches, glaring at Miranda while she stuffed the biscuits frantically into her near-toothless mouth. Saliva, mixed with soggy white crumbs, trickled down her chin. Miranda found herself wondering how Crazy Sally could have bitten anyone, let alone inflicted serious damage.

"All right, miss, you done it," the wagon driver said. "You proved whatever you wanted to prove. Now let me give you a hand up and we'll be headin' on to the fort. You don't want to be out here after dark."

Miranda glanced up at him, still hesitant. The early spring wind, tasting of snow, plucked tendrils of her light brown hair and whipped at the folds of her woolen cloak as she turned back toward the old woman. Crazy Sally was still crouched against the rocks, her small black eyes narrowed to slits against the blowing dust.

"For the love of Pete, what is it now?" the wagon driver demanded.

Miranda's eyes took in the old woman's threadbare dress and exposed limbs. "We can't just go off and leave her. There's a storm blowing in. She'll freeze before morning. Help me get her into the wagon. We've got to take her back to the fort."

None of the soldiers moved.

Miranda's gazed darted from one impassive face to the next. Some of the men averted their eyes, avoiding her furious gaze. Most of them did not bother. Had she pushed them too far this time?

"Beggin' your pardon, miss." The first outrider spoke up at last. "Ain't none of us goin' to lay a hand on that old squaw, let alone put her in the wagon."

"If she ain't got the sense to take shelter, let 'er

freeze," the corporal chimed in. "Good riddance to one more Navajo, that's what I'd say. It's what we'd all say."

Miranda glared up at him in helpless rage. Phillip, her fiancé, had once accused her of being a flaming do-gooder who never knew when to leave well enough alone. He was undoubtedly right. Even so, she could not just walk away and leave a fellow human being to die.

"Very well." She squared her shoulders and folded her arms across her chest. "If Sally stays here, then so do I. You can tell my father—"

"The major would hang us if we was to go off and leave you here," the outrider interrupted. "We got orders to bring you safely back to Fort Sumner. With all due respect, miss, if we have to hogtie you and toss you in the wagon bed, that's exactly what we'll do."

Miranda's heart sank as she realized she had backed herself into an impossible corner. If she refused to get in the wagon, it would be an easy matter for nine men to move her by force. And, given the circumstances, her father would likely excuse their actions.

Her shoulders sagged in acquiescence. But there was one small victory yet to win, one last thing she could still do for poor old Sally, and this time, she vowed, no one was going to stop her.

Lifting her chin in defiance, she began unbuttoning the front of her long, hooded cloak. A birthday gift from Phillip's family, the cloak had been woven in France from the finest blue merino wool and had likely cost a small fortune. Even now, the lush fabric

caressed her fingers as she worked the buttons
through their satin-bound holes. The wind was numb-
ing in its chill. But she would be at the fort within
the hour, Miranda reminded herself. And she could
always buy another cloak, just as warm if not as elegant.

She waited for the soldiers to protest, but none of
them spoke as she released the last button and slid
the cloak off one shoulder. By now they probably
thought she was as crazy as old Sally. Well, let them
think whatever they wished. She would do the right
thing, the moral thing, and the whole contemptuous
lot of them could go to blazes.

The icy wind struck, penetrating to Miranda's
bones as the cloak slipped free of her body. She
gasped with the sudden shock of it, then forcefully
brought her reaction under control. This was no time
to show weakness, she lectured herself. If old Sally
could endure the cold, so could she.

Clenching her jaw against the urge to shiver, she
turned back to the old woman, opened the cloak and
wrapped it around the ravaged body. The garment
was far too large for the tiny Navajo crone. Its elegant
folds pooled around her where she squatted on her
bony haunches, the lining already gathering dust. In
no time at all the beautiful cloak would be filthy. But
at least Sally would be warm. Heaven willing, she
would survive the cold night with its blowing wind
and snow, and many more nights to come.

"And just what do you think you're doing?"

The voice was not loud, but its deep resonance,
coming from behind and above her, made Miranda
gasp. She turned so sharply that she lost her balance

and stumbled to one side, wrenching her ankle. She caught herself against a jutting boulder, just managing to avoid an all-out sprawl.

"I asked you what you thought you were doing." The voice was laced with a fury so cold that it made the raw wind seem as gentle as a southern breeze. Still clinging to the rock, Miranda looked up to see a tall, mounted figure, starkly outlined against a sky that had deepened to the color of flowing blood.

The man was not a soldier—that much was clear at once. He was hatless and swathed in a long, fringed poncho that swirled around him in the stinging wind. Only when his horse snorted and turned, the new angle flooding his features with crimson light, did Miranda see the high, jutting cheekbones, the obsidian eyes, the long raven hair, bound with string into a knot at the back of his head. Only then did she realize he was Navajo.

And for all his angry tone, he had just spoken to her in very passable English.

"This woman was hungry and freezing!" She shouted above the wind in response to his question. "I did what any decent soul would do. I gave her something to eat and something to keep her warm."

"And tomorrow she'll be out here begging again!" he snapped. "She and a half dozen others who've seen what you gave her. Begging is not the way of my people! We may be poor, but we take care of our own!"

"So I see!" Miranda pushed herself fully erect, seething with indignation. "Is this how you take care of your helpless old people? By sending them out in the winter to starve or freeze?"

"My mother's sister is not well. She wandered away from camp and I came looking for her." He seemed somewhat taken aback by Miranda's outburst, but only for an instant. Then his chiseled face darkened as he swung off his horse, seized the cloak and jerked it none too gently from around the old woman's frail body.

"No!" Now it was Miranda's turn to be indignant. "I gave her that cloak to save her life! You've no right to take it from her!"

The man's thin upper lip curled in a grimace of contempt, showing a flash of white, even teeth. "You," he snarled, dangling the garment from his long, brown fingers. "Teachers, missionaries, do-gooders of every damned kind! You're as bad as the army—no, worse! They only kill our bodies! You kill our spirits, our traditions, our pride!" The wind caught the cloak, swirling it high just before he flung it into the dust at Miranda's feet.

"Pride?" She made no move to bend and pick it up, even though the cold was cutting like a knife through the thin serge of her suit jacket. "Will pride keep an old woman from freezing? Will pride keep a young child with an empty belly from crying in the night?"

For the space of a long, tense breath he glared at her. Then, without a word, he reached up and worked the opening of his own thick woolen poncho over his head. Bending down from his imposing six-foot height, he wrapped the poncho around the old woman's shivering body. When he spoke to her in Navajo his voice was low, almost melodious. Miranda found herself straining her ears to catch the odd, birdlike tones of a language she was hearing for the first time. But he spoke only a few phrases. Then he lifted his head and glared at her with hate-filled eyes.

"We take care of our own," he said in an icy voice, "and we would rather steal than beg. We don't need your kind here. Get in that wagon and go back to where you came from, *bilagáana* woman! If you want to help us, write to your president in Washington and tell him to let the Diné go home to their own land!"

Miranda's attention had been fixed on the old woman and the tall Navajo. She did not realize, until the first one spoke, that two of the outriders had dismounted and come up behind her.

"I'd watch my mouth if I was you, Ahkeah," one of the men drawled. "This here ain't no Bible-thumpin' missionary lady. This is the major's own daughter, come to pay her pa a visit."

The revelation seemed to make no difference to the man the soldier had called Ahkeah. He stood his ground, the wind whipping his faded cotton tunic against his lean, hard body. Only by chance did Miranda notice that his hand had moved to rest protectively on old Sally's humped shoulders.

"I say this uppity Injun ought to apologize to Miz Howell here and now." The second outrider gripped his rifle, his swaggering stance challenging the unarmed Navajo to defy him. "Go ahead, Ahkeah, we're all waitin'."

Tension hung dark and leaden on the wintry air. In the wagon, the corporal slipped his rifle bolt into fully cocked position. The faint click splintered the icy silence, but no one else moved. Even the mules seemed

to be watching, waiting, their white breath steaming
from their distended nostrils.

Miranda had forgotten the cold wind that knifed
through her clothing. She had almost forgotten to
breathe. Her eyes were on Ahkeah. He had stepped
in front of the old woman, shielding her with his body
as he faced the soldiers. Under different circumstances his size and strength would have been more
than a match for any two of them. But here and now
the odds were nine against one, and all the cavalry-
men were armed.

The Navajo's flinty eyes narrowed like a puma's
as he measured his enemies. The man was proud, but
no fool, Miranda surmised. He would choose his bat-
tles, and this was neither the time nor the place to
take a stand. His throat rippled lightly as he swallowed, then spoke.

"My apologies, Miss Howell." His voice dripped
contempt. "In the future, kindly save your charity for
those who appreciate it. Please enjoy your visit to this
fair country."

Without another word he turned a defiant back on
the soldiers, and, shepherding the old woman before
him, strode toward his emaciated horse.

"Not so fast!" the first outrider snapped. "If that
was an apology, I'm the king of France, you smart-
mouthed redskin bastard. Come on back here and say
it like you mean it, or somebody's gonna be pickin'
lead out of your backside!"

Ahkeah turned only when the second man cocked
his rifle. His eyes glittered like black ice in the twilight. "I'm unarmed and here under treaty," he said,
his cold, flat voice implying that any soldier's firing

on a defenseless Navajo would raise a cry that would be heard all the way to Washington.

"Piss on the treaty," the soldier growled. "I've shot plenty of your kind, Ahkeah. Too many for a piece of paper to make a dime's worth of difference. Now, do you want to apologize to the lady again or do I pull this trigger and blow your stubborn head off?"

"This is ridiculous!" Miranda flung herself between the two antagonists. "No one is going to shoot anybody, Private. Now get back on your horse and let this man take his poor old aunt home."

Distracted by her outburst, Ahkeah did not see what was coming next—nor did Miranda, until she heard the sickening thunk of a rifle butt against flesh and bone. The tall Navajo crumpled to the earth, felled by a third soldier, who had crept up behind him. He lay sprawled on his face, the blood seeping from his shattered temple onto the frozen ground.

Chapter Two

The old woman was first to reach the fallen Navajo. She crouched over him, pawing at his face with her hands and making the frightened little mewling noises. As Miranda approached, she scuttled backward and, still wearing the poncho he'd flung around her shoulders, vanished into the swirling darkness.

"Son of a bitch!" the private swore, jerking his rifle bolt back into safety position. "What'd you go and clobber him for, McCoy? That Ahkeah's been nothin' but trouble since the day he come in! Always stirrin' things up! I coulda shot the bastard and been rid of him once and for all!"

"I did it to save your fool hide," the other man retorted. "Pull the trigger on a Navajo, with so many government bigwigs snoopin' 'round here, and your ass would be in a sling for the next twenty years! You'll thank me for it once you simmer down."

"Maybe." The private wiped his runny nose with the back of his hand. "Come on, let's get outa here. With luck, the bastard won't even remember what hit

him when he wakes up." He spun on his heel and
strode back toward his horse.

"Wait!" Miranda had dropped to the ground beside Ahkeah. Her urgent fingers probed his neck,
groping for signs of life. Beneath her touch the Navajo's skin was as cool and smooth as ivory, stretch-
ing taut over ropy cords of muscle and sinew. Pressing deeper, she found his pulse. The beat was thready
and erratic. She remembered the sound of the blow,
the crack of bone. Dread tightened like a clenched fist
around her heart.

She crouched lower, laying her ear against his back
to catch the labored rise and fall of his breathing. The
aroma of mesquite smoke rose from his threadbare
tunic, lingering at the edge of her awareness. Why
should she care about this man? she found herself
wondering. He was a stranger, almost an enemy, and
he had spoken to her as if she were a troublesome
child.

The rifle butt had struck just above his temple. She
fingered the wound, felt the swelling flesh and the
wetness of blood. "We can't leave him here," she an-
nounced to the soldiers. "Help me get him into the
wagon."

None of the men moved. "He's just an Injun,
miss," the wagon driver said. "Injuns got hard heads.
Afore long, this 'un will wake up sore and stumble
on home."

"And what if he doesn't wake up?" Miranda
flared. "There's a storm blowing in! If you refuse to
take him and he freezes or dies of his injuries out

here, I'll hold every last one of you accountable! Every newspaper and congressman in the country will hear about how you struck down an unarmed Indian and left him to die!''

None of the men responded, but she could sense their minds working, weighing her threat. Her father was a powerful man, and her influence on him could make life uncomfortable for them all.

At last the senior outrider, a sergeant, cleared his throat and spat in the alkali dust. ''Load him in the damned wagon. When we get to the fort, we can dump him off at the Injun hospital.'' He glared irritably at two of the men. ''You! Move!''

''Watch his head.'' Miranda hovered anxiously as the two soldiers lifted the unconscious Navajo and carried him toward the buckboard. His length sagged between them, one limp hand dragging in the dust. They hefted him high and rolled him onto the bed like the carcass of a freshly killed buck.

Miranda stifled a little cry as his body struck the planks. She paused to snatch up her discarded cloak from the ground. Then, without waiting for assistance, she scrambled up beside him and gathered his battered head into her lap. ''Go,'' she said to the driver. ''Hurry.''

The wagon jounced over the rutted road as the mules broke into a trot. Miranda covered Ahkeah's chilled body with the cloak and cradled his head to lessen the jarring. Tending injured men was nothing new to her. Her maternal uncle, Dr. Andrew Cavanaugh, who'd taken her in when her mother died, had

spent the Civil War stationed at a Boston military
hospital. With so many wounded to tend, he'd had
little choice except to press his young niece into service. There was little in the way of grief and misery
that Miranda had not seen. Perhaps that was why,
when the war ended and she was able to resume her
schooling, she had chosen to train not as a nurse, but
as a teacher.

"Just think of it!" she had exclaimed to her disappointed uncle. "If we can teach children kindness
and tolerance before they're grown, perhaps there'll
be no more need for war!"

Miranda's own words came back to haunt her now
as she nestled the fallen Navajo's head between her
knees. His head wound had stopped bleeding, but his
eyes were closed and his breathing was ragged. His
pulse fluttered like the wings of a dying bird beneath
her fingertips.

She remembered the sight of him, standing in the
twilight beside his horse. His gaze had pierced her
like a blade, touching deep, secret places that had lain
undisturbed for all the twenty-two years of her life.
Even now that he lay helpless in her lap, the power
of his presence left her shaken. No one had ever
looked at her with such pure hatred—a hatred that
had chilled Miranda to her bones. What chance did
her own beliefs stand against such deeply bred hos-
tility? Why hadn't she stayed in the East, where little
more was expected of her than to be sweet, pleasant,
ladylike and studious?

One of the outriders had caught Ahkeah's horse

and tied it to the back of the buckboard. When the clouds swept clear of the moon, Miranda could see the barred shadow of its rib cage below the tattered saddle blanket. When they reached the fort she would order the poor creature stabled and fed, she resolved. An animal, at least, would not be too proud to accept a bit of human kindness.

Ahkeah's head rolled in her lap. He moaned softly, but his eyes did not open. Miranda gazed down at his moon-chiseled features—the jutting ledges of his cheekbones, the fine, straight nose, the long jawbones that met in a prominent, stubborn chin. His eyes lay in deep pools of shadow within the sockets of his skull. There was nothing to his face but skin and bone, and little more to his rangy body. All the same this Navajo was a riveting figure of a man—a wild hawk, lying broken and wounded in her arms, exuding a savagery that burned behind the lids of his closed eyes, searing her senses.

His limbs twitched like a dreaming animal's as he moaned again, struggling in the depths of his darkness. Miranda's fingers brushed back a tendril of night-black hair from his forehead. His skin was like polished jade, the hair stiff with alkali dust.

She thought of Phillip, his blue eyes, his fine, pale hair and his gentle ways. Dear heaven, what she wouldn't give to be with him now, away from this bleak desert and this frightening man.

"It's all right," she whispered, remembering that seemingly unconscious people had been known to hear what was said to them. "You've got a head injury—perhaps a serious one. We're taking you to the hospital at the fort. You'll be looked after properly there."

Had she felt his body jerk? The slight, convulsive shudder passed like a ripple beneath the woolen cloak and was gone.

"Ahkeah?" Could he really have heard her speak? Bending closer, Miranda gazed at him intently, but he did not move. Only his ragged, shallow breathing and the elusive flutter of his pulse told her he was alive.

Why did you hit him so hard? she wanted to scream at the soldier who'd crashed the rifle butt into Ahkeah's dark head. *Was it hatred, fear or simple stupidity?* Miranda kept her silence, knowing that it was too late for outrage—and knowing, too, that this man could not be lost to his people. Whatever it took, whatever influence she could wield, she would see that he got the best possible care.

"Beggin' your pardon, miss." The driver's twangy voice broke into her thoughts. "If there's any chance that Injun can hear you, you'd best not say nothin' 'bout the hospital."

"What do you mean?" Miranda glanced at him sharply.

"Navajos got some odd beliefs. They don't like to go where a body's died, somethin' about ghosts. Hell, I've seen 'em burn a place to the ground 'cause a body's died there—and the whole family just standin' round with no place to live. Sometimes, if they know ahead, they'll haul the poor soul's bed outside so's he won't have to die in the house."

"And that's why they don't like the hospital? Because people die there?"

The corporal laughed, a raw, humorless sound. "We hafta drag 'em there at gunpoint. Ain't no use tryin' to do nothin' for 'em, miss. Navajos ain't got no more gratitude than they got sense!"

"I see." Miranda sank back into her own silence. The stars had come out, diamond pinpoints spilling across a black velvet sky. So far away. So cold.

The road was straighter and more level here, as if it had been recently graded. Bare cottonwoods, their skeletal branches clawing skyward, lined the road on both sides. This, Miranda realized, would be the final approach to Fort Sumner.

Straining her eyes into the darkness ahead, she could make out glimmers of light, lower and brighter than the icy stars. Soon she and her weary escorts would be safe within the boundaries of the fort. Soon she would be greeting the tough, taciturn near stranger who was her father.

Major William Howell, known as Iron Bill to his troops, had already made it clear that he could not leave his post to travel East for Miranda's June wedding. Dear Uncle Andrew would be the one to walk her down the aisle and give her to Phillip in marriage. All the same, Bill Howell was her father. Even though she had seen him less than half a dozen times in the fifteen years since her mother's death, Miranda felt a need to close the tenuous circle that bound them together. With Phillip planning to take over the London office of the family shipping business, who could say whether she and her father would ever meet again?

The man in her lap stirred and moaned. His moon-silvered eyelids twitched as if he were dreaming, but his eyes remained closed in the shadowed pits of their sockets. Miranda studied the proud, sharp planes of his sleeping face. The proud Navajo was pure trouble, she knew. By all rules of common sense, she should let the soldiers deliver him to the Indian hospital. He was certainly in no condition to protest or even to be frightened.

In any case, Ahkeah and his people were none of her concern. She had come to Fort Sumner to see her father, not to aid the downtrodden. Two weeks from today she would be leaving by this very road. She would be going back to her own familiar world, to finish out her school year at Radcliffe and prepare for her marriage to Phillip. Two weeks—why, that was hardly any time at all, certainly not enough time to make a difference in this miserable place. She would be foolish to try, foolish to get involved.

Miranda squared her jaw, her decision made. She would instruct the men to leave Ahkeah at the hospital where he belonged. Then she would put the tall Navajo firmly and permanently out of her mind.

Ahkeah drifted below the brink of consciousness, struggling again and again toward the surface, only to tire and sink downward once more into the enfolding darkness. Images floated through his mind—faces from the past, scenes of misery, horror and unspeakable sadness. The broken bodies on the floor of Canyon de Chelly…wise old Ganado Mucho lying in his own blood…the rocky earth falling onto Ahkeah's wife's lovely, cold face….

Surrounding everything was the aura of pain, spreading outward in quivering rings from his temple, like ripples on still, black water. He moaned, struggling to break into the light, then spiraling helplessly downward once more.

The fragrant softness that surrounded his body was alien to his senses, yet strangely familiar. Even in his semiconscious state he felt the nearness of the young *bilagáana* woman, the lean firmness of her thighs supporting his head and shoulders, the touch of her fingers like warm snow on his face. She smelled faintly of lilacs—an aroma he remembered and hated. Now he was floating in a lilac sea, drifting in scented warmth, in and out of awareness, in and out of pain. The scent was repellant, and yet, somehow, so arousing that he felt his body respond with a deep, stirring heat.

He had never considered *bilagáana* women attractive. The ones he'd known had been stringy, washed-out creatures with eyes like sheep and voices like wild crows—women like Mrs. McCabe, whose husband had bought him as a small, terrified boy from a Mexican slave trader. The nine years he had spent in the McCabe household still gave him bad dreams—the whippings to "break" his spirit, the crushing labor, the stream of shrill tirades from Mrs. McCabe's hatchet tongue when he failed to speak English perfectly. And every spring the cloying scent of the blooming bushes that ringed the McCabes' front porch. The scent of lilacs.

Now Ahkeah floundered in the shallows of a lilac sea. His efforts to break the surface were exhausting, even though he sensed the reality that his body had not moved. His eyelids were leaden, his limbs like stone, able to feel the jarring motion beneath them but with no strength to obey his will. He was trapped in this scented dream where pain swirled and dipped like a dancer in a floating skirt. And something else was wrong—an awareness that lay like a sheet of ice beneath the dream's liquid warmth. What was it? Some word, something the *bilagáana* woman had said—

The sudden chill penetrated to Ahkeah's bones as he remembered. They were taking him to the hospital, to that place of terror and pain where the ghosts of the dead lingered and the Holy People would not go. His fears were pure superstition, the *bilagáana* would say. But he had visited friends who'd been taken there, and on every visit he had felt the evil in that place, and had sworn he would never allow himself or any of his family to be taken there.

Wildly now, he began to jerk and thrash, willing his limbs to move, his voice to cry out in protest. But the lilac dream held him fast. He felt the woman's soft, cool hand stroking his forehead, heard her whispering voice as he fought his way upward, struggling into the cold night air.

* * *

The Navajo's head jerked in Miranda's arms. His body twitched, quivering agitatedly along its length in the wagon bed. He muttered random words—at least she supposed them to be words—in his strange language.

"It's all right," she repeated, soothingly, her hand brushing tendrils of coarse, black hair away from his forehead. "You're hurt, but you'll be well taken care of. We're going to—"

Her words ended in a gasp as his eyes shot open.

Miranda's heart seemed to stop as the full fury of his anthracite gaze struck her. It was as if a sleeping tiger had suddenly awakened in her arms.

"What happened?" His voice was thick, the words slurred.

"You were hit. Your head is injured, and you need to keep still." The words tumbled out of her as the heart that had frozen an instant before broke into a frenzied gallop.

"Where am I?" he demanded. "What happened to the old woman?"

"Nothing. She ran away." Miranda's outrage flared at the distrust his question implied. "No one would have harmed her, Ahkeah. I would never have allowed that to happen." Her gaze flickered away as his cold eyes reminded her that she hadn't stopped the soldiers from harming *him*. "One of the men struck you down to keep you from being shot. But the blow was harder than he'd intended. It was an accident, truly…."

Good heavens, she sounded like a fool, stumbling around in the morass of her own silly words. She shook off the condemnation in his hard black eyes and forced herself to continue. "You'll be well looked after. I can assure you of that."

"In the hospital?" He uttered the last word with the vehemence of a curse. Then, without waiting for her to respond, he rolled off her lap into the wagon bed and pushed himself to a shaky sitting position.

The lights from the fort were much closer now. Miranda could make out the low, blocky outlines of buildings and see the flare of torchlight on adobe walls.

"Stop the wagon," Ahkeah said, looking as if he were about to faint. "I'm getting out right here."

"Don't be ridiculous!" Miranda snapped, reaching out to steady him. "You're badly hurt. You need to be examined by a doctor."

"I'll be fine. If not, my own people can take care of me." He shook off the clasp of her steadying hand. His jaw tightened as he gripped the side board of the bouncing wagon and struggled to stand. "I know my rights, Miss Howell. I've broken no rules, and you can't force me to—"

The driver glanced back over his shoulder. "Everything all right back there, miss?"

"Yes. Fine." Miranda's upward glance confirmed that he wasn't reaching for his rifle. "Just get us to the fort. Hurry!"

Spurred by the urgency in her voice, the young corporal slapped the reins down on the backs of the mules. *"Ha!"* The buckboard shot forward as the tired animals broke into a trot. Wheels bounced and flew along the rocky surface of the road as they pushed the outriders ahead of them.

When Miranda's gaze returned to Ahkeah, she saw that he had gained his feet and was standing in a half crouch, his leather-clad legs braced apart to support him in the jouncing wagon. His face was ashen in the moonlight, his mouth a grim line of tightly controlled pain.

"Tell your driver to stop," he muttered between clenched teeth.

"Don't be a fool!" Miranda snapped, glaring up at him. "You need medical attention. You need—"

"Tell him to stop! Tell him now, damn it, or I jump out on the count of three!" The whites of his eyes glittered in the moonlight. "One...two..." His legs quivered unsteadily, and his eyes had taken on a glaze. "Three..." Ahkeah's voice trailed off as he reeled and tumbled forward into Miranda's arms.

Chapter Three

Miranda reacted instinctively, bracing herself against Ahkeah's falling weight and reaching up to protect his head. Having cared for men with head injuries, she'd known what to expect when he tried to get up too soon. Ahkeah's fainting had not surprised her.

Now, as the buckboard careened down the road, the tall Navajo lay across her lap, his head on her bosom, her arms supporting his chest and shoulders. His gaunt ribs were as distinct as the tines of a pitchfork through the thin cotton tunic. Wildness was in the feel of him, in the smoky scent of his hair, the sharpness of his bones and the wind-burned tautness of his skin. Miranda cradled his unconscious form gently, aware of his face pressing against her breast. She felt the tightness in her body, felt the liquid heat that pulsed from the deep core of her womanhood, stirring, strangely restless.

What was wrong with her? At the hospital, when she'd held injured youths in her arms to ease their pain, she had felt nothing but pity. And Phillip—yes, she had embraced him, kissed him ever so chastely on the lips and felt a safe, abiding sweetness that she judged to be love. But holding Ahkeah in her arms was like holding a broken eagle that, at any moment, might wake up and fly at her with its deadly beak and talons. The sense of danger shimmered like wine in her blood.

He stirred against her, moaning softly, his chin pressing her nipple through the thin serge of her jacket. Miranda's lips parted in a little gasp as hot, tingling sensations flooded her body. Oh, this was wrong—she was engaged, almost married. And this man—he was a savage who'd likely pillaged and murdered and done heaven knows what. She had to put a stop to what was happening. But the exquisite pressure of his touch held her captive. She was powerless to move. Heat and color crept upward to flood her face. She struggled to breathe. A moment more, and—

"Say, looks like we got ourselves a welcomin' party!" The corporal leaned to one side and spat over the side of the wagon. "Good thing we didn't git you here any later, Miss Howell, or we woulda' been strung up by our hocks like a passel o' spring hams."

Straining upward, Miranda peered past him over the seat of the buckboard. Her searching eyes caught the glint of moonlight on metal a quarter mile ahead, and then, as it materialized out of the night, a solid, moving black shape that she judged to be a close-riding troop of cavalry. As they came into full view she recognized the unmistakable tall-in-the-saddle frame and outsize Stetson of her father, Major Iron Bill Howell. He was riding at the head of the column, pushing his rangy buckskin mount to a gallop.

Miranda's arms had frozen around Ahkeah's inert body. As the outriders hailed the column, her first impulse was to roll the Navajo discreetly away from her, onto the planks. But the buckboard was bouncing crazily and the man was injured, she reminded herself. She could not risk his coming to further harm for the sake of appearances.

Carefully she eased his dark face away from her breast. Then, still supporting him in her arms, she steeled herself against the coming onslaught.

"What the hell took you so long?" Bill Howell's voice boomed above the swirl of dust, wind and horses as the two groups mingled. "You were supposed to be back before nightfall! And where the devil is my daughter?"

"I'm here!" Miranda called out from the back of the wagon. "There's nothing to be concerned about, Father. Everything is perfectly…fine."

The all-too-familiar knot in Miranda's stomach tightened as she saw him pushing his mount through the swarm of men and animals. As a child she had always been a little afraid of her father. He was so large and forceful, always looming above her like the giant in "Jack and the Beanstalk." Not once in her memory had he ever bent down to her eye level or lifted her up to his. He had been—and was—a tower of authority, gruff and unbending. Maybe that was part of the reason Miranda's gentle mother had remained in the East, refusing to follow him to his remote postings as many officers' wives did.

Someone had lit a torch. In its blazing yellow light she saw him looming above her once more—older now, by nearly four years, than when she'd last set eyes on him. The leathery creases around his eyes had deepened and the bristling sideburns that failed to hide his outsize ears were streaked with gray. But his penetrating granite eyes were exactly as Miranda remembered them.

Now those eyes were staring down at the man Miranda held in her arms—a man he undoubtedly knew and probably hated.

"What in blazes is going on here, Miranda?" he growled without so much as a nod of greeting. "What are you doing with this Indian?"

"He's hurt." Miranda forced herself to meet her father's angry gaze. "If we'd left him by the road with a storm blowing in, he could have died of exposure."

"Not the worst thing that could happen, by a long shot!" Iron Bill snapped. "If you ask me, the whole damned reservation, even the Navajos, would be better off without the troublemaking bastard!" Before Miranda could respond, he turned abruptly to the sergeant. "What happened, soldier? And who allowed my daughter to get involved with this vermin?"

The sergeant's Adam's apple quivered as he swallowed and spoke. "Ahkeah, here, insulted your daughter and refused to apologize, sir. Things were getting out of hand, and—''

"And just as your men were about to shoot him, someone crashed a rifle butt into his head!'' Miranda interrupted. "The entire episode was completely uncalled-for, Father. If your soldiers had left well enough alone, Ahkeah would simply have ridden away without—''

"I can speak for myself.'' The Navajo's sharp voice sliced into the flow of her own words. Startled, Miranda glanced down into the jet-black pits of Ahkeah's eyes.

"The sergeant was right,'' he said, twisting away from her and pushing himself, with effort, to a sitting position in the wagon bed. "I did insult your daughter. She was meddling where she had no business. I told her as much, and when I was ordered a second time, I did refuse to apologize. Now, since the matter of blame is settled, I'll be taking my leave.''

Miranda watched the pain ripple across his face as he flung the cloak aside and staggered to his feet, then turned to catch the reins of his horse, which had been tied to the back of the buckboard. A vehement protest sprang to her lips. The man was in no condition to ride. If he passed out again he could lie unconscious all night, exposed to the coming storm. But one glance at his stubbornly set face confirmed that arguing would do no good. Not with a man like Ahkeah.

Grimacing with effort, he brought the rack-ribbed animal alongside the wagon. No one made a move, either to assist him or to hinder him, as he eased one leg over its back and slid awkwardly into place. The wind whipped his raven hair as he swung away from the wagon and turned, for the space of a heartbeat, to lock his gaze with Miranda's. His contemptuous eyes ignited sparks of black fire through a glaze of pain. Then, as lightning forked across the sky with an ear-splitting crack, he wheeled his mount and galloped into the darkness.

The silence that hung over the small company lasted for the space of a long breath. Then another bolt of lightning ripped the gathering clouds, and the full fury of the storm burst out of the sky. Lashing sleet, driven almost sideways by the wind, pelted them like buckshot. Mules brayed. A horse screamed and reared. Galvanized to action, the cavalry and wagon formed a column and headed like an arrow for Fort Sumner.

Teeth chattering, Miranda gathered her dusty cloak from the wagon bed, flung its sheltering warmth around her head and shoulders and clambered onto the jouncing seat beside the driver. The thick, soft wool still carried the pungent wood smoke scent of Ahkeah's body. As she closed her eyes against the stinging sleet, the aroma stole into her senses, evoking the memory of his obsidian eyes piercing her defenses, his sharp-boned features molding the shape of her breast.

She pictured him now, galloping his half-starved mount through the icy storm, his water-soaked clothes freezing to his skin. She imagined the horse stumbling, startled, perhaps, by a fleeing animal or a sudden clap of thunder. She saw the reins slip from the frozen bronze fingers…

Stop it! Miranda admonished herself. *You can't allow yourself to fret over the man! You're not responsible for what happens to him!* And yet she knew in her heart she *was* responsible. If she had not stopped to help a pathetic old woman, none of this ongoing debacle would have taken place. If Ahkeah came to further harm tonight, the blame would be squarely on her own shoulders. That awareness weighed on her, darkening her thoughts as the buckboard and its escort thundered through the flying sleet toward the shelter of the fort.

Miranda awoke the next morning to the cold, gray silence of the spare room in her father's quarters. For a long moment she lay quietly beneath the flannel sheet and thick woolen army blankets, watching the play of light beams through a crack in the shuttered window. Her gaze wandered to the rough-timbered ceiling and down the plain adobe walls, bare, even, of whitewash. She inspected the peeling wardrobe, standing askew as if it had been hauled in from some dusty storage room for the purpose of her visit.

As her mind roused to full wakefulness, she remembered last night's arrival—the flaring torchlight, the steaming breath of the mules as she dismounted stiffly from the buckboard. She remembered the strained, hasty supper of cold beans and bread in the officers' mess, and her father's brusque silence, which she'd tried to fill with chatter about her long trip. She'd wanted to ask him about Ahkeah, but had decided against it. Things were too unsettled between the two of them, too raw and confusing. Oh, why had she come here? Why had she placed so much importance on making peace with the man who'd fathered her, when it would have been so much easier to simply let go? Why had she allowed Iron Bill Howell to matter so much to her, when she clearly mattered so little to him?

As she turned onto her side, she saw her leather trunk, standing open as she'd left it last night after rummaging for a clean nightgown. She had fallen into bed, too tired even to brush her hair or wash her face. Now she felt rumpled and gritty-eyed, her hair damp and coarse with alkali dust. What she wouldn't give for a bath! But this was no time for self-indulgence. It was time to get up, pull herself together and face whatever the day might bring.

Tossing back the covers, Miranda swung her legs out of bed. Her serge traveling suit lay damp, dirty and hopelessly rumpled where she'd spread it on the single wooden chair last night. She took a moment to smooth out the worst of the wrinkles and rearrange the folds. Then she selected another gown from the chest, a simple, dark brown twill, its severity softened by a white lace collar. Hastily she dressed, then splashed her face at the washstand and twisted up her hair.

The silence from the other two rooms told her, even before she opened the door, that her father had already risen and left. His bedroom stood open, the simple bunk made up with military precision. There was no fire in the potbellied stove, and the rudimentary cooking facilities looked as if they had never been used. A quick inspection of the cupboard revealed nothing but a few dishes and not so much as a crumb of food. Clearly Iron Bill took his meals in the mess hall and expected his daughter to do the same—if indeed he'd given any thought to the matter.

Miranda's blue cloak hung neatly on a rack beside the door. As she lifted it down, she saw that it had been brushed free of dust; but even now the faint aroma of wood smoke clung to it, whispering of Ahkeah. The scent enfolded her as she slipped the cloak over her shoulders, worked a single button through its satin-bound hole and opened the door.

The morning breeze was chilly, but not really cold. Once the sun was high, she realized, the cloak would be too warm. Stepping back into the room, she replaced it on the hook and selected a cashmere shawl—another of Phillip's gifts—from her trunk. With the shawl's airy warmth wrapped around her shoulders, she stepped outside and closed the door behind her.

Miranda had glimpsed the lay of the fort last night in the darkness. Now the vista of open desert and low-slung adobe buildings spread before her, not enclosed by walls, as she might have expected a fort to be, but sprawling over acres of barren land, unconstrained by factors of space and safety. Clearly the small military unit that remained here to keep order and protect the

Indian Agency had little to fear from their captives or from outside attack. Her eyes picked out what she guessed to be barracks, stables and offices, and one large building that resembled a warehouse—some kind of commissary, she surmised. The ground was still glazed with a thin coating of sleet. Bare earth steamed and glittered in the morning sunlight. There was little or no grass, and the few trees she could see were stunted and bare. How did her father stand this desolate place?

Lifting her skirts above the frozen mud, Miranda strode across the empty square of land that passed for a parade ground toward what she remembered to be the mess hall. The few soldiers who were loitering outside the door straightened to a semblance of attention, tipping their hats as she passed. One of them, a quiet young man who'd been part of her escort from Santa Fe, smiled shyly and held open the door. With a nod of thanks she stepped over the threshold.

Her heart sank as she surveyed the long mess hall with its sea of empty tables and benches and the more genteel officers' section at the far end. Where was her father? Couldn't he at least have waited for her to join him for breakfast? Did he think she'd traveled all this distance to wander around this desolate place alone?

"So here you are, my dear."

Startled by the sound of a feminine voice, Miranda turned to see a plump, birdlike woman hurrying toward her from the direction of the kitchen. She was well into middle age, her badly dyed brown hair sculpted into rigidly upswept curls. Her wine-colored gown was elaborately ruffled at the neck, sleeves and hem, giving her the look of a drooping garden peony.

At closer range Miranda saw that the woman's childlike face was webbed with lines, but traces of faded beauty lingered in her molasses-brown eyes. Those eyes sparkled as she seized Miranda's fingers in her small, lace-mitted hand. "Your father had pressing duties this morning and couldn't be here. I offered to wait and show you around—after you've had breakfast, of course. My name is Violet Marsden. My husband is quartermaster here at the fort, and I..." She caught her breath, as if the very effort of speaking had strained her. "I can't tell you how very pleased I am to welcome you here!"

Still a bit dazed, Miranda allowed the woman to lead her to a table in a corner of the deserted officers' mess. It was cheerlessly set with a threadbare linen cloth, chipped but serviceable white porcelain and heavy silver plate that bore a patina of long use. But someone had placed a sprig of tiny yellow spring wildflowers in a spare cup. Who had it been? Her father? This woman, perhaps?

"I've just been to the kitchen to make sure the cook saved you some porridge." Violet Marsden settled herself across the table, adjusting her gown like a preening sparrow. An undertone in her fragile voice spoke of cotton fields and magnolias and the gracious manners of a time forever gone. What was she doing here in this barren place that seemed to have had every trace of gentility parched, burned, starved and frozen out of it?

"Did you have a difficult journey?" she asked, lifting the china teapot and pouring a cup for Miranda, then one for herself. There was no sugar or cream on the table, but the tea was fresh, its warmth curling pleasantly in Miranda's stomach.

"The trip wasn't bad," she replied, dismissing what she remembered of last night's arrival. "But I do have a question. Am I just imagining things, or is my father avoiding me?"

"Avoiding you?" Violet glanced up, her eyes wide with surprise. "How on earth could you imagine such a thing? Of course Major Howell isn't avoiding you!"

"Then where is he? We've barely exchanged a dozen words since I arrived last night!"

"But, my dear, there's a perfectly logical explanation for that," Violet protested. "Last night you were exhausted and needed your rest."

"And this morning?"

"Why, it's simply the usual Saturday. He needed to be at the issue house early to make certain there's no trouble with the Navajos!"

"Trouble with the Navajos?" Miranda asked, dimly aware that she sounded like a trained parrot.

"Why, bless you, this is the day they come in to get their rations. Thousands of them! The line goes all the way from the issue house to the road and beyond. With so many Indians about the place, a strong military presence is needed."

Miranda glanced down at the bowl of gluey oatmeal laced with canned milk that had appeared on the table before her. "And my father couldn't be spared for a single morning?" she asked, stirring the grayish mess with her spoon.

"The commanding officer of the fort is required to be in attendance." Violet dabbed at her little rouged mouth with her napkin. "With the care of the Navajos passing from the army to the Bureau of Indian Affairs, this fort has come under a good deal of public scrutiny, my dear. If there's trouble and some impulsive young soldier fires at unarmed Indians, it could make the army look very bad. Do you understand?"

"I do." Miranda remembered the rifle butt crunching into Ahkeah's skull. Evidently it was all right to hit Navajos but not to shoot them.

"It's the major's responsibility to make sure nothing happens that would open the army to criticism," Violet said, brushing away an imaginary crumb from the lace edging on her bodice. "That's why your father couldn't delegate the job to anyone else, not even to be with you."

"I see." Miranda forced herself to eat, knowing she would be hungry later. Questions about the Navajos—and the disturbing man she had held in her arms last night—milled in her mind, clamoring for answers, but she cautioned herself to hold her tongue. The last thing she wanted was to trigger unpleasant gossip by showing too much interest in a man she had no business knowing.

"Will I be allowed to go to the issue house and watch?" she asked casually.

"I suppose so." Violet's patrician nose crinkled with distaste. "But don't expect to like what you see. The Navajos are a filthy, treacherous lot, far worse than the slaves on my daddy's plantation ever were. Their young girls hang around the fort and offer themselves to the soldiers for a few crusts of bread! Some of our boys have caught the most dreadful diseases from them! A gentlewoman isn't supposed to know about such things, but one can't help hearing talk!"

She frowned, then brightened as her eyes fell on Miranda's empty teacup. "Would you like me to read your fortune, dear? My old mammy back in Louisiana taught me how, and I'm really quite good at it! I read for all the officers' wives before they left."

"Then, by all means, go ahead." Miranda set little store by fortune-telling, but she had no wish to be rude. She watched skeptically as the small woman took the cup and stared intently into it, studying the pattern of the tea leaves in the bottom.

"Please don't tell me I'm going to fall in love with a tall, dark stranger," Miranda said, striving to keep things in the spirit of fun. "I'm getting married in June, and my fiancé is neither dark nor particularly—"

"Hush!" Violet whispered urgently. "Something's coming to me!" She lifted the cup closer to her face, knitting her brows and pursing her small mouth. "It's not terribly clear," she said, "but I see a great change coming into your life."

"Of course," Miranda said with a little smile. "As

I told you, I'm getting married, and after that Phillip and I will be living in London.''

"No." Violet's fragile voice rasped with conviction. "The change I see is one you're not expecting and can't prepare for. This change will shake your very soul. It will challenge all the things you've ever believed in!"

Miranda forced a good-natured laugh. This was all nonsense, she reminded herself. No one could look into a scattering of soggy tea leaves and read the future.

"And how will I deal with such a change?" she asked, humoring the woman. "Do the leaves tell you that?"

Violet's eyes seemed to darken. Then she sighed and shook her head. "No. But be careful, my dear. I see danger in the leaves...and death—the death of someone close to you, perhaps, or even your own!"

"Oh, come now, my future can't be as bleak as all that!" Miranda crumpled her napkin, tossed it down beside the half-finished bowl of porridge, and rose to her feet. "Look through the window. The sun's come out. It's going to be a fine morning, and I want to see the Navajos!"

"Very well, my dear." Violet set the cup on the table, stood up, then bent to straighten her ruffled skirts and snatch up the parasol she'd left propped against a chair. "But don't forget what I told you. When my old mammy read tea leaves, she was never wrong. She even foretold that one day I'd elope with a Yankee and be disowned by the whole family, right down to the Georgia cousins! I didn't believe her at the time, but two years later her prediction came true!''

Miranda's gaze lingered on the sad little figure as they crossed the mess hall and walked toward the door. Yes, the puzzle of Violet Marsden was slowly coming together. Had her marriage been worth the pain of losing her family? Glancing at the woman's careworn face, Miranda could only wonder.

Sunlight dazzled her eyes, warming her face as they stepped onto the porch. Violet opened her parasol, frowning as she noticed that Miranda had not brought a parasol for herself.

''And no bonnet, either!'' she clucked disapprovingly. ''You really must take care of your skin in this desert climate, my dear girl, or the sun and wind will shrivel you like a raisin!''

But Miranda scarcely heard the well-meant advice. Her gaze was already leaping across the parade ground to the long, dark line that was forming up outside the doors of the issue house. Deny it though she might, she knew she was searching—first casually, then urgently—for a single tall, proud figure. She needed to know that he had survived the terrible night and that her interference had done him no permanent harm.

With growing desperation she scanned the line. Where was he?

Where was he?

Chapter Four

Miranda was halfway across the parade ground, holding back her stride to keep pace with Violet's mincing steps, when she caught sight of him.

He was standing near the front of the line, his height towering a full head above the Navajos around him. A strip of crimson cloth bound his temple, more like a badge of defiance than the dressing for a wound.

Had he seen her? Miranda's pulse skipped erratically at the thought of that sharp obsidian gaze following her across the open ground. But what did it matter? she berated herself. Last night's encounter had been humiliating for them both. He would not welcome the sight of her—no more than she should welcome the sight of him.

"Violet, where are the other officers' wives?" she asked in an effort to make polite conversation. "I thought we might be meeting some of them this morning."

"Why, bless you, they're gone. What few there

were could not abide this place. They transferred out with their husbands when the garrison was cut back here. Now there's only me. And, frankly, my dear, I'm counting the days until those filthy Navajos are shipped off to the Oklahoma Territory so Mr. Marsden and I can leave, as well.''

''And when's that to happen?'' Miranda asked, her interest suddenly roused.

''Who knows?'' Violet shrugged daintily. ''The rumors have been flying for months, dear, ever since General Carleton left. No one believes it's possible to keep the Navajos here another season, not when their crops have failed three years' running. The poor wretches are starving here, and the Indian Bureau can't afford to keep feeding so many thousands of them! Something's got to change, and soon, or they'll all be dead!''

We take care of our own!

Ahkeah's defiant words echoed in Miranda's memory as she recalled his proud refusal to accept her cloak for his elderly aunt. What was it costing his pride to stand in line, as he was standing now, waiting with his people for his handout from the U.S. Government?

Miranda's gaze wandered down the wretched line of people. Many of the Navajos lacked coats or blankets to protect them from the biting desert wind. The children were thin and ragged, the old men and women little more than hollow-eyed human wrecks with barely enough strength to walk. The sight of them tore at her heart.

"What are you looking at, Miranda?" Violet's childlike voice broke into her thoughts. "Your father's over there, at the end of the table. Do you see him?"

"Yes." Miranda had already spotted Iron Bill, seated at the long plank table set up in front of the issue house. Behind him a platoon of blue-clad soldiers stood at rest, carbines ready in case trouble should break out and their commander gave the order to fire.

Other figures, as well, milled about the table. A bespectacled clerk was spreading pens, inkwells and a huge ledger in his allotted space. Navajo youths, pressed into service as helpers, scurried back and forth fetching chairs and supplies.

A cynical-looking man in a houndstooth check jacket stood to one side, scribbling with a pencil in an open notebook. Miranda had seen plenty of newspaper reporters during the war, and she bore them no liking. They were like hyenas, slinking along the sidelines of history, watching for the strong to fall so they could swarm in for the kill. What would a reporter be doing in a place like this? What was he waiting to see?

"We can sit just inside the door," Violet said. "That way we'll be out of the sun and wind. I'll have one of Mr. Marsden's assistants get us some chairs."

"Thank you." Miranda's awareness bristled as she followed the plump figure toward the door of the vast adobe building. Her decision to come here and watch the Navajos get their rations had been a reckless impulse. Now, too late, she realized she was guilty of the same insensitivity she had so long despised in others. She should never have come here. But trying to leave now would only make matters more awkward. She had little choice except to sit and watch the humiliation of a proud man and his people. Ahkeah would hate her for it, but that was his choice, something she could not change.

Feeling his gaze on her, she raised her chin and strode toward the open doorway of the issue house.

Ahkeah's eyes narrowed as he watched Big Hat's daughter cross the parade ground. He should have known she would come to watch—to see the grim spectacle of eight thousand people lined up for food. Well, let her watch! She was bored here, most likely, and this was the only entertainment in fifty miles!

He watched her follow the small, plump sparrow woman to the issue house and disappear inside. He hated ration days, hated the shame of seeing his people lined up like so many sheep, swallowing their pride for the sake of their children and old ones, who would starve without these weekly handouts from the government storehouse.

Most days the quantity of food they had was barely enough to keep a dog alive. That it be wholesome and appetizing as well was far too much to ask. Lately, more often than not, there was nothing but moldy flour, which the Diné had difficulty cooking because they had so little firewood. They had been given flour for the first time just before the start of the Long Walk. Never having seen it before, they had made it into gruel, like the familiar ground corn it resembled. The gluey mess, which they'd had no choice except to eat, had sickened them so severely with cramps and diarrhea that many had died or been shot by the soldiers because they were too sick to march.

Even now, the memory of those hellish days caused Ahkeah's jaw to tighten, triggering a throbbing pain in his injured temple. He would have been better off resting, he knew. But duty compelled him to be here.

Glancing toward the issue house, he saw that the two women had settled their chairs in the shadow of the doorway, where the desert sun would not burn their delicate skins. They were chatting animatedly, as if eager to watch the sad spectacle. His gaze lingered on the major's silver-eyed daughter, as prim as a preacher-lady in her dark dress and white lace collar. *Go ahead and watch,* bilagáana *woman,* he thought. *See us for what we are and for what your people have made us!*

He was still struggling with his anger when he felt a light tugging at his sleeve. Something tightened around his heart as he glanced down into the liquid eyes of his six-year-old daughter. She did not speak, but her small fingers crept into his palm, seeking reassurance.

"Nizhoni." He murmured her name as his hand tightened around hers. Nizhoni was too young to remember their life before the Long Walk; too young, even, to remember her mother's smile and the sound of her voice. This white man's purgatory was the only life that she, and so many other Diné children, knew.

What would Nizhoni's life be like if the Diné were sent to the Oklahoma reservation? Would she ever know the joy of standing between the four sacred mountains and watching the morning sunlight steal over the peach-colored walls of Canyon de Chelly? Would she celebrate the dawn of her womanhood by blessing her people as Changing Woman?

Or would she go to the white soldiers, as so many had done, and offer her young body in exchange for a meal and a warm bed?

Instinctively he drew his little girl closer, as if to shield her from sight. She was only six, little more than a baby. But the years would fly, and before he knew it she would be a beautiful young woman. How long would he be able to keep her safe?

"Ahkeah!" Someone near the front of the line had hailed him. Trouble already, and, as usual, he was being called upon to straighten it out. The new Navajo agent, Theodore Dodd, was the first decent administrator to serve at the fort, but Dodd was a white man and, for all his good intentions, he was no miracle worker. For the Diné, little had changed. The problems continued as always.

"Ahkeah!"

"Here." He thrust Nizhoni toward his aunt, then broke from the line and hurried forward.

Miranda edged her chair back into the shadows as Ahkeah strode toward the table. She had seen some kind of argument break out between the first Navajo in line and the small, efficient-looking man in civilian clothes who was seated at the table and appeared to be in charge. Clearly, there was a problem, but the two of them could not speak enough of each other's language to make themselves understood.

"The man at the table is Theodore Dodd, the new Indian agent," Violet whispered. "The Navajos call him Little Gopher. You can certainly see why, can't you?"

Miranda nodded, straining to hear what was going on at the table.

"They have their own names for many of us," Violet continued. "Your father is Big Hat. My husband is Lame Bear because he has a bad knee. Even I have a name. They call me Sparrow Woman."

Again Miranda nodded, her attention on the dispute. The elderly Navajo was arguing vehemently, pointing to the burlap sack into which one of the soldiers had just dumped a measure of flour from a large barrel. More than a hundred similar barrels were stacked outside the issue house. How many would it take to feed all these people, Miranda wondered, even for a few days?

"Blast it, I'm aware of the problem, but this is what they sent us! It's all we could get!" Dodd looked up in relief as Ahkeah broke through the crowd of Navajos and made his way to the table. "Tell him, Ahkeah. Tell them all! I've sent scores of wires to the bureau! They promised us beans and corn, but, blast them all to hell, this is what they sent!''

Dodd was interrupted by an outburst from the man with the sack, who then turned his outpouring of anger on Ahkeah. Ahkeah listened calmly, then turned back toward the agent. ''Are you aware that this flour is full of worms?'' he asked.

Dodd swore under his breath. ''It wouldn't make any difference if I had been aware. There's nothing I could have done. I'm sorry, Ahkeah, but your people will just have to clean the flour as best they can. Now tell your friend to take his family's share and move on.''

Ahkeah did not move. ''Do the soldiers at the fort have to pick the worms out of their flour?'' he demanded. ''Or do the *bilagáana* think themselves too fine to eat what they provide for us?''

Dodd looked pained. The Navajo who'd first complained turned around and began talking to others in the line. The soldiers behind the table shifted nervously, fingering their carbines.

Miranda felt her throat tighten in apprehension. Ahkeah, she knew, was using this incident to make a statement of pride. But pride would not feed eight thousand starving people. If the Navajos didn't accept the flour, they would go hungry. Was that what Ahkeah wanted? To trigger an incident for the benefit of that sleazy reporter—an incident that would call public attention to the plight of his people? Or was he merely a troublemaker, a reckless firebrand with more pride than common sense?

"You, Major." He wheeled suddenly to face Miranda's father. "You have a daughter. So do I. How can you ask me to feed my daughter what you would not feed your own?"

The silence that followed was broken only by the raucous call of a passing crow. Miranda saw Iron Bill's neck and ears redden, a sure sign of rising impatience.

"I asked you a question, Major." Ahkeah's voice was as flat and as cold as the blade of a knife. "I've met your daughter, and I know her to be a fine and proper lady. Would you expect her to eat bread made from this flour?"

Miranda could sense her father's anger welling. She could see it in the bristling eyebrows and in the clenched fist that rested on the table. She could feel her own tension building as she waited for the explosion...

The explosion that would be exactly what Ahkeah wanted.

"Why don't you ask *me* that question?" The words burst out as Miranda rose to her feet. All eyes were suddenly on her—Ahkeah's eyes, coldly challenging; her father's eyes, startled and outraged; the reporter's eyes, narrowing as he flipped to a fresh page in his notebook.

"Miss Howell?" Ahkeah's voice dripped ice.

"Ask *me* your question," she said. "I can answer for myself."

"As you like." His contemptuous gaze measured her, testing her mettle. "Would you eat *this?*" He filled a scoop from the open flour barrel and thrust it under her nose. Miranda fought the urge to recoil as the surface of the flour stirred slightly and a small, tan insect fluttered upward, past her face.

"If I were starving and there was nothing else, yes, I would eat this flour!" Miranda declared. "And if I had hungry children, yes, I would give it to them! I would give them anything to keep them alive!"

"Very passionately spoken." Ahkeah glanced at the circle of listeners, playing to them with the skill of a politician. "But you aren't starving, are you, Miss Howell? I saw you come directly here from the mess hall. Is *this* what you had for breakfast?"

"No." Miranda remembered the gluey, tasteless oatmeal. Ahkeah, she knew, was intent on using her. He would take advantage of her natural squeamishness to make fools of Agent Dodd, her father and the U.S. Government. There was just one way to stop him—a way that lay before her now in a scoopful of weevil-infested flour.

Swallowing hard, she forced herself to meet his cold eyes. "If I show you that I'm not too proud to eat this flour, will that satisfy you, Ahkeah? Will you then be still and allow your people to get their rations without shame?"

A spark flickered in the depths of Ahkeah's obsidian eyes, but his face remained as impassive as granite. "You, a *bilagáana,* would dare such a thing?"

Without answering him she turned to one of the soldiers. "Take a cup of this flour to the kitchen and ask the cook to make one flapjack—"

"No," Ahkeah interrupted sharply. "We will do the cooking right here, where all the people can see." Turning to the openmouthed private, he ordered firewood, an iron skillet, salt, baking powder, a spoon and a measure of lard. Spurred by the authority in his voice, the young soldier scurried to do his bidding.

Miranda glanced toward her father. Iron Bill's rigid face was flushed like an overheated stove. His lips were pressed tightly together as if to hold back an outburst of ill-timed rage. He would not be so foolish as to speak out, nor would Agent Dodd, who was staring at Miranda as if she'd just sprouted wings and a tail. The news reporter was waiting, pencil poised to scribble down every reckless word, giving Ahkeah just the ammunition he needed for his publicized incident—an incident that would cause a whole nation of men, women and children to go hungry for the sake of pride.

By the time the ingredients and utensils arrived from the kitchen, Ahkeah had started a small, crackling fire in a shallow pit. Miranda watched in grim silence as he measured the flour, salt and baking powder into the bowl. She had hoped he would take time to sift the weevils out of the flour, but she should have known better. He would not make this easy for her.

Glancing up, he added a splash of water and a scoop of lard and began to knead the fist-size mass with his fingers. "This is how we make our bread," he said. "With no yeast and no ovens. If the flour is fresh it isn't so bad. But with this…"

Letting the words trail off, he dropped the rest of the lard into the skillet. As it melted, he made a flat circle of the dough, as broad as his hand was long, and dropped it into the sizzling fat.

"Don't worry about the worms, Miss Howell," he said, "the heat will kill anything living in that flour. Besides, you look as if you could use a little meat in your diet."

The flat bread browned swiftly. Ahkeah turned it with his knife, then used the point to lift it free and hold it in the cool air for a moment.

"Here you are." He thrust the bread toward Miranda with a mocking flourish.

Miranda accepted it gingerly between her fingertips. The fried bread was hot, but not hot enough to burn. She forced her eyes to blur so she would not have to look at it too closely. It would not be so bad, she reassured herself. She had surely done more distasteful things than this in her lifetime. And if she felt anything crunch between her teeth she would simply pretend it was a nut or a raisin.

Struggling to appear nonchalant, she sank her teeth into the warm, crisp dough. Every eye was on her as she moved her jaws in a semblance of chewing, then swallowed the small wad of dough in a single gulp.

"All of it," Ahkeah growled, close to her ear. "You're to eat every last crumb."

Miranda tore off another small bite, meeting his gaze as she forced herself to swallow. His eyes held hers so intently that she could see her own reflection in the depths of his jet-black pupils. She could un-

derstand now why her father hated this man and why
the soldier had been on the verge of shooting him last
night.

Now he was waiting for her to slip—to gag, to
choke or to fling the bread to the ground in disgust.
But no, she would not let him win. Pride was one
thing. Letting children go hungry was quite another.

Bit by bit she finished the bread, swallowing each
piece as an act of sheer will. She avoided biting down
or even touching the dough with her tongue. If she
were to find a weevil in her mouth, her hard-won
control would be lost. Ahkeah watched her every
move, his eyes smoldering, his mouth twisted in a
thin, humorless smile.

A gasp of relief broke over the assembly as the last
bit of bread disappeared into her mouth. Miranda
forced it down her convulsing throat. Done.

Flashing Ahkeah a defiant look, she glanced around
frantically for water. It was Ahkeah himself who
passed her a canteen. ''Right from the Pecos River,''
he murmured. ''Just like the water we drink. Well
done, Miss Howell. You've proved your point.''

He jerked his head in an affirming nod, and the
Navajos at the front of the line spread out along the
stations at the table, sacks open to receive their ration
of tainted flour. Miranda gulped the brackish water,
her stomach churning as people milled around her.
Had she done the right thing, or should she have allowed a stubborn man his pride? Never mind, what
was done was done. And suddenly she wanted noth-

ing more than to get as far as she could from this
miserable place.

"Miss Howell?" The reporter shouldered his way
into her path as she turned to leave. His eyes were a
watery blue, and a splintered hickory toothpick jutted
from between his thin lips. "My name is Hyrum
Blount, Miss Howell. Your quick action prevented an
incident that could have turned very ugly. What do
you have to say to readers of the *Denver Post?*"

Bile rose in Miranda's throat as she turned on him.
"Are you disappointed, Mr. Blount?" she flared.
"Would you rather have seen a hunger strike, or better yet, a bloodbath? Would that have made a more
sensational story to wire home to your paper?"

The reporter's startled face blurred in Miranda's
vision as she felt the greasy bread and alkaline water
welling up into her throat.

"Miss Howell, are you all right?"

Shoving the man aside, she stumbled around the
end of the table and bolted for the back side of the
issue house.

A ghost of a smile teased Ahkeah's lips as he
watched her go. It did not surprise him that Miranda
Howell was sick. But his amazement at her boldness
and tenacity warmed to a grudging admiration. For a
bilagáana, the woman had courage.

Would he have pushed a confrontation over the
flour if she had not come forward? He shrugged—a
white man's gesture that he had never quite managed
to lose. His people had eaten far worse than infested

flour in their four years at the fort. Perhaps it was just as well that nothing more had happened. At least their bellies would not be empty this week.

He stood at the corner of the long table, aching as his gaze wandered down the long, sad lines of his people. Even the great warriors, Manuelito and Barboncito, were here. They had surrendered with their starved little bands only a few moons after the main body of the Diné had reached the fort. Now they stood gripping their ration sacks with the others, the cold spring wind whipping their threadbare clothes against their bones.

On ration day, all the Diné at the fort were required to come in and be counted, to make sure none had slipped away. Not that the bureau had any reason to worry. Of the few families who'd attempted to leave, all had either returned, starving, on their own or been hauled back on a wagon bed, their frozen bodies stacked like cordwood.

Would life be like this in the Oklahoma Territories, or would conditions be even worse? The only thing the Diné knew for certain was that they would be even farther from their four sacred mountains—so far that the Holy People would never bless them again.

Shaking off his gloom, Ahkeah scanned the line for his own small family. He glimpsed his aunt, standing where he'd left her, bundled in the woolen poncho he'd placed around her shoulders the night before. She looked lost and weary. Maybe it was time he found someone else to help care for Nizhoni. The old woman was growing too frail to keep up with an active little girl.

Glancing around, he concluded that there would be no more trouble with the rationing. The major's strong-willed daughter had seen to that. It would be safe to relieve the old woman of Nizhoni and walk the little girl around the fort. She loved seeing the horses in their corrals and the colorful American flag fluttering from its pole on the parade ground. There was so little color in her own drab life—no blooming wildflowers against warm russet sand, no flash of silver jewelry, no bright ribbons in her long black hair. He had no heart to deny his child the little pleasure she found in this dismal place.

Pushing other concerns aside, Ahkeah shouldered his way through the milling crowd toward the place where his aunt stood. Nizhoni would be close by, probably clinging to the trailing poncho. Like most Diné children his daughter tended to be shy in the presence of strangers. He'd never had to worry about her wandering off on her own.

All the same, a shadow of foreboding crossed his mind as he approached his aunt. She was huddled in the line, her wizened face staring straight ahead, eyes focused on some inner vision that only she could see. This trancelike state seemed to be coming upon her more and more of late.

No, he acknowledged sadly, he could not trust her to care for Nizhoni any longer. It was time he took someone else into his household—perhaps his recently widowed cousin Naahooyéí, and her two young sons. They could use his protection, and he could use their help. He would begin digging another dugout for them as soon as—

Ahkeah's thoughts scattered as the line shifted, suddenly giving him full view of his aunt, from her scraggly head to the worn remnants of her dusty moccasins. Only then did the realization hit him like a blow—the old woman stood alone, her hands dangling listlessly at her sides.

Nizhoni was nowhere to be seen.

Chapter Five

White-faced and quivering, Miranda pressed her forehead against the cold adobe wall. The fried bread had come up so fast that she'd barely made it around the back of the commissary before the retching heaves had struck. Now the worst of the nausea had passed, but she still felt weak and shaky. Never again, she vowed, gagging on the vile aftertaste; not for any cause on earth would she let herself be bullied into eating such revolting food!

The brackish water in the canteen Ahkeah had passed her had only made matters worse. Straight from the Pecos, he'd said. Good heavens, was that all the Navajos had to drink? Had he offered it to prove yet another of his wretched points? Oh, what she wanted to say to that arrogant, insufferable—

Her thoughts scattered as she felt a light tug at her skirt. She was too dizzy to look around, but her heart lurched with dismay. She had hoped, at least, to be alone in her disgrace. Maybe if she paid no attention, whoever it was would go away.

But no—at a second, more demanding tug, Miranda swallowed her nausea and turned her head. She found herself looking down into a pair of luminous black eyes, framed with long silken lashes and set in an exquisite little pansy face.

Complaints forgotten, Miranda dropped to a crouch. The tiny Navajo girl was clad in a threadbare woolen shift, a miniature version of the garment the old squaw had worn last night. A faded poncho, cut from the corner of a worn blanket, hung loosely over her shoulders, its fabric far too thin to keep out the biting wind. Her dusty little feet were clad in moccasins that looked as if they'd been painstakingly pieced from the remnants of a larger pair.

"Well, now," Miranda said, trying not to frighten her. "Where on earth did you come from?"

The Navajo child only stared, eyes wide, lips softly parted. Her long hair was sloppily braided and her face was none too clean, but nothing could mask the little girl's heart-melting beauty.

"It's all right," Miranda whispered, hoping the tone of her voice would convey what words could not. "You needn't be afraid of me. I won't hurt you."

The dark eyes narrowed thoughtfully. One chapped hand reached up to brush a damp spot on Miranda's cheek as the child spoke in a questioning voice, her language like the piping call of a desert wren.

"I'm all right," Miranda replied, guessing at the meaning of the words. "But somebody must be looking for you. We need to go back around the building and find your mother."

The little girl did not move. Her gaze dropped shyly to Miranda's cashmere shawl. Slowly and carefully one small hand reached out and brushed the creamy knit fabric. Her eyes widened as she stroked it, fingering the lushness of the costly imported wool.

Pity tugged at Miranda's heart. A child of this age would remember almost nothing of her life before the Long Walk. This dreary place would be her whole world—a world with no beauty, no warmth, no pleasure.

Impulsively she slipped the beautiful shawl off her own shoulders and wrapped it around the little girl. A quiver passed through the tiny body. Then, as she snuggled into the soft warmth, her little flower face broke into a smile of pure delight.

Miranda found herself smiling back. Ahkeah would disapprove, she knew. Well, let him! The man did not own her, nor did he own this precious little girl! Who was he to tell her she could not give a present to a needy child?

We take care of our own. Once again his angry words echoed in her mind. No, Ahkeah, she thought, your people *can't* take care of their own. Not under such miserable conditions. The Navajos need more help, and the only thing keeping it from them is the ridiculous pride of men like you!

Rising, she held out her hand. Wary as a fawn, the little girl hesitated. Then the frigid, trembling little fingers crept into Miranda's palm. Miranda's throat tightened as she made a warm cocoon around them. "Come on," she said, punctuating the words with a smile and a gentle tug. "We need to go and find your mother."

She had been looking down at the little girl as she spoke. Only when she straightened and began to walk did she see the rangy figure rounding the far corner of the commissary. A lump of dismay congealed around her heart as she recognized Ahkeah.

His body stiffened as he caught sight of her with the little girl. She squared her chin in response, bracing for a confrontation as he approached. No, Miranda resolved, she would not let this man intimidate her. Not this time.

Like two opposing armies, they closed. Miranda was dimly aware of the child pulling eagerly at her hand, drawing her forward into the fray.

Ahkeah's face was a thundercloud. The ends of his crimson head cloth fluttered like battle flags in the morning breeze as he glared down at her.

"What," he demanded roughly, "are you doing with my daughter?"

Miranda felt her heart drop into the pit of her queasy stomach. Her throat went dry as she groped for something to say. Not in a million years would she have guessed that this beautiful child would be *his*.

"I'm taking your daughter back where she belongs," she declared, finding her voice. "To her mother!"

Something flickered in Ahkeah's hard, black eyes. Then he glanced away, his gaze coming to rest on the cashmere shawl that swathed the child's thin shoulders.

"What's this?" he growled, glaring at Miranda. "Didn't I make myself clear last night? We don't want your charity!"

"She was shivering," Miranda said, meeting his angry gaze. "The wind was blowing right through her clothes. Would you let your child suffer from cold for the sake of your pride, Ahkeah?"

A muscle twitched in his cheek, and Miranda sensed she had wounded him—as she had meant to wound him. She allowed time for the sting to penetrate, her palm still enfolding the cold little hand of Ahkeah's daughter. Where was his wife? she wondered. Probably waiting in line with the others for her ration of weevil-infested flour—a woman as beautiful as the child she had given this proud man. No wonder Ahkeah had never stopped fighting for them.

Seconds passed before he spoke into the strained silence. "If you were to give equally fine gifts to all the children of the Diné, then perhaps it would be allowed. But how can I let her have what others do not? It would set her apart from her people and lead to bad things—perhaps, one day, even the kinds of things that are happening to our young women. I know you mean well, Miss Howell, but don't spoil our children and old ones. Don't teach them to be envious or entice them to become beggars!"

Without waiting for Miranda to respond, he bent to a crouch, so his eyes were on a level with his daughter's. When he spoke to her in Navajo his voice was low and gentle. Her eyes grew large as she listened.

For a moment she hesitated. Then, her hand slipping free, she unwound the precious shawl from her shoulders and thrust it up at Miranda. When she spoke it was in Navajo, the words like the speech of a little windup doll.

"Nizhoni thanks you for your kindness but she cannot accept your gift," Ahkeah translated. "She asks you to please take it back."

Miranda looked down at the little girl, her heart contracting as she caught the glimmer of a tear in the luminous black eyes. "Can't your daughter speak for herself?" she demanded, glaring at Ahkeah. "Surely you've taught her a few words of English, since you speak it so well yourself."

"Nizhoni speaks no English," Ahkeah said curtly. "And I do not plan to teach her."

Miranda gaped at him, making no effort to hide her outrage. "But that's foolish!" she declared. "Your daughter strikes me as a very bright little girl! She could go to school and make something of herself— become a teacher, perhaps, or even a doctor. Think, Ahkeah, what she could do for her people with a proper education—"

"Nizhoni will have a proper education." Ahkeah cut her off coldly. "She will have the education of a Diné woman."

"A Diné woman, indeed!" Miranda retorted, her patience snapping. "I see your Diné women! I see them waiting in that wretched line, cold and dirty and ragged, with no way to lift themselves out of their misery! Is that what you want for your daughter—to have no better life than her mother out there—''

''You know nothing!'' Ahkeah snatched the cashmere shawl from the little girl's hands and flung it at Miranda's chest. ''Nizhoni's mother died on the Long Walk. She was beautiful and wise and full of courage—everything I would wish our daughter to be! All that without your white man's education!''

The silence that followed his words was as deafening as the rumble of an earthquake. Miranda was dimly aware of the wind flapping the folds of the half-frozen flag on the parade ground and, muted by distance, the cacophony of crows settling on an empty field. Nizhoni had retreated to the safety of her father's side. She clung to his leg, her eyes wide and tremulous.

''I—I'm sorry,'' Miranda blurted, finding her voice at last. ''Truly, I didn't know.''

''There's a great deal you don't know about us, Miss Howell.'' Ahkeah's voice was like granite, flat and hard. ''You know nothing about the things we value, nothing about the things we honor and respect. What you see in this place—the ration lines, the rags, the sickness—this is not who we are. It is only an illusion, a mirror that reflects the injustice of your people. Look into it—you will see only your own white face!''

''But even here there are opportunities!'' Miranda had recovered and was on the attack again, striking out with the zeal of a missionary. ''Don't you see?

The world is changing. If your people don't change with it by learning civilized ways, they'll never survive.''

Ahkeah shook his head, the ends of his crimson head cloth blowing across his stormy bronze face. ''No—you could not be more wrong. Only by remaining true to our own beliefs will the Diné survive as a people. Take those away and we will have nothing. We will vanish like rain into the desert sand.''

''I don't understand you at all!'' Miranda flung the words into the wind.

''At least we agree on something.'' Ahkeah's voice was thin with sarcasm. His eyes glittered like flints.

Goaded to fury by his manner, Miranda clenched her quivering fists. Only Nizhoni's small, shy presence kept her from recklessly striking him. ''You,'' she said, flinging the words like a gauntlet, ''are the most unreasonable human being I have ever met!''

''And you,'' Ahkeah replied in a voice as soft and frigid as winter snow, ''are nothing but a misguided, meddling woman who needs a lesson in minding her own business.''

Dizzy with outrage, Miranda stood her ground. Her eyes stung with the bitter salt of unshed tears. She had only meant to help, but this man—this *Indian*—had cut her down, humiliating her with his haughty manner and making her look like a fool!

And the worst of it was, she was right and he was wrong.

Struggling to ignore her queasy stomach, she glared

up at him. "You..." she sputtered, groping for the precise words. "You arrogant, mule-headed—"

"Oh, there you are, dear!" Violet's voice floated on the wind as her squat figure, ruffles aflutter, came bustling around the far corner of the building. "Are you all right, Miranda? Your father was worried when you didn't come back after eating that filthy Indian bread. He asked me to..."

Her words trailed off as Ahkeah turned his head and she finally noticed him. "Oh, my dear girl!" she exclaimed. "Has this vile creature harmed you?"

"Miss Howell is quite safe. We were just about to leave." Ahkeah reached down, lifted his daughter in his arms and settled her against his shoulder. Turning to go, he swung his head back toward Miranda. His gaze lanced her like a shaft of ice. "You ask why I refuse to let Nizhoni learn English. Ask yourself this, Miss Howell. Why should I want her to understand words like the ones your friend just spoke?"

Without waiting for a reply, he turned and strode away, his daughter's small brown hands clinging to the back of his neck.

Miranda stared after them, the cashmere shawl dangling from her fingers, as Violet fluttered toward her.

"Oh, my dear, thank heaven I came looking for you when I did! The very thought of you back here with *that man*..." She left the sentence unfinished, as if the implications were too dire to be spoken aloud. "You must be more careful of your reputation, Miranda. To be alone with such a person—"

"We weren't alone." Miranda flung the shawl impatiently around her shoulders. "His little girl was here. You saw her."

"His little girl, indeed!" Violet dabbed at her moist nose with a tiny lace handkerchief. "You can't be so naive as to think he wouldn't take advantage of you with a child present! Why, those savages live all in one room, just like the slaves on my daddy's plantation—men, women and children all together, with no privacy at all! If a man wants a woman, he just takes her right there in front of the whole family! It's no wonder their girls grow up to be little more than prostitutes, creeping into the barracks at night—"

"Really, now, Violet!" Miranda took the woman's arm, steering her back toward the crowd at the front of the commissary. Violet Marsden was her only friend in this place, she reminded herself. Even so, she had no wish to continue this unsettling line of conversation.

"Instead of finding fault with these poor people, we should be doing something to help them," Miranda said. "If the Navajo children were properly educated, they could grow up to lift their people out of this morass. The terrible conditions we see here would be nothing but a memory."

"Educated?" Violet's rosebud nose twitched imperiously. "Voicing such high-minded ideas is one thing, Miranda. Putting them into practice is quite another. These people have no classrooms and no teachers. And even if they did, they're far too lazy to bring their children to school, let alone allow them to learn anything outside of their own dark superstitions!"

"How do you know that?" Miranda asked, her pulse leaping, as it was wont to do when a new idea struck her. "Has anyone ever tried starting a school here at the fort?"

Violet sidestepped a thawing puddle, lifting her skirts above the mud and mincing like a cat with damp feet. "Of course not! If you'd lived around Navajos as long as I have, you'd know better than to ask such a question! It would never work!"

"But why not?" Miranda caught the woman's sleeve, stopping her before she could move around the corner of the building and rejoin the noisy, milling crowd. "Why not, Violet? With so many officers leaving the fort, there must be some space available for a classroom. And as for a teacher—"

"Good heavens, don't look at me!" Violet sputtered. "I'm no schoolmarm! And even if I were, I wouldn't stay in this godforsaken spot a day longer than Mr. Marsden's duty required! In any case, the Navajos themselves won't be here much longer. The Indian Bureau plans to ship them off to Oklahoma as soon as the weather's warm enough for them to travel."

"But there's so much that children can learn, even in a few weeks," Miranda argued, flushed with excitement. "The beginnings of English! Hygiene! Arithmetic! Geography! Why, if I delayed my return to the East, I could teach them myself!"

"But, my dear girl, you're planning your wedding! You're getting married!"

''Not until June—and most of the planning's done, even my gown! There's plenty of time!''

''Don't even think about it!'' Violet seized Miranda's elbow and steered her firmly toward the crowd at the front of the building. ''You'll exhaust your strength and break your heart, my dear. And all of it for nothing!''

''But if I could light the mind of even one child…'' Miranda thought of Nizhoni, with her little flower face and bright, eager gaze. Ahkeah had said that if she, Miranda Howell, could present a gift equally, to all the Navajo children, it might not be refused. Dear heaven, what if she were to actually offer such a gift?

''That revolting Indian bread has addled your mind,'' Violet huffed, dragging Miranda toward the two empty chairs they'd left in the shelter of the doorway. ''Sit down. Give yourself time to come to your senses!''

Miranda settled onto the rigid wooden seat, her mind racing. Could she really do it—kindle the spark that would light the path out of darkness for this suffering nation?

Her gaze wandered down the long line of human misery. Ahkeah's proud figure was missing, but she could see his elderly aunt, old Sally, shuffling forward in the line, clutching her empty flour sack. And there were others, so many others, with ragged clothes, jutting bones and vacant eyes. What had they seen? What had they lost?

Even the children did not tease and play as white children might. They clung to their elders in silence, their dark eyes taking in everything around them. What would happen' to these children if their young intellects were never awakened? What would happen to this people?

Violet was chattering away, some long, involved story about a Creole woman who had lived at the fort. Miranda scarcely heard her. She was gazing at the line, her eyes picking out one child, then another and another—here a small boy, there a baby in its cradle-board, each one more beautiful and more needy than the last. So many children.

What would happen if no one cared enough to help them?

Ahkeah balanced his daughter on the corral fence, relishing her excitement at the sight of so many sleek, well-fed horses. The few mounts the Diné had managed to keep alive were little more than skin and bones, with scarcely enough energy to lift their pitiful heads. But these…yes, these were horses!

Such animals reminded him of the old days, the good days, when a man could straddle a mount and ride like the wind across Dinétah, the land between the four sacred mountains. He ached now for the feel of it—the wind sweeping through his hair, the surge of the horse's powerful body between his legs, the beauty of sun-burnished mesas and clear turquoise skies.

Major Howell's meddlesome daughter would never understand such freedom, he mused, his thoughts lingering on the image of her storm-colored eyes and square-jawed face. Like so many of her kind, she was bound on all sides, as much by her misguided sense of Christian duty as by her rigid clothing and tightly pinned hair.

How would it feel to loosen that hair? he wondered idly. How would it feel to slip the tortoiseshell combs from that tawny brown mass and let it tumble like water over his hands as he filled his senses with its warm lilac aroma? How would it feel to brush it aside and, with his fingertips, touch the creamy skin at the nape of her neck?

But what was he thinking? He had never touched a *bilagáana,* or even wanted to. In their own way, such women were even worse than their menfolk— shrill, overbearing and quick to judge. Ahkeah had never met a *bilagáana* woman he liked, let alone desired.

Miranda, the sparrow woman had called her.
Miranda…

"Look, Father," Nizhoni piped, pointing excitedly. "That yellow horse—the white mark on its face looks like a half-moon! And look at that spotted horse, the one with white feet! Which one would you ride if they let you choose?"

Ahkeah's arm squeezed her waist. "I would let *you* choose, small one. Which horse do you like best?"

She frowned, her brows knitting pensively. "That white…no, that one over there! The black one! It looks strong and swift. We could jump on its back and ride all the way to Dinétah!"

"And what would we do in Dinétah?" he asked,

knowing these dreams of her homeland might be all she would ever have.

"We would build a hogan with the door facing east to meet the rising sun," she said, her voice like a little silver bell. "And we would live as the Holy People taught us to live."

"And that is?" Ahkeah prompted her gently.

"With respect for the land and all who live on it." She glanced up, seeking and receiving her father's approving smile. "Why were you angry with the *bilagáana* woman?"

"I was not angry with her," Ahkeah replied, speaking perhaps too quickly.

"You sounded angry."

"I only wanted her to understand that she must not give you what other little girls could not have." He paused, sensing unspoken questions. "Did you like the shawl?"

"It was pretty. So soft. So warm."

"But you gave it back willingly. I was proud of you, Nizhoni."

"No," she corrected him. "I did not give the shawl back, Father. I held it out, but the woman only took it when you threw it at her. You *were* angry. I could tell."

"My anger was wrong. If I wish to teach you patience, then I must show patience, even with the *bilagáana.*"

"Did you think she was beautiful, Father?"

Beautiful? Ahkeah's heart seemed to stop.

"That is not for me to say," he answered, forcing

the words. "Beauty dwells inside a person, not out-side, for people to see."

"She gave me her shawl because I was cold. I be-lieve she was beautiful inside and outside." Nizhoni's small, clear voice carried a note of finality.

"As you say—" Ahkeah broke off as he glimpsed movement out of the corner of his eye. Glancing around, he saw a uniformed soldier striding toward them, brandishing a heavy-caliber rifle. Ordinarily, Ahkeah would not have been concerned by such an approach. He was well-known on the post and, while few people liked him, no one had found reason to stop him from going where he wished.

But this man, Sergeant Jethro McCree, was a trou-blemaker and an avowed Indian hater. Ahkeah's arm tightened around his daughter as the sergeant strode closer.

"Touch one o' them horses, you thievin' redskin, and I'll blow you to kingdom come!" he growled, cocking the rifle. "Go on! Try somethin'! I'd truly enjoy riddin' the world of one more Navajo bastard!"

"You know better than that, McCree," Ahkeah said guardedly. "I'm unarmed and no threat to any-one here. And even if I were reckless enough to take one of your horses, I wouldn't do it in broad daylight under the eyes of the sentries."

Nizhoni had turned around to look at the squat, pugnacious figure. McCree's bulldog face widened in a malicious grin as he noticed the child's interest.

"Say, now, that's a right purty young-un. Hope I'm still ready an' able by the time she's old enough to come scratchin' 'round the barracks and crawl into my bed.'' He gave a low whistle. ''Yessiree Bob! She'll be a hot tamale, that one!''

The rage that exploded upward from Ahkeah's chest was so intense it made his vision swim. He knew the sergeant was deliberately baiting him, goading him to attack so he could have an excuse to fire the rifle. That, or he was planning to call in his cronies, who would be happy to stomp an unarmed Navajo into the mud or slam him in the stockade. Even so, it was all Ahkeah could do to keep from leaping on the man and pounding his face to a bloody pulp. Only the thought of what might happen to Nizhoni without him kept his fury under control.

Bells of pain rang in his injured head as he willed his face to become an impassive granite mask. Moving cautiously, he lifted his daughter off the fence, turned a disdainful back on his tormentor and strode off toward the main gate.

''Come back here, you sneakin' redskin coward!'' McCree's hooting laughter rang out behind him. ''Come back an' face me like a man if'n you got the guts for it!''

Ahkeah kept walking, praying with each step the sergeant would not shoot. There would be no flour ration for him today. Much as his family could use it, he could not bear the humiliation of standing in line under the contemptuous gaze of the soldiers—or even worse, the pitying silver eyes of Miranda Howell.

"Father..." Nizhoni tugged at his ear, then pointed. "Over there! The line is that way!"

"I know." His arms tightened protectively around her. "No line for us, small one. Not today."

Chapter Six

Miranda faced her father across the table in the dimly lit mess hall. The hour was so late that the other diners had long since finished their meals. But she had waited there for him, reminding herself that Iron Bill could not avoid her forever. Sooner or later he would have to come in and eat.

Her own supper sat cold before her, the fat-coated mutton chop, greasy fried potatoes and baked Mexican beans congealing in the lamplight. Miranda had long since abandoned any thought of eating. She had far more urgent matters on her mind.

"How do you know that a school won't work if no one's ever tried it?" she persisted. "All I'm asking for is a chance!"

The major's jaw worked as he chewed the tough, overcooked mutton. His salt-and-pepper eyebrows bristled as they met in a scowl above the bridge of his jutting Roman nose. For much of the meal, the conversation between father and daughter had been strained and stilted, confined to trivialities between bites of food. Only when Miranda broached the subject of a school had he shown any degree of emotion.

"Hell's bells, girl, didn't your mother raise you with a lick of sense?" he rumbled, swallowing the last of the mutton. "First you make a spectacle of yourself by eating that wormy flour, and now this!"

"You didn't answer my question." Miranda fixed him with a level gaze, forcing herself to speak calmly and clearly. "How do you know that starting a school for the Navajo children wouldn't work?"

Iron Bill gulped the last of his coffee and slammed the empty mug onto the table. "First off, they wouldn't come. Why should they? If you've talked to that hothead, Ahkeah, you know how they feel about having their children learn white men's ways—"

"But that has to change!" Miranda interrupted. "Their old life is finished! If they don't learn English and adopt civilized ways, they'll be as badly off in Oklahoma as they are here! And when those children grow up, they won't have a chance in this world!" She shoved her plate to one side and leaned across the table, meeting the storm-colored eyes that were so like her own. "What if we were to offer them something they needed—like food? A good healthy meal for every child who comes to school. What parents would refuse that for their little ones?"

Iron Bill leaned back in his chair. "Strikes me as a mite like baitin' skunks," he drawled. "And where would you get the food? Are you looking to see it fall out of the sky like manna?"

"There's plenty of canned and dried food in the army storehouse, more than enough to feed your troops and a handful of Navajo children. We could—"

"Now, wait just a blessed minute!" he snapped, cutting her off. "Those Navajos are no longer the responsibility of the U.S. Army! If you want to feed them, go talk to Theodore Dodd!"

"You know Mr. Dodd's position even better than I do," Miranda said, refusing to budge. "His resources are stretched to the limit. But as for the army stores, Mr. Marsden himself told me that once the Navajos are gone and the garrison is reduced, most of the food will have to be hauled out on wagons. Why not use it now and save the expense?"

All of what she had just told him was true. Miranda had spent much of the past two days working out a plan, checking on resources and talking with people who might be able to help. Agent Dodd, harried to distraction by more pressing concerns, had given her permission to do anything she pleased as long as she stayed out of his way. But even with that obstacle removed, she knew she would have to depend on the army for food and classroom quarters—and that meant persuading Major Iron Bill Howell himself.

"Please," she said. "Is it so much to ask?"

Her father's gaze narrowed, deepening the leathery furrows at the corners of his eyes. He looked odd without his hat, the skin on his balding pate stark white above his sunburned face. The contrast made him appear strangely vulnerable, almost childlike. How old was he? Fifty-five? Sixty? Miranda suddenly realized she did not know.

From the kitchen she could hear the faint clatter of dishes and the sound of rough laughter. A silent eternity seemed to pass before he shifted in his chair and slowly shook his head.

"Go home, Miranda. Marry your young man. Have a family, a fine house, all the things you deserve. Forget this crazy scheme of yours. Forget these miserable people and this crusty old soldier who doesn't need you here, messing in his business!"

She stared at him as if he had dashed hot coffee in her face. "Father—"

"I mean it," he said. "I was never much of a father to you, girl, and you can't change that—not any more than you can change the condition of those poor Navajo devils out there. There's no point in your staying the full two weeks when I can arrange an escort back to Santa Fe tomorrow."

"But I don't understand…" Miranda's balled hands pressed hard into her lap, fingers cold and trembling. "I came all this way just to be with you—"

"If I'd gotten your letter in time to reply, I'd have told you not to come," he said. "As it was, I barely had time to send a detail to meet you in Santa Fe. There's nothing for you here, Miranda." His features contracted sharply. For the space of a breath, he gazed down at his empty plate. The face he raised to her looked pale and strained. "No amount of good intent can make stew out of rocks and horse manure, girl. I don't want you here. I can't say as I ever—''

His body crumpled in the chair as he doubled over, his right hand clawing at his chest, his features contorted with pain.

Miranda was already out of her chair, lunging around the table to seize his shoulders. "What is it?" she demanded, her mind rifling wildly through the things she knew about heart failure and apoplexy.

"It's—nothing." Iron Bill spoke through clenched teeth. Drops of sweat beaded his forehead, catching glints of amber light from the lamp overhead. "Help me stand," he rasped. "Quickly—before somebody comes in!"

"Are you mad?" Miranda struggled to drag him to the floor. "You need to lie down while I go for help! Is there a doctor on the post?"

"No, damn it!" He fought her efforts, staggering to his feet by sheer willpower. "Help me back to my quarters—there's medicine there. Do it!" he snapped when she hesitated. "Don't you understand? If anybody sees me like this, I'm finished!"

Miranda worked herself beneath his arm so she could lift against his body, supporting him as they made their way toward the door.

"Tell me what's wrong," she insisted. "Is it your heart? Your stomach?"

"That's none of your blasted business!"

"Have you seen a doctor?"

"What for?" He stiffened against her as a fresh jolt of agony shot through him. "Damned quacks with their prodding and poking—got no use for 'em! Just get me my medicine, and I'll be—right as rain!''

They crossed the parade ground, where sentries walked their posts in the lamplit darkness. Iron Bill held himself painfully erect, his body taut with the effort. Miranda strained against his weight, aiding, for now, in the deception her father was so desperate to maintain. She understood that he was hiding his illness to save what remained of his army career. But she could not allow the pretense to continue. He needed good medical care, but where could he get it in such a place? Aside from a small infirmary, there was only the crude Navajo hospital, which was dark, cramped and not much bigger than a shed.

They reached the door of his quarters and staggered across the threshold. Miranda closed the door behind him, and would have helped her father to his bed, but he stopped beside the plain wooden rocker that faced the potbellied stove. ''Here,'' he grunted. ''I'll sit here. You get my—medicine...''

Grimacing, he lowered himself into the chair. His hands gripped the armrests, his fingertips whitening from the pressure.

''Where is it?'' She glanced urgently around the room.

''Top drawer—my dresser...'' He jerked at the tight collar of his military tunic. One brass button popped loose and clattered to the floor as Miranda raced for the bedroom.

She had no trouble finding the brown-tinted pint bottle, half filled with a dark, syrupy liquid. As she snatched it up, she caught sight of the label and her heart sank.

Dr. Hagopian's Pain Elixer, the gaudy gold lettering proclaimed. Dear heaven, it was nothing but cheap patent medicine—molasses or corn syrup laced with alcohol, bitters and probably enough laudanum to stun a full-grown mule. Miranda battled the urge to fling the bottle and shatter it against the wall. Her father was in terrible pain, she reminded herself, and there was no other remedy at hand.

Heavyhearted, she walked back into the parlor. Judging from the level of liquid in the bottle, her father's body had at least developed a tolerance for the vile stuff. But in the long run it would only do him harm.

When Iron Bill's eyes fell on the medicine, he reached out and snatched the bottle from her hand. Twisting off the cap with desperate haste, he tipped the opening to his lips and took a single long, hard gulp.

Lowering the bottle, he slumped in the chair. His eyelids jerked slightly as the drug began to work against the pain. Miranda reached down, lifted the medicine from his clasp, replaced the lid and set it on the cabinet.

"What you're taking is no better than poison," she said. "You need to see a doctor."

"No!" His head wobbled on his neck. "No doctor. Can't let...anybody know. They'll send me away... ship me off to some damned hospital...."

"But you need good care," she argued. "You'll die if you stay here!"

"Better here, in the saddle, than tied to a stinking bedpan in some louse-ridden old soldiers' home!" His hand caught hers in a bone-crushing clasp. "Promise me you won't tell—not a word—"

"But you could be dying. If treatment could save your life—"

"No!" His grip tightened. "The army is my life. Take that away from me and I might as well be dead." His storm-gray eyes drilled into hers, the pupils already dilating from the effects of the drug. "If you have a drop of human kindness in your heart, Miranda, promise me you won't say anything. Promise…!"

Miranda gazed at him, struggling to keep an emotional distance. Was this the reason he had avoided her, the reason he had urged her to leave? Or had he spoken the truth when he'd said he simply didn't care for her?

"Can you make it to bed?" she asked.

He kept his grip on her hand. "Promise!" he rasped. "Promise me before I go."

Miranda sighed. "Very well. For now."

Releasing her hand, he shifted forward in his chair. Miranda reached down to help him, but he ignored her proffered hands and, cursing softly, rose to his feet. She held her breath as he staggered into his room and closed the door behind him. A moment later she heard the double thud of his boots hitting the floor. The bedsprings creaked heavily. Then there was only silence.

* * *

April 5, 1868

My dearest Phillip...

Miranda's pen paused above the paper as she groped for the words to begin. So many unsettling changes had taken place since she'd last written to her fiancé. How could she even begin to explain them all?

It appears I won't be coming home as soon as I'd planned. My father is ill, how seriously I can't be sure, since he ignores my urgings that he see a doctor. In any case, he is fading before my eyes, losing weight and color, and the laudanum he takes for his pain only seems to make his condition worse....

Again Miranda's pen paused as she stared into the guttering flame of the candle that sat on the kitchen table. Every night Iron Bill took the pain elixir and fell into a laudanum-induced sleep that allowed him to rise the next morning and resume his military duties. But the pain was worsening daily. How much longer could he go on? And how much longer could she continue helping him cover his illness?

I know you will understand, my dearest, when I say that I cannot leave him just yet. My father has not asked me to stay—he is far too proud for that. But I know how much he needs me.

She rested the pen against the inkwell and pressed the center of her forehead in an effort to rub away the day's built-up tension. She had already begun making excuses for Iron Bill's haggard appearance. He had a cold…an upset stomach…a headache. No one knew about the laudanum. She was part of his conspiracy now, and the guilt was telling on her. If only Uncle Andrew were here! Surely he would know what to do.

Determinedly now, she dipped the nib into the inkwell and took up her letter again.

But on to happier news. I have received permission to start a school for the Navajo children! Through a great deal of faith and more than a little wheedling (you know how persistent I can be) I have secured a vacant officer's quarters, furnished it with spare benches from the mess hall, and even commandeered some food for the children's lunches! Tomorrow we begin. Think of it, Phillip, my first real teaching position! I can hardly wait!

Restless, Miranda laid the pen on the table, stood up and walked to the small, curtainless window. Her muscles ached from the long day of lifting furniture and scrubbing floors to ready her little classroom, but the work had been a labor of love. She massaged the small of her back, sighing as the pressure of her fingers penetrated through her stiff corset.

In truth, it was not persistence but subtle extortion

that had finally secured the room and the food. Her knowledge of Iron Bill's illness had given her an unspoken power. While she would never have threatened him with exposure, the possibility had hung between them like a suspended weight, and when the crusty major had granted permission for her school, the implied promise on her part had carried equal gravity. Their bargain was sealed, and they both knew it.

What would it be like, her first day as a teacher? Would she even have any students? Miranda had sent out a Navajo youth, one who spoke a little English, to carry the word to nearby families, but there was no guarantee the boy had done his job or that anyone had listened to him. For all she knew, even though the Navajos would be coming in for their Saturday rations, she could be facing an empty classroom tomorrow.

Miranda pressed closer to the glass, gazing up at the thin crescent moon that hung above the far mesa. Would the children come? she wondered.

Would *he* come?

She had not seen Ahkeah for nearly a week, but she already knew how he would feel about her school. Would he come, if only as an enemy to stop her? Would he sear her with his anger? Freeze her with his contempt?

Would he come?

She turned away from the window, away from the deep night sky that was almost as black as Ahkeah's eyes. Her letter to Phillip lay on the table, candlelight flickering on the half-filled page. Miranda wandered back to the chair, sat down and closed her eyes. The image of Phillip's pale, noble face formed, then blurred in her memory. He seemed so far away tonight, like an inhabitant of some distant world—a world of refinement and gentility, where old people did not freeze by the roadside, where children did not starve for want of food and learning, and where tainted flour was thrown out to feed the pigs and chickens.

She took up the pen and dipped it into the inkwell, hoping that if she continued writing, the tender words she wanted to say would fall into place. But no more words would come. She was too tired, too drained of emotion and too restless to finish the letter tonight.

Miranda capped the inkwell and rose wearily to her feet. Taking up her cashmere shawl, she flung it around her shoulders as she drifted toward the door. The air in the small quarters was rank with the scent of Iron Bill's evening cheroot. A few moments outside might at least clear her lungs and her mind.

Clasping the warm shawl around her, she opened the door and, closing the latch softly behind her, stepped onto the front stoop. She had expected the night to be cold, as the day had been, but the air was surprisingly warm. A gusty wind struck her face, smelling of long-delayed spring. She closed her eyes, filling her senses with the moist, dusty sweetness.

Ahkeah's craggy face appeared unbidden in her mind, every detail in perfect clarity—the sharp cheekbones jutting beneath golden-bronze skin, the deep-set eyes above them, jet-black, as keen and angry as a hawk's. Did those eyes ever sparkle with humor? she wondered. Did the grim line of his mouth ever curve in a smile? Was there any laughter in the man? Any remnant of tenderness?

And perhaps the most perplexing question of all— why should it matter to her? Who was this man, this dark, angry, half-wild stranger, that her thoughts should fix on him with such persistence?

Miranda's reverie was cut short by the sound of drunken laughter echoing across the parade ground. Three figures, leaning on each other for support, staggered into a pool of lamplight. Although they were a good sixty paces off, Miranda could make them out clearly. The taller one in the center was a soldier, his hat missing, his shirt open down the chest. Clinging to him were two Navajo girls who looked to be about fifteen. One of them giggled as the soldier twisted his hand downward and squeezed her breast.

"Whee—oo!" he whooped, laughing. "Ol' Jethro McCree sure got lucky tonight! You two wantin' to take turns with me, or try it both at once?" The question ended in a hiccup as the trio reeled, laughing and giggling, into the shadows and vanished from sight.

Miranda gripped the porch railing, her throat muscles knotted with suppressed rage. It was all she could do to keep from running after the three revelers, jerk those poor, foolish girls away and give Jethro McCree a tongue-lashing he would never forget.

But that would make no difference, she knew. The girls were hungry, and even if she diverted them tonight, they would be back tomorrow, and the next night, and the next....

Miranda understood now why Ahkeah refused to expose his daughter to so-called civilized ways. But Ahkeah was wrong! Only education could change the terrible conditions she had seen among his people. Only education could give girls such as these a sense of their true worth and teach them the skills they would need to make their way with dignity.

And right now, providing that education was up to Miranda.

She turned into the breathy spring wind, one hand catching her tightly pinned hair to hold it in place. Her eyes closed as she filled her lungs with the scents of wood smoke, alkali and damp earth.

"I know you're out there," she whispered, imagining Ahkeah's tall presence somewhere in the darkness. "And I know what you think of me and my little school. But I'm going to prove you wrong, Ahkeah. So help me, no matter what you might do, or try to do...I'm going to prove you wrong!"

Ahkeah stood outside the entrance to the dugout, watching the first fingers of dawn creep over the desert. Below, in the darkness, Nizhoni still slept, curled with the old woman beneath the woolen poncho that served as their only blanket. The morning was chilly, and for a moment he was tempted to light a fire so they could be warm when they awakened. But no, the precious store of mesquite roots was needed for cooking. In any case, the smell of spring was in the wind.

By the time the march to the fort for rations was underway, the sun would be warming the land.

Perhaps the spring weather would bring more children to Miranda Howell's school. Nizhoni would not be going, of course, but other parents had told him they would be sending their children for the promised food. How much harm, after all, could one *bilagáana* woman do, they reasoned, especially one who could not speak the Diné language?

How much harm? Ahkeah's mind conjured up a vision of Miranda arguing, her pert face thrusting up toward him, her fists planted at her slender waist. Those who considered her a harmless nuisance did not know her as he did. They had never glimpsed the granite spark of determination in those cool gray eyes or the stubborn jut of that finely squared chin. The woman was the daughter of Iron Bill Howell, and she had inherited the full measure of her father's bull-headed toughness.

As for her ideas… Ahkeah shook his head ruefully. Miranda Howell, and well-meaning people like her, could do more damage to the Diné way of life than a whole detachment of Kit Carson's army regulars.

She had even invaded his dreams last night. Ahkeah felt his member stir and begin to harden at the memory of it. Some dreams, he knew, carried messages. But not this one. Its vivid images and sensations had been spawned by nothing more than unslaked physical need.

He had dreamed that he was back in Dinétah, riding alone at night up a windswept desert canyon. Above him the moon had hung like a golden peach, ripe and full and sweet. The stars had glittered like drifts of shining sand—the same sand that sang and murmured beneath the hooves of his galloping mount.

On either side of him, pale sandstone ledges, sculpted by wind into flowing shapes like the curves of a woman's body, rose into the darkness. Ahead of him they had joined, to form a deeply shadowed cleft that beckoned him to dismount, enter and climb upward toward the hanging orb of the moon.

As he climbed, Ahkeah had realized he was naked, but the night had been warm, the rocks in the cleft as smooth as polished marble. Higher and higher he'd climbed, drawn by a silent voice that seemed to call him upward, whispering into his heart, singing in his blood. Only when he had reached the top and stepped into an open hollow had he seen her—lying on a bed of the softest furs, her honey-brown hair flowing over her breasts, her skin pale gold in the moonlight. His lips had formed her name—*Miranda.*

There had been no need to ask if she had called him. Her arms had reached out to him, beckoning him close, pulling him down beside her onto the furs. Her bare skin had smelled of moonlight and peach blossoms, with an erotic undertone of lilac—the scent he had always hated but now found wildly arousing. Even then his body had been ready for her, his shaft swollen hard, aching with need.

The tips of her breasts had been small and pink, like sun-kissed raspberries. She had moaned softly when he touched them, brushing them with his fingertip until they puckered into taut little nubs. He might have pleasured her further, with his mouth, perhaps, but she had taken his hand and guided it downward to the damp nest of curls between her thighs. He had stroked her pulsing cleft and felt the shudder of response beneath his palm, and he had known she was ready for him—that she had been ready all along.

Her wetness had eased his way as he plunged into her in one long, smooth stroke. Her pale legs had wrapped around him, pulling him deeper, deeper, until he was lost in her, lost in her warm, moist sweetness, in her whimpering need. Again and again, deeper, harder, faster, he had thrust into her, feeling her shuddering response, hearing her small moans of need urging him on until the very stars had exploded, swirling around the moon in the dark night sky....

He had awakened damp and sweating behind the leather flap that separated his bed from the rest of the dugout where his aunt and daughter slept. The dream had been real. Too real. Pah! He needed a woman.

Ahkeah had never wanted to take a wife in this hellish place. His people had so many needs, it was all he could do to take care of them, along with his daughter and his poor old aunt. He had no time to devote to a husband's duties. Worse, the very thought of bringing more children into the grim world of Bosque Redondo filled him with sorrow. Marriage was out of the question—as was dallying with the foolish young girls who followed the *bilagáana* soldiers. He was bound by duty and circumstance to remain in this state of private torment.

The sun was coming up now, painting the clouds with flame above the eastern horizon. The alkaline landscape glowed like heaped embers in the morning light, parched and barren even in this season of awakening spring. For the past three years his people had planted crops and watered them by way of the long ditches they'd dug from the river. Every year the maize and beans had sprouted, only to be ravaged by drought, wind, hail and cutworms. This year the Diné would not plant again. They would leave this place or starve.

Ahkeah felt the touch of small, cold fingers creeping into his palm. Nizhoni stood beside him, pressing close to his legs for warmth. Bending down, he wrapped her in his arms and lifted her into the sunlight. "Did you sleep well?" he asked.

She answered him with a sleepy little yawn. "Father, my friends Deshna and Chee are going to the new school at the fort. They say the *bilagáana* woman will give them food."

Ahkeah sighed, pained by the eagerness in her beautiful dark eyes. "Are you unhappy because I won't let you go to the school?" he asked.

Her silence answered his question.

"Do you understand why I don't want you to go?"

"You think the *bilagáana* woman is bad," she said.

Ahkeah pushed the dream from his thoughts. "Not bad. I know she is trying to help us. But she is wrong, Nizhoni."

"She promises to give us food," Nizhoni argued. "How can that be wrong?"

"Because while she fills your belly with food, she will be filling your mind with poison."

Nizhoni stared at him. "How can this be so? She was kind to me. She would have given me her shawl if you had—"

"Listen to me." Ahkeah touched a silencing finger to her soft lips. "Am I not your father?"

"Yes."

"And do I not know what is best for you?"

Nizhoni lowered her feathery lashes. "Yes, my father," she murmured, submissive, as Diné children were raised to be.

"Then trust me when I say this. The new school is not a good place for you."

"But you will take me to the fort today, yes?" She was bright and eager once more, her smile plucking at his heart. He hesitated, pondering the lure of Miranda Howell's school and remembering, also, last week's encounter with Sergeant Jethro McCree. No, this would not be a good day for his daughter to be at the fort.

"Today I will take the horse and get the rations for all of us," he said, anticipating her crestfallen look. "You stay here and take care of Hedipa. If she tells me you behaved well, I'll take you for a ride when I come home."

"Can we go down in the wash and see the coyote puppies again?" Nizhoni was making an effort to hide her disappointment. Ahkeah was proud of her.

"If they haven't left their den, yes, we will go."

"And will you tell me a Coyote story?"

His arms tightened around her. "No more Coyote stories until winter, small one. To tell stories about the animals when they are awake would be disrespectful."

"Why?" She nestled her silky head beneath his chin, snuggling into his warmth.

"Would you like to hear someone telling stories about you?"

"No. That would be rude," Nizhoni agreed.

"The animals give us many things. And even when we must kill them, we treat them with respect. That is our way."

Our way.

Ahkeah lifted his eyes to the beauty of the rising sun, thinking of the day ahead. Miranda Howell would do her misguided best with her little school. But she would never understand the way of the Diné. She would never understand the knowledge that came, not from books, but from generations of living wisdom. She would never understand the importance of keeping that wisdom alive.

Her ways were wrong, and it was up to him to protect his people from her influence.

Ahkeah willed the strength of earth and sky to flow into his spirit. Today's battle, he knew, would be the first of many. For the sake of his people, he could not let Miranda win.

Chapter Seven

There were nineteen Navajo children in the classroom, ranging in age from five or six to, perhaps, eleven. Ragged and unwashed, they sat crowded together on the high wooden mess-hall benches. Their feet dangled above the floor, some bare, some clad in worn moccasins or wrapped in rags.

Miranda's pulse danced nervously as she stood before her very first class. She had come braced to tame a roomful of rowdy little hooligans, but the silence was broken only by the slow ticking of the clock on the wall. None of the children had spoken so much as a word. They sat with their eyes downcast, their hands in their laps. Only their feet moved, swinging restlessly where they hung below the benches.

She glanced toward the open doorway, as if expecting to see a tall, proud figure blocking the morning sunlight. But no one was there. She should have known Ahkeah would not come—not even as an enemy.

Facing the class, Miranda cleared her throat. ''My

name is Miss Howell,'' she said, pointing to her chest.
''Miss Howell. Can you repeat that after me? *Miss
Howell.*'' She gestured, palm-up, toward the children,
her spirits sinking as she realized no one was going
to respond. What now? she wondered. How on earth
could she teach these children English if they would
not even look at her, let alone speak?

Taking a different tack, she planted herself before
one of the older boys. ''My name is Miss Howell,''
she said, emphasizing each word and pointing to her
chest. ''Now, you tell me *your* name. Say, 'My name
is—''' She left the inflection open, praying he would
understand.

The boy did not look at her, but his throat worked
with effort. Miranda held her breath as his lips moved.

''My…name Miz…How.''

No one else spoke, laughed or even moved. Miranda knew she should correct him, but at least the
boy had spoken. Her instincts told her to leave well
enough alone.

Giving him a nod of approval, she moved to another student, a small, pretty girl wearing what looked
to be a cast-off man's shirt, tied at the waist with a
piece of rope.

''What is your name?'' Miranda asked gently.
''Tell me. Say, 'My name is…'''

Again, the child did not look at her. ''My…nem
Mis 'Ow.''

The class remained silent. Grateful that she'd decided to limit today's session to a couple of hours,
Miranda moved on to question other students. Their

responses were the same. This was not an encouraging start. But at least they were talking.

Fearing the children might be getting restless, she strode to the front of the room and pulled down the roll-mounted wall map, a treasure she'd unearthed in a dusty storeroom. "This is your country," she declared, pointing to the map, "the United States of America!"

The students gazed blankly at the colored shapes that represented states. The idea of a map meant nothing to them, Miranda realized. But she had little choice except to continue what she'd started.

"New Mexico!" she exclaimed, pointing to the irregular pink rectangle. "We are right here!" She jabbed at the location of the fort with her index finger. "And here—" she traced a meandering blue line "—this is our river, the Pecos."

The faces of the students reflected no comprehension at all.

"The river..." Miranda gestured toward the window, making wavelike motions with her free hand. "River!" Did they understand? She singled out one of the older girls. "Say it—*river!*"

"Riv...er," the girl repeated. Was there any spark of understanding? There was no way to tell because she did not raise her eyes. Miranda ached for the presence of someone who could bridge the gap between herself and these needy children—even Ahkeah.

Abandoning the map, she seized the remaining object she had brought—a printed portrait she had taken from the wall of her father's office.

"Students," she said, holding up the picture of Andrew Johnson, "this is the president of the United States. Say it. *President!*"

The final hour of class had been a struggle at best. The young Navajos had learned to parrot whatever Miranda told them to say, but even when she fell back on simpler concepts—eyes, hair, arms, feet, colors— she saw no indication that they understood. After meeting Nizhoni, she could not believe these children were any less intelligent than whites. Perhaps they simply didn't trust her—or worse, maybe they just didn't care about learning.

Only when she'd brought out the big basket of roast mutton sandwiches she'd made early that morning did her students show any interest. They had pounced on the sandwiches like hungry little animals, tearing at the bread and meat, stuffing their mouths, ignoring Miranda's demands for order. As soon as the food was gone, they'd scattered to the four winds. School was over for the day.

Miranda slumped onto an empty bench with her back to the door. She should have known it would be like this, she lectured herself. She had dreamed of planting seeds of learning in fertile young minds, but the Navajo children had come to school for only one thing—food. Take that lure away, and she would have no students at all.

But she could not give up after one class. Tomorrow was another day, and she would face them with new plans, new determination. There had to be a way to make these children want to learn. Somehow she would find it.

She glanced up as a shadow fell across the rectangle of sunlight from the open doorway behind her. Was it Ahkeah at last? She held her breath as she pictured his tall, proud figure filling the doorway, his eyes blazing their dark fire. No one else in Miranda's small world had seemed to care what happened this morning—not her father, and certainly not Violet. But Ahkeah would care. He hated her school, but yes, he would care with a passion that equaled her own.

"I got somethin' to say to you, teacher lady."

The drawling voice startled Miranda. She whipped around so abruptly that the motion sent a hot dart of pain shooting down the back of her neck. For a moment she could not place the squat, pugnacious-looking soldier who had ambled into her classroom. Then she remembered. She had seen him last night, crossing the parade ground with the two Navajo girls.

"Scared you, did I?" He grinned, showing tobacco-stained teeth. "Well, that ain't the worst thing that could happen. Somebody needs to scare you right good, missy. Might as well be me."

"Do I know you, Sergeant?" she asked coldly.

He leered down at her. "Jethro McCree's the name, and you might say I come to give you a friendly warnin'."

The man's manner tightened a coil of apprehension in the pit of Miranda's stomach, but she held her fear in check as she rose to her feet. "What do you want?'' she demanded. "Speak your piece and be gone. I've got work to do."

He took a step forward, bringing himself so close that Miranda could smell the stale liquor on his breath. She willed herself not to back away.

"Just wantin' to save you some trouble," he said. "I got friends that don't much like what you're doin' with the Injun kids. It's a waste of time tryin' to teach them stinkin' Navajos anything. They're too stupid and lazy to learn."

"If that's really so, then why should it matter what I do?" Miranda retorted. "Your so-called friends are out of line, Sergeant. Navajos deserve the same rights as any other Americans, and that includes the right to an education."

"Listen!" He hissed the word, spraying her cheek with drops of spittle. "Injuns got their place here. But you try puttin' your uppity ideas in their heads, and pretty soon you got your hands full! Next thing you know, they'll be thinkin' they're as good as us—like that bastard Ahkeah!"

"And you don't like that, do you, Sergeant?" Miranda snapped, quivering with rage. "You want to keep them in the ration lines! You want to keep their daughters sneaking into the post to sell their bodies for a few bites of food! I saw you last night—you and those pitiful young girls—"

"Hell, I gave those two little squaws the time of their lives!" McCree growled. "Maybe you shoulda joined us, teacher lady. You look like you could use a good pony ride yourself. Maybe it'd even put a smile on that prissy face of yours—''

"Get out!" Miranda was dizzy with anger. "Get out, before I call my father and—"

"Is this man bothering you, Miss Howell?" The steel-edged voice cut through the tension in the room as Ahkeah stepped through the open doorway. He was here. He had come. But even as her pulse leaped in response, Miranda realized she could not allow the tall Navajo to be her rescuer. She had to defuse this situation any way she could.

"The sergeant was just leaving," she said, forcing a polite smile. "Weren't you, Sergeant?"

But it was as if she had not spoken. The hatred between the two men was almost palpable, its acrid presence filling the small classroom.

McCree's eyes narrowed. "Filthy Injun! If I had a gun, I'd blow your smart-mouthed head off here and now!"

"But you don't have a gun," Ahkeah replied icily. "And I don't have my daughter with me." The implied challenge could not have been more clear. Miranda held her breath as the two men glared at each other—McCree solid as a barrel and surly as a mastiff; Ahkeah tall and lean, steel in his nerves and quicksilver in his veins.

Who would have the advantage in a fight? McCree would be heavier, stronger and probably more vicious. Ahkeah would be sharper and quicker, with the cool instincts of a cougar.

But there would be no confrontation today. Miranda saw the sergeant's gaze flicker toward the floor, and she realized that, like most bullies, he was a coward who would not take on an enemy without a solid advantage. Ahkeah knew it, too. Most likely he had known it all along.

"I'm lettin' you go this time, Injun!" McCree sneered, backing toward the door. "But one of these days you'll go too far, an' then you'll pay for it. Your people are the lyin', thievin' scum of the earth, and the fact that you talk like a white man don't make you no different!"

He took a step toward the door, then paused and swung back toward Miranda. "An' you, missy—if I was you, I'd watch who I was seen with. Folks 'round here don't think much of Injun lovers, 'specially a white woman who lets one of the red-skinned bastards between 'er thighs!"

He swaggered out the door, slamming it shut behind him before Miranda could react. But the ugliness of his words hung in the silence. The low ticking of the clock echoed off the walls of the room as she stood facing Ahkeah, her legs trembling beneath her skirts.

"He's…a terrible man," she said, staring at a frayed spot on his worn cotton tunic.

"But there is truth in what he said." Ahkeah's own voice sounded ragged and unsteady. "People will judge you badly for this."

"For this?" She willed herself to look up at his face. "For my harmless little school?"

His black eyes flashed in warning, but when he met

her gaze Miranda was overcome by the strange tenderness she saw there. Something moved inside her, warming, unfolding like the bud of a flower. Her lips parted as she struggled to break the silence with words that would not come.

"Not just your school," Ahkeah said. "I know your heart is good, Miranda Howell, but your efforts to help the Diné will only make enemies for you—dangerous enemies, on both sides."

"Including you?"

Time froze as he loomed above her, his eyes smoldering with unspoken secrets. His thin lips were sensually curved, his sharp bronze face much too close to her own.

"Including me?" His husky voice echoed her question as his gaze held her captive. "Make no mistake, *bilagáana* woman. You and I have been enemies from the first moment we set eyes on each other."

His words struck Miranda like a dash of cold water. She reeled, then countered angrily, "So why did you come here? To insult me? To gloat over this morning's rough beginning? It *was* rough, you know. I tried everything I could think of, Ahkeah, but I could not reach those children. I couldn't even get them to look at me, let alone learn. They only came for the food."

Ahkeah had stepped backward, distancing himself physically and emotionally from her tirade. He stood watching her, his arms folded across his chest, his eyes black slits of disdain.

"Go ahead!" she snapped. "Laugh at me! Say you

told me so! Just don't stand there…looking at me that way.'' Her voice had begun to quiver. She blinked back furious tears.

"Stop it, Miranda. I did not come to laugh at you.'' He spoke without moving or changing his expression.

"Then why?''

"I came to apologize for the children of my people.''

She stared at him, too dumbfounded to speak.

"I saw them leaving, and I stopped them. They needed to be told there was no excuse for such bad behavior, even toward a *bilagáana*.''

Miranda swallowed, freeing her constricted throat muscles. "But I don't understand! You've opposed me at every step!''

"As I do now. If I had my way, I would close your school, burn these benches, this white man's map and this ugly picture of the man you call your president. This very day, I would put you in a wagon, hitch up the mules and drive you back to Santa Fe myself.''

"I still don't understand.'' She sank onto a bench, her knees refusing to support her. Who was this man, that he could reduce her to quivering jelly with a word or a look?

"Do you understand honor?'' He glared down at her, his elegantly long hands clenched into fists. "Once the Diné were proud people. Our enemies feared us, and we took what we wanted from them. Now those days are gone, and honor is all we have left. Surrender that, and we have nothing.''

"That's what you told the children?''

"I reminded them, yes. And I told them that if they did not come to school to behave and learn, they were not to dishonor themselves by accepting your food."

"And they listened."

"Some listened. The others will not be back."

So he had already succeeded in reducing the size of her class. What was he planning to do next? Miranda glanced up at him. "Are you battling me with kindness, Ahkeah? Is that your plan?"

Ahkeah's stern expression did not change. "I cannot forbid my people to send their children to your school. They are free to decide such things for themselves. But telling the children they must behave in class is a different matter."

"And it makes the whole idea of school less alluring, doesn't it?" Miranda smiled for the first time that morning. "I do know a few things about children, after all."

"But not Diné children," Ahkeah said. "How can you presume to teach them when you know nothing about their lives and their customs—for example, the belief that it shows discourtesy to look directly at people when you speak to them?"

"Oh…" Miranda's lips parted as the truth struck home. In keeping their eyes averted when they answered her questions, her students had meant nothing more than politeness. "But *you* look at me when you speak."

"I was raised in the *bilagáana* world, and I know your customs. With my own people, I speak looking away."

"And your daughter—she looked at me, too."

"She learns from me."

"She could learn from me, too! Nizhoni is such a bright child, Ahkeah! Let me teach her!"

"No."

A wall had slid into place behind his obsidian eyes—a wall that Miranda was suddenly determined to breach. "Then let me learn from you!" she demanded. "I want to see how your people survive in this wretched place. I want to see these customs and beliefs you're fighting so hard to preserve."

"Why?" His eyes were wary, his expression guarded.

"Because what you told me is true. If I'm to give these children what they need, I have to understand them."

"And if I don't want you to give them anything?"

"What *you* want is of no more consequence than what *I* want! Your people are going to change! For better or worse, things outside their world are going to influence them! If I give up and walk away, it will simply leave a path open for someone else—perhaps someone who cares nothing for who they are or what they believe! Show me how I can help your people, Ahkeah! That's all I ask!"

Drained by her own outburst, Miranda watched his face—the subtle tightening of lines and creases, the conflicts that flashed and seethed in the depths of his eyes. Had she overstepped herself this time? Had she said too little? Too much?

An eternity seemed to pass before he spoke. "You won't find it pretty."

"I know," she said, reining in her excitement. "When?"

"Not today. I have a promise to keep. Tomorrow?"

Miranda hesitated, then nodded. Tomorrow was Sunday, but on an isolated post like this one, it would be like any other day. She had even planned to hold school, fearful that skipping a day would discourage her students from coming at all.

Ahkeah frowned. "You father will not approve of your going."

"No, I fear he won't," Miranda agreed. "And neither will men like Sergeant McCree. I'll take a horse and meet you somewhere outside the fort. If I leave during lunch, I should be able to get away without being seen. My father will be too busy to miss me until dinnertime, and by then I'll surely be back, won't I?"

His gaze impaled her, triggering fierce little whorls of sensation that spiraled downward to pool in the warm, dark depths of her body. "Are you sure you want to do this, Miranda Howell?" he asked.

"Yes." Her reply came without hesitation. "Yes, I'm sure."

"Then I will wait for you in the dry gulch beyond the trees—you will see it if you ride parallel to the road. But if there is any sign of trouble, you must not come."

She felt the power of his eyes—wise, sad, angry

eyes that made a shambles of all her defenses. She could never lie to this man, Miranda realized. She could never flirt or tease or pretend to be anything she was not. One look at her, and he would know the truth.

"Why are you helping me?" she asked.

"Helping you?" A bitter smile tugged at his lips. "I have no intention of helping you. My only purpose here is to show you how wrong you are and to keep you from doing more harm to my people."

His face was close to hers, his mouth grim, his beardless cheeks as smooth as polished leather. What would happen, she found herself wondering, if she were to reach up, catch his knotted hair with her hand and pull that thin, sensual mouth down to hers? Would he taste like the desert, of wind and salt and alkali? Would he be shocked, even angry? Or would he return the kiss with all the wild hunger of his savage spirit?

But what in heaven's name was she thinking? She had never done such an impulsive thing, not even with Phillip. She was, after all, a lady, and a calm, sensible person. Rashness was not in her nature.

"I should go." His voice was thick and husky.

"Yes," Miranda whispered, looking up at him. "Yes, you should."

"Tomorrow, then?" His six-foot height loomed above her, disturbingly close.

"Yes." Miranda's lips moved, forming the words, but no sound emerged from her tight throat. He was so large and powerful, and so near. Without conscious thought, she strained upward toward his stern bronze face....

"Miranda!" Violet opened the door, causing them both to spring backward. "My dear girl, I've been looking all over for—"

The words died in her throat as she caught sight of Ahkeah, who had stepped back toward the wall. Her mouth dropped open, her rouged lips forming a little rose-pink O of surprise.

"I was just leaving," Ahkeah said, with a formal nod. "Good day to you, Mrs. Marsden." He was gone before she could answer, departing not in haste, but with the fluid silence of a shadow.

Violet stared after him. "Well," she said, clucking her tongue. "Well, indeed!"

"We were just discussing my students," Miranda said, aware that her face was burning.

"With the door closed?" Violet raised one thinly pencilled eyebrow. "My dear girl, I may not be schoolteacher material, but I'm smart enough to know when a woman's hell-bent for trouble!"

Miranda forced herself to laugh. "The door was closed because Sergeant McCree was here, and he slammed it shut when he left. Really, Violet, you're imagining too much! We were talking, that's all."

"That's all?" Violet shook her mahogany-colored curls. "Maybe. But regardless of that, you're dragging your reputation through the mud when you allow yourself to associate with that—that *creature!* He's an Indian, for heaven's sake—a murdering savage with no more regard for a woman's virtue than—"

"That's enough." Miranda spoke quietly, but she could feel herself trembling. "I've done nothing wrong, and neither has Ahkeah. Anyone who believes otherwise can say so to my face."

Violet's plump bosom rose and fell. "Miranda, they're already saying it," she said with a sigh. "And not to your face."

Chapter Eight

Miranda arrived to find her students waiting outside the classroom, some leaning against the adobe wall, others squatting in the dust, watching her as she strode across the parade ground carrying the picnic hamper she had filled with sandwiches. She counted thirteen children, six less than yesterday, no thanks to Ahkeah. Given a choice, she would have elected to keep them all.

The children averted their eyes as she came closer. One of them—an older girl who had not been there the previous day—stood up and came forward, looking directly at her. She looked to be about fifteen, pretty, slightly plump and clad in a dirty calico dress.

"I come help missy," she said in broken English. "Ahkeah, he send me."

Only then did Miranda recognize her as one of the girls she had seen crossing the parade ground with Sergeant McCree.

"Juana." The girl pointed to her ample chest. "Speak damn good English. Learn from soldier." She grinned, showing crooked white teeth. "Ahkeah, he say I come help—you give food."

"Yes," Miranda answered, swallowing her surprise. "The sandwiches are in this basket. Tomorrow, come to the mess hall and help me prepare them, and you can have an extra for breakfast. Do you understand?"

"Damn good!" Juana's smile broadened. "We go in now. You talk me. I talk them." She nodded toward the children. "Make 'em learn like hell."

Miranda unlocked the door, mentally shaking her head. What kind of "help" would Ahkeah, her avowed enemy, send her next—a swarm of locusts? But of course—the revelation came to her at once— Ahkeah had not done this for *her*. It was the poor girl he'd been thinking of—a means for her to get food without having to sell her body.

Miranda suppressed a smile as she strode into the classroom. Ahkeah's tactics might be subtle and mysterious, but she was beginning to understand them.

The Navajo children shuffled into the room and clustered on the back benches like forlorn sparrows. Only Juana sat in the front row, her hands clasped on her knees, her broad face creased in an expectant smile. She was probably thinking about those mutton sandwiches in the picnic hamper, Miranda mused darkly. The idea that the poor, silly creature had come to learn was far too much to expect.

As she took her place before the class, Miranda struggled to ignore the leaden lump in the pit of her stomach. Would the morning class go as badly as yesterday's? Would she accomplish something good here, or was she only wasting her time and breaking her heart?

Swallowing the tightness in her throat, she resolved to begin again. "My name is Miss Howell," she said, pointing to her chest. "Say it. Miss Howell."

"Miz 'Ow," the children parroted, their gazes fixed on the tile floor.

"Now…" She took a deep breath and glanced toward the girl on the front bench. "What is your name?"

"I tell you before. Juana." The girl's smile did not waver.

"Say 'My name is Juana.'"

"My…name…is Juana." The girl's mouth worked with effort, but in the end she pronounced all the words correctly. She gazed anxiously at Miranda, waiting for some sign of approval.

"Again," Miranda said. "What is your name?"

"My name is Juana." The girl's dimples deepened as Miranda nodded and turned toward a small boy who sat at the end of the back row.

"What is your name?" she asked gently.

He stared at the floor. "My…name…Chee."

"My name *is* Chee. Again."

"My…name…is…Chee." The boy gave her a timid smile.

Miranda felt the nervous lump in her stomach dissolve and float away. *Hallelujah!* This was going to work after all! She was going to teach these children!

She was going to open their minds to new ways and new ideas, and no one was going to stop her!

Not even Ahkeah.

The sun blazed high and hot in the midday sky, its reflection glittering on the alkali flats that dotted the desert like patches of stark, white snow. A flock of crows circled against the turquoise sky, their cries carrying far on the still spring air.

Ahkeah rested his horse in the lee of a boulder, shading his eyes against the glare as he gazed toward the fort. He had seen the children leaving school, with Juana shepherding the little flock safely down the road. Juana was a good-hearted girl, cheerful and intelligent. In that better time, the time of Dinétah, she would have been preparing herself for marriage, not selling her body to the soldiers.

Was it too late to save her and the others, these child-women with shattered pride and diseased bodies, whose only crime was trying to survive in this place of hunger? Ahkeah had no answer to that question—unless, perhaps, the answer was Miranda.

He had counted it as a victory, persuading Juana to attend the school. Perhaps if the girl did well, others like her, already hurt and tainted by the *bilagáana,* would follow her. If Miranda could help these damaged children, he would take back every bad thing he had said or thought about her.

Once more his eyes scanned the empty road. Would she really come out to meet him? Did he want her to come?

He had lain awake all night debating the wisdom of this adventure. Why had he agreed to show her the way his people lived? The whole idea was a reckless mistake. Even if they didn't venture far, there were dangers—not the least of them the consequences of their being seen together. If it became known that Miranda had stolen away to meet a Navajo she would become a pariah, with no friends in this place.

Toward morning he had made up his mind. He could not afford to be responsible for Miranda's safety or her reputation. If she came here, to their meeting place, he would send her back to the fort.

He checked the road again, his spirits unexpectedly sinking when he failed to see her. Maybe she had come to her senses and decided not to ride out. That would be for the best, he knew. In fact, he was only here to make sure she returned to the fort and didn't go wandering off in search of him.

Ahkeah stiffened reflexively at the sound of approaching hoofbeats. His pulse leaped as he turned and saw her riding from the direction of the river. Evidently she had taken time to leave the fort from the far side and circle the unplanted fields to make certain no one had followed her.

His admiration swelled as he watched her ride, mounted on a tall bay whose galloping legs ate up the fallow ground. She rode astride, her fawn-colored riding habit fitting every curve of her trim figure. Her tightly bound hair was covered by a man's broad-brimmed hat that Ahkeah found more appealing than all the beribboned bonnets he had ever seen on white women. She rode expertly, leaning forward in the saddle, her small, compact body balanced as easily as a boy's.

For a long moment Ahkeah sat and watched her. Then, as she came closer, he nudged his horse out into the open where she could see him. There, in silence, he waited.

Miranda slowed her horse to a trot as she approached the wash. Her escape from the fort had left her strangely exhilarated. She could feel the high color in her cheeks, the dampness of sweat at her hairline. Her pulse drummed recklessly, fueled by the thought of the adventure to come.

She had feared Ahkeah would not be waiting. Now she caught her breath at the sight of him seated astride his spotted mustang, looking as wild and savage as the desert itself. Only now did Miranda realize how much she had wanted him to be here.

He rode out to meet her, stern-faced, with no word of greeting. "I was hoping you had changed your mind," he said.

Miranda recoiled as if he had slapped her. "Then why did you wait for me?" she retorted.

"To send you safely back. You shouldn't be here, Miranda. This can come to no good for either of us."

She held her ground, reining in the high-strung bay. "You said I needed to understand how your people live. How can I do that if you won't show me?"

"Not all things are necessary for you to understand." His face was a chiseled mask. "Go home,

Miranda, back to the life you were made to live. Forget your high-flung ideas about saving a downtrodden race. My people are none of your concern.''

"You're saying you won't ride with me? You're breaking your promise?''

"If it truly was a promise, yes. When you come to your senses, you'll thank me.''

"Fine.'' She thrust out her chin, her temper seething. "Then I'll just take a ride by myself. There's no law against that, is there?''

She swung her mount sharply around and was shifting her weight when the menacing buzz of a rattlesnake exploded almost under the horse's hooves. The startled bay shot up and sideways, dodging the snake's lightning strike, but throwing Miranda partway out of the saddle. She grabbed for the horn, dropping the reins as the horse screamed, bucked wildly, then bolted for the open desert.

Miranda gripped the horn with one leg as she struggled to regain her seat. Ahkeah had responded instantly and was thundering along behind her, but he was already losing ground. The cavalry-bred bay was bigger, faster and better nourished than Ahkeah's wiry desert mustang. There was no chance he would be able to catch her.

Gripping the bay's mane with one hand, she groped frantically for the reins, which had fallen forward and caught between the bridle and the horse's ears. Balanced over the horn, she stretched and teetered, gaining a fearful half inch, then another.

Miranda's fingertips had just brushed leather when

the horse lurched down the slope of a wash, flinging her off balance again and forcing her to seize the beast's slippery neck with both arms. By the time she'd secured her leg hold on the saddle once more, the terrified animal was running full out along the meandering bed of the wash, and Ahkeah was nowhere in sight.

She gasped in pain as the horse passed under the prickly skeleton of an ocotillo that jutted outward from a sheer wall of rock and mud. The long thorns clawed her cheek, snagged her hat and tangled in her hair. The horse's speed jerked her onward, leaving pins and light brown strands of hair fluttering from the dead black spikes. Ignoring the pain and the blood that trickled down her cheek, she held on, still fighting to reach the reins.

Just ahead, the wash curved and narrowed, its walls so close that Miranda feared she would be crushed against the horse's side. Praying the cinch would hold, she focused all her effort on pulling upward against the horn to gain a secure seat on the saddle. Fear lent her strength as, with a final heave, she twisted her leg over the far side and wrenched herself upright just as the galloping horse reached the narrows and plunged into the shadowy depths.

Numb with terror now, Miranda pressed forward, keeping low to avoid the thrusting rocks that threatened to shatter her skull. Not far ahead, she glimpsed a shaft of light where the wash opened upward. In the next instant she passed into the blinding glare.

Her heart stopped as she felt the impact of a large,

lithe body landing behind her on the horse. Was it a cougar? Miranda pressed forward, cringing away from the teeth and claws that any second would rip into her unprotected back. Then Ahkeah's sinewy arms reached forward on either side of her. At the sight of his lean, bronze hands, her body went limp with relief. He had cut a straight course that paralleled the curving wash, she realized. The shorter path had put him ahead of her, so he could wait for the horse to pass beneath him and make the dangerous drop to its back.

"Get the reins. I'll hold you." His voice rasped in her ear. "Do it!"

He clasped her waist, gripping the horse with his knees. With little choice except to trust him, Miranda released her hold on the saddle and strained forward along the horse's neck. The sides of the wash flew past her vision in a blur of mud and boulders. She knew she would fall and die if he let her go, but strangely, she was not afraid.

Her fingers reached out, touched, then seized the bouncing strip of leather. As she twisted it around her hand, she felt Ahkeah dragging her back to the saddle. She gasped as he jerked her over the horn and onto the seat. Then his powerful hands were reaching past her to pull on the reins, while he murmured calming Navajo words to the panic-stricken horse.

Dust swirled as the animal fought the pressure of the steel bit in its frothing mouth. It snorted and reared, its hooves knocking showers of loose sand and rock from the sides of the wash. Miranda was flung back against Ahkeah's chest. She felt his arm catch her as the horse reeled, dropped forward and came to a shuddering rest with its four feet on the ground, its head down, its sides heaving like giant bellows.

Speechless, Miranda lay back into Ahkeah's lean, solid strength. He clasped her fiercely, his wrist pressing below her breasts, his heart slamming against her back and his breath rasping in her ear. Only now did she realize how afraid for her he must have been.

"Are you all right?" The question was little more than a whisper.

"Yes..." she murmured, sensing the warm movement of his throat against her temple. "Yes, thank you."

"You should never have come here, Miranda."

His voice blended tenderness and anger. Did he mean she should never have left the fort today, or that she should never have come to New Mexico? Either way, Miranda had no answers to the questions that churned in her mind. She only knew that she felt safe and protected here in the circle of Ahkeah's arm, her heart thudding in counterpoint to the strong pulse at his wrist. Nothing else was making any sense at all.

Without a word he pulled away from her and slipped lightly to the ground. Without letting go of the reins, he moved toward the front of the trembling horse. Stroking the lathered neck, he murmured soothing phrases in Navajo. Miranda felt the tall bay's muscles relax beneath her. Its ragged breathing slowed and deepened. She gazed down at the knot of

Ahkeah's raven hair and realized this man had powers she could scarcely imagine, let alone understand.

Feeling shaky, she eased herself out of the saddle and dropped to the ground. Her legs buckled on impact, refusing to hold her. Ahkeah turned and caught her elbows as she sagged, pulling her upright. She stood between his supporting arms, her hair wildly disheveled, her heart pounding.

"You're bleeding." His hand brushed her cheek and she saw that his fingers came away stained crimson with her blood.

"It's just a scratch—" she started to say, but he was already reaching for the canteen that she'd filled and slung from the saddle before leaving the fort. Wetting his fingers, he rubbed away the blood and cleaned the long, stinging scratch, the contact strangely intimate against her raw flesh. Miranda's nipples tightened beneath her blouse, almost as if he had touched them. The sensation trickled lower, stirring slow ripples of liquid heat in the depths of her body. The eyes that blazed into hers were as fierce and hot as a golden eagle's.

"We should get you back to the fort," he said huskily.

"Yes. I suppose…we should." Miranda broke eye contact and lowered her gaze, forcing her mouth to form the words. It would be the safest course for both of them if she simply mounted and rode back to Fort Sumner by herself. Coming in alone, she could easily explain that the horse had run away with her. No one would have reason to question her story.

Then she remembered. "Your horse—"

"My horse should be waiting where I left it. We can go back for it. Then I'll ride with you until you're safely within sight of the fort." Turning away from her, he removed the stopper from the canteen and poured a little water into his cupped palm for the thirsty bay. The big, velvety mouth dipped into his hand, lipping up the water as Ahkeah added more.

Miranda stood watching the tall Navajo, feeling as if a mountain had sprung up between them—a mountain of differences that would never go away. Ahkeah hated the white man's world and all it stood for. He hated the people in it. He probably hated *her*.

"I can make it back to the fort by myself," she said. "There's no reason for you to escort me."

He shot her a stern glance. "This place is more dangerous than you know. You're not riding back alone."

"Very well, then." She ran an impatient hand through her tangled hair. "We should go. The sooner the better."

Ahkeah stoppered the canteen and swung back into the saddle without a word. His curt nod toward the rear of the horse clearly indicated that she should climb up behind him. As she hesitated, he bent down from the saddle, caught her waist and swung her up as if she were a child. She scrambled into place, her knees fitting into the bend of his legs, her arms circling his rib cage. His body was as lean and solid as cordwood, the muscles sharply defined beneath the worn cotton shirt. He smelled of wood smoke and desert wind.

"Are you ready?" He spoke as if to a stranger. When Miranda did not answer, he nudged the bay forward, guiding it down the wash to a place where the bank had caved in, leaving a fan of loose sand and gravel.

Miranda's arms tightened around his ribs as the horse lurched upward. Her thumb brushed his nipple through the thin fabric. The feel of that taut little nub sent a jolt of unexpected heat through her body. She jerked her hand lower, her face flaming as they gained level ground and turned to gaze back along the winding path of the wash.

Ahkeah's spotted mustang was nowhere in sight.

He muttered something that sounded like a curse, then kicked the bay to a brisk trot. Miranda could sense the anger in him, and also the worry. He needed the horse, she knew, to serve his family and his people. Getting another mount would be difficult, perhaps impossible.

"Could your horse have wandered off?" she asked, clinging tightly to keep from being jarred off the bay's bouncing rump.

"I dropped the reins. He couldn't have gone far on his own. I don't know what—"

He broke off suddenly and reined in the bay. His muscles tensed as he gazed at the ground.

"What is it?" Miranda asked.

"Tracks. Unshod horses. Several sets of prints."

He scowled down at the rocky earth. "Comanches, I'd say. Small party—maybe four or five of them."

"Comanches?" Miranda felt her stomach drop. "But this is Navajo territory!"

"Not according to the Comanches. They raid us anytime they get the urge, and we don't stand a chance against the illegal guns they get from white traders. The government agents look the other way because they believe the raids help keep the Diné in line."

"But that's terrible!"

Ahkeah ignored her naive outburst. "They can't be very far ahead of us," he said, then paused and muttered something under his breath. "We've got to get you back to the fort. Now."

"Now?" She stiffened against him. "But what about your horse? You have to go after those Comanches or you'll never catch up with them!"

His body tensed beneath her hands, then he exhaled sharply. "Miranda, it's too dangerous. They'll have guns, and I don't even want to think about what will happen if they get their hands on you. I can't risk your safety for—"

"No, listen!" she interrupted. "They don't even need to see me. We can track them, staying of sight. Sooner or later, they're bound to drop their guard."

"That's crazy," he growled, but Miranda knew he was thinking about the horse and how much he needed to get it back.

"At least we can track them long enough to find out which way they're headed," she argued.

He made a small, irritated sound. "All right, we'll track them from a distance, but just to make sure they're headed for their own territory, not bent on more raiding. Then it's back to the fort for you."

"Your horse—" Miranda started to protest, but his dark, backward glance silenced her. Ahkeah would not risk her safety for a horse, no matter how precious that horse might be. This whole debacle was her fault. He knew it, and she knew it, too. Arguing would only make matters worse.

"Can you keep still?" He nudged the bay to a careful walk.

"Of course." She mouthed the words, breathing them into his ear. "I'm not a complete fool! Is there anything else you want from me?"

"Yes. In case of trouble, do you promise you'll do exactly as I tell you?"

She hesitated.

"Promise or we don't go another step."

Miranda sighed. "All right, I promise."

"Fine, then. Don't say another word. Don't even breathe if you can help it." He moved the horse ahead, leaning slightly forward in the saddle, eyes and ears alert for any sign of the Comanche raiders. Miranda listened, too, but she could hear nothing but the wind and the harsh, scolding cry of a desert bird. Her heart was a leaping drum that pounded against her ribs, its sound filling her head even as she willed herself to keep still.

Ahkeah stiffened slightly, head up, like a wolf on

the scent. "Stay with the horse," he whispered, mouthing the words. "I hear something."

Guiding the bay behind a sheltering rock, he slipped to the ground and glided forward like a shadow. Ahead and to the east the ground crested in a low escarpment that dropped to the open desert on its far side. Miranda watched as Ahkeah sank to a crouch, crept forward and vanished among the rocks.

She waited in the long afternoon silence, her fingers gripping the reins he'd handed her. For a time she looked up and watched two long-winged vultures circling in the sky. Then she looked down and watched a big horsefly crawl up the sleeve of her jacket.

Where *was* he? What if something had happened to him? She twisted the knotted leathers in her hands, growing more worried by the minute. Her mind began playing cruel tricks as she imagined him impaled by a Comanche arrow or sprawled on the ground with rattlesnake venom pumping through his veins.

How long had it been? she wondered. Ahkeah had told her to stay here with the horse. But what if he was in trouble? What if he needed her help?

Miranda gazed desperately toward the spot where he'd disappeared. No, she could not wait another minute. Ahkeah would probably be furious with her, but if he was in trouble, she needed to know.

Quietly she slid off the back of the horse and looped the reins securely over a jutting boulder. Then, scarcely daring to breathe, she crouched low and crept toward the line of rocks where he had gone.

Chapter Nine

Ahkeah heard her approaching well before she scrambled up behind him. With a sigh he glanced back at her and, turning where he lay, motioned her down and forward. He should have known Miranda would not stay put.

Her eyes were wide and frightened, but she was clearly relieved to see him. He knew he should scold her, but this was no time for words—not with so much danger lurking on the flats below the rocks.

She bellied forward, coming up even with him below the brink of the escarpment. Her body brushed his as she wriggled into place. He gazed straight ahead, struggling to ignore the prickles of sensual warmth that stirred wherever she touched him. He fought against the memory of holding her in his arms on the horse. Everything about this situation was wrong, but there was no longer an easy way out.

She nudged his shoulder to make him look at her. *What's happening?* She mouthed the words, making no sound.

"Down there. You can look, but be careful," he whispered. The distance was safe enough for now, and this, he realized, was something she should see.

She scooted forward, the light contact of her body triggering yet another hot jolt of arousal. Unaware of what she was doing to him, she moved closer, to peer between the concealing rocks. As the view opened below her, Miranda's mouth formed a round, silent O.

Sixty or seventy paces below the escarpment, the desert leveled off into a broad alkali bed that was as white as winter snow and as flat as the surface of a lake. At its edge, looking like a bizarre mirage, sat a gaudily painted patent medicine wagon, enclosed like a small house above the bed and drawn by a team of four dusty mules.

Two men sat on the high seat. The smaller of the pair, a ratty little man who was evidently the driver, clutched the reins in one hand and a heavy lever-action rifle in the other. The second man, also armed with a rifle, was portly and bearded, wearing a stovepipe hat and a boldly checkered jacket. Even from a distance the two men looked nervous, and with good reason. The four mounted Comanches Ahkeah had been trailing were bunched on the near side of the wagon, along with his missing horse. They were arguing with the man in the stovepipe hat. Their voices, loud and belligerent, carried on the clear spring air.

"What are they doing?" Miranda whispered, close to Ahkeah's ear.

"Negotiating a trade, I'd say," he answered

through clenched teeth. "Right now they're offering him my horse in exchange for two jugs of whiskey. But he wants silver, that's what he's telling them. No silver, no whiskey."

"But that doesn't make sense," Miranda argued, caught up in the drama. "Where would those Indians get silver?"

Ahkeah tasted bitterness as he gazed into her innocent gray eyes. "From the Mexicans, Miranda. They get it in exchange for the Diné children they capture and sell as slaves."

Her breath caught in an outraged gasp, and for an instant he feared she would raise her voice and give away their presence. His finger touched her lips, reminding her to keep still.

"It's been going on as long as anyone can remember," he said. "Back in Dinétah it was the Mexicans who came and captured our children. Here it's the Comanches, but in the end it's the same. My sister and I were no older than Nizhoni when we were taken. I was sold to a *bilagáana* family..." He stared down at the rocks, haunted by the memory of two small, terrified children, screaming as rough hands dragged them apart.

"What happened to your sister?" Miranda's eyes were gentle, her voice sympathetic. She wanted to care. But how could she imagine what it had been like—this pampered woman who had never known fear or want in her life?

"I never saw my sister again," he said. "I spent the next eleven years as a slave in your world."

"Not *my* world!" she protested vehemently. "I was raised by abolitionists! I would never—"

"Shh!" Again he touched a finger to her lips, silencing her. Her gaze followed his to where the Comanches and the medicine show man were concluding their business. Mexican silver flashed in the afternoon sun as the man in the checkered jacket handed over a single large clay jug. The Comanche leader seized it and, with a bloodcurdling whoop, waved it aloft.

Ahkeah lay a restraining arm across Miranda's shoulders as the four raiders wheeled their mounts and galloped away, the mustang still in tow. Their shrieks of anticipation quivered on the desert air, sending a chill of icy hatred along his spine.

The driver of the medicine wagon waited long enough to make sure the Comanches were on their way. Then he slapped the mules to a trot, turned the wagon and headed off in the direction of the fort.

"Give them a few minutes," Ahkeah cautioned as Miranda stirred beside him. "No sense in moving out till it's safe."

She settled into place once more, soft and warm against his side. The fragrance of lilacs crept into his nostrils, churning up a whirlwind of conflicting emotion.

"There's something I don't understand," she said. "Those Indians outnumbered the white men two to one, and they had guns, as well. Why didn't they just ambush the wagon, take the mules and whiskey, and be off?"

Ahkeah turned onto his side to study her at leisure. Her hair was loose and windblown, its color as rich and tawny as the pelt of a cougar. His hands ached with the urge to reach out and stroke it, to smooth the wind-tangled waves, to feel those silken strands gliding between his fingers. But no, even the idea was dangerous. This woman was not of his world. He would have to be crazy even to think of touching her.

"Everyone around here knows that big white man," he said, taking refuge in her question. "He makes a good living selling bottled concoctions and rotgut whiskey in these parts, as well as illegal guns and whatever else will make him a dollar. He's been warned by Agent Dodd to stay off the reservation, but that's never stopped him."

She crinkled her nose to dislodge a fly that had settled on its delicate tip. "You still haven't told me what kept those Comanches from killing him and his driver," she said.

Ahkeah squinted at the sky, taking his time. "Hagopian's no fool," he said, noticing that her eyes widened at the mention of the name. "He never carries more than a few jugs of whiskey in his wagon. The Indian who kills or robs him cuts off any future supply. It's a tight game, and the fat old buzzard plays it well."

"But what does he get in return for all that risk?" Miranda persisted. "There can't be that much money to be made out here!"

"True." Ahkeah eased away from her and sat up. "But Hagopian has powerful friends—men who want to keep the Diné on their knees. They wanted our land in Dinétah because they thought they'd find gold there." He felt his hands clench into fists as his anger surged. "There's no gold in Dinétah. Only beauty. More beauty than the eye and the spirit can hold. But that doesn't matter to these people. Now they want to wipe us out, to make sure we never return there. They pay men like Hagopian to poison our warriors with whiskey, and to sell guns to the Comanches so they can raid us and keep us weak!"

She was staring at him, her soft silver eyes brimming with pity. But Ahkeah didn't want her pity. He wanted Miranda Howell to take her maddening sweetness, her noble intentions and her lush temptress's body and go back to where she'd come from!

"Isn't there anything your people can do?" she asked.

"The Diné headmen try to stop the whiskey, but so many of our young men drink it that it's like trying to stop a river from flooding. They'll do anything to get it, and men like Hagopian are always ready to help them."

"But there must be laws against such things!" she protested. "Surely the government—"

"Your government does nothing!" he snapped, pushed beyond the limits of his patience. Why was he wasting words on this woman? She would never understand the pain of his people. No *bilagáana* could ever understand!

"Remember the first time we met?" he said. "I told you then to go home and tell your president to send us back to Dinétah! That's the only place we can heal, the only place where we can be a whole people again!''

She touched his arm, her fingers light and cool. ''Ahkeah, I don't have the president's ear, but I'll do anything I can. I'll talk to people, write letters....''

She stopped speaking and withdrew her hand as she realized he had closed himself to her words. He could feel her hurt in the awkward silence that settled between them. She stared out across the alkali bed, her small, strong chin jutting stubbornly forward. None of this was her fault, Ahkeah knew. But he could not bring himself to apologize where there had been no wrong, or to offer comfort where there was none to be found.

In the distance, off to their left, a plume of dust lingered above the trail the Comanches had taken. Miranda's gazed narrowed as she watched it. ''What do you think they'll do now?'' she asked. ''Will they go home?''

Ahkeah shook his head. ''They've got whiskey, and only one thing on their minds. As soon as they find a sheltered spot, they'll open that jug and drink themselves senseless.''

The sparkle in her eyes gave her away even before she spoke. ''Then we still have a chance to get your horse back!''

He scowled at her. ''We aren't going to take any more chances. I'm taking you back to the fort. Now.'' He rose to his feet and, without bothering to brush the alkali dust off his clothes, thrust out a hand to help her up. "The Comanches are gone, and so is Hagopian, so we should be safe enough. Let's get going."

"No." Challenge flared in her eyes.

"No?" he retorted. "Are you saying I'll have to pick you up, carry you to the horse and sling you across the saddle like a sack of flour? That's exactly what I'll do if I have to, Miranda. This has gone far enough."

She glared up at him, her face spattered with dust, her tangled hair a wild, glowing mane in the afternoon sunlight. "Take me back now, and you'll lose those Comanches for good! Why give up now, when you could simply follow them, wait for them to get drunk and pass out, then sneak down and get your horse? I'll stay out of the way, I promise. You won't even know I'm there!"

Ahkeah groaned inwardly as he weighed her words. He knew he should get her back to the fort, but her plan made sense. So did the other, more urgent thought that flashed into his mind. What if the Comanches didn't pass out from the liquor? What if it only made them crazy and mean, and they set out with their brains on fire to murder the first Diné family they could find?

He owed it to his people to learn what these raiders were up to, and to warn anyone in their path. Miranda was a hindrance, and he knew he would be better off without her. But he needed her horse, and he could not send her back to the fort alone and on foot. He would have no choice except to take her with him.

"All right," he said, seizing her wrist and yanking her to her feet. "We'll trail them, but only at a distance. Any sign of trouble, and we turn back. I don't want to be responsible for what four drunken Comanches would do to a white woman. Do you understand?"

Miranda twisted her wrist out of his clasp. "I understand," she said in a small, stiff voice. "And I won't hold you responsible for anything that happens to me!" She turned away and marched past him, head high, toward the spot where she'd left the bay.

For the space of a long breath, Ahkeah stood gazing after her, thinking he'd been too harsh and should, perhaps, apologize. But this was for the best, he reminded himself. Keeping Miranda angry and at a distance was the safest course for them both.

He heard the big cavalry horse snort as she approached. Forcing himself to move, he hurried after her. In her present state of mind, Miranda was capable of vaulting into the saddle and riding off alone. He couldn't afford to let that happen.

The sun hung low above the western horizon, searing the clouds with crimson and casting long shadows across the flatland. A lone red-tailed hawk circled one last time, then banked and flapped its way homeward, its hunting curtailed by the vanishing light.

Miranda stifled a moan as she shifted her aching buttocks behind the saddle. Ahkeah had been trailing the Comanches across the desert for what seemed like hours, keeping the bay to a plodding pace that would not raise telltale dust. For most of that time she had clung to his back in silence. At first she'd been angry because of his high-handed treatment. Now she was simply tired. Why on earth had she suggested this madness? For a good deal less trouble, she could have found a way to replace Ahkeah's mount from the ample supply of horses at the fort. Now it was too late.

What was happening at the fort? she wondered. Surely she had been missed by now. Her father would be furious. He would have every man on the post looking for her. She felt sick as she thought of the trouble she had caused. She had always been such a *good* girl....

"There." Ahkeah's back tensed, its sudden hardness startling Miranda from a doze. She blinked herself awake, her weary gaze following the line of his pointing arm.

At first she could see nothing through the desert twilight. Then, as she stared, her eyes made out a faint curl of smoke against the deepening sky. Her heart crawled into her throat as she watched it rise. Trailing hostile Indians hadn't seemed like such a dangerous idea—until now.

"That would be where they've stopped," Ahkeah said. "We'll move in a little closer, then I'll leave you with the horse and go in on foot."

His words triggered a puckering sensation in the pit of her stomach. Why hadn't she taken him at his word and allowed him to escort her back to the fort? Now he was about to put his life on the line—and for a horse!

Not far ahead, a large mesquite bush cast its eerie shadow across the sand. Out here on the open desert, it was the best shelter they were likely to find. Ahkeah brought the horse to a stop in its shadow and slid lightly out of the saddle. His eyes reflected a bloodred glimmer of sky as he handed her the reins.

"Stay here," he ordered. "I mean it, Miranda. And if you hear any commotion, forget about me and get the blazes out of here."

"You're saying you can hold off four liquored-up Comanches on your own?" Her tremulous voice betrayed her attempt at lightness.

"I'm hoping I won't have to," he said grimly. "But if it comes to that, I'll have my hands full without you to worry about. I need to know you'll be safe. Is that clear?"

"Clear." She gazed down at his beautifully chiseled face, wishing with all her heart she'd had the sense to leave well enough alone. Ahkeah was a leader among his people and the father of a helpless little girl. If anything were to happen to him...

"We don't have to do this," she said, and caught the unexpected flash of his smile in the darkness. She knew, then, that it was too late to stop him. Ahkeah was a warrior, and the excitement of taking on an enemy was already a fire in his blood. Blast the man, he was *enjoying* this!

"Be careful," she whispered, quelling the impulse to reach out and touch him. Ahkeah was already beyond her reach. He had become a wild desert creature, stealthy and alert, eager for the hunt.

She watched him slip away, biting her lower lip as he disappeared into the twilight. What if there was trouble? Could she really do as he had ordered and ride to safety, leaving him to face terrible odds?

The light was fading fast now. In the sky, darkening clouds were sweeping over the horizon, driven by a breeze that carried the smell of rain. From somewhere out on the desert, the wailing cry of a lone coyote send a chill along Miranda's spine. Her heart was a fluttering moth, trapped against the wall of her ribs. She lifted the reins to turn the horse deeper into the shadow of the mesquite, then suddenly stopped herself.

What was she doing—quaking and wringing her hands like a silly little fool? She was a grown woman, resourceful and reasonably intelligent. If danger threatened, she would be ready for it. All she needed was a plan—and a weapon.

Fumbling in the half-light, she checked the saddle. What a fool she'd been, bringing nothing with her from the fort except the canteen! Even that might have served as a weapon had it been full. But by now two-thirds of the water was gone, and with it the weight she needed. The horse was a weapon in itself, as long as she could keep the nervous animal under control. But she needed something more—a rock, perhaps, or a limb; something solid.

Looping the reins over a branch of the mesquite bush, she slipped to the ground and began a cautious search.

* * *

Ahkeah crept forward, slipping from shadow to shadow as stealthily as a cougar. In one hand he clutched a small, sharp knife, the only weapon he possessed. Against four guns, or even one, the knife would be of little use. But if there was trouble he would give a good account of himself. He would fight and die like a warrior.

Like a warrior. A bitter smile flickered across Ahkeah's taut lips. He had ceased to be a warrior when he came down from the mountains of Dinétah to join his people on the Long Walk. Now he was only a desperate man, trying to recover a badly needed horse. One single, small, skinny horse—when he had once owned the finest herd in all Dinétah.

As he crept toward the enemy, he thought briefly of Miranda, waiting for him in the shelter of the mesquite bush. He remembered the fear in her beautiful gray eyes as she'd watched him go. Had that fear been for herself, alone in the desert night, or had it been for him?

What would she do if something went wrong?

He had ordered her to take her horse and run at the first sign of trouble. But he was beginning to know this woman and her reckless heart, and he knew better than to assume she would obey. To risk himself would be to risk Miranda—that thought sobered him as he made his way through the gathering darkness. He knew exactly what those Comanches would do to a pretty young white woman. The very thought of it left him dizzy with rage and horror. He would slit

Miranda's throat with his own knife before he let her fall into their hands.

But he was letting his mind jump ahead, when his full attention needed to be fixed on the task at hand. He would act with careful judgment, Ahkeah resolved. If he sensed that the odds were against him, he would abandon the horse, return to Miranda and rush her to safety.

A cool, moist breeze was blowing in from the west. The evening air quivered with squeaks and chirps as a myriad of creatures awakened to the night. A foraging bat whirred past Ahkeah's ear, its velvety wingtip almost brushing his cheek. He welcomed the near encounter as a blessing, a sign that, even though he was far from home, these desert creatures were his brothers and would do him no harm.

His nostrils caught the smell of mesquite smoke, bittersweet on the fresh night breeze. His straining eyes could not see the fire, but he suddenly realized that the Comanches had chosen a shallow wash for their whiskey drinking. The sloping sides would shelter them from the wind and hide their fire from approaching eyes. It was a clever hiding place. They were almost below him, even closer than he had realized.

Dropping to the earth, he bellied toward the edge and peered cautiously into the wash, where the fire had burned down to glowing coals. By the reddish glow, he could see the four Comanches. The first was slumped at the base of a boulder. Two more were sprawled on the far side of the fire, and the fourth lay in the shadow of a rock, the whiskey jug still clutched in his hand. All of them appeared to be fast asleep.

Ahkeah's fingers closed on a pebble that lay beneath his hand. With exquisite care he raised up and tossed it into the fire. It landed in the coals, sending up a shower of sparks. He held his breath, muscles tensed for flight. But no one moved.

As the seconds passed, he began to breathe again. Edging closer, he could see the horses bunched together a little way down the wash. They stood with drooping heads, still wearing their bridles. The Comanches would have been too thirsty to care for their animals properly—a small thing, but it fed the anger that already seethed beneath Ahkeah's icy surface.

As he glided down the slope into the wash, the temptation gnawed at him. He had his knife. He could kill them all, so swiftly and silently that they would not even scream. He could leave them for the buzzards and take everything—horses, guns, all the riches they possessed—back to his own people.

He held the thought for a moment, then discarded it. Past experience had taught him well. Any strike against the Comanches would bring terrible reprisals down on the helpless Diné. The suffering of his people was too high a price for four horses, four rifles and a warrior's pride. He would take back his own property and leave his enemies in peace.

Lightning flashed above the western horizon as he moved toward the horses. The rumble of thunder was faint, but he could tell the storm was moving in fast.

He needed to reach his horse quickly and get Miranda to shelter before the rain struck.

The horses snorted nervously as he approached. The Comanches had hobbled their front legs with rawhide thongs, and they moved with small, stumbling steps, shifting one way, then another. Ahkeah spoke softly to them, soothing them with his voice as he edged closer. Spooked by his presence—or perhaps by the coming rain—they tossed their heads and rolled their eyes, the whites flashing in the darkness.

Finding his own spotted mustang, Ahkeah caught its bridle. As he bent to slash its hobbles, a sudden idea struck him. Why not cut the other hobbles, as well? The horses would scatter on their own, leaving the Comanches on foot. Any raid they might be planning against the Diné would have to be called off.

Thunder rumbled again, closer this time, as he hacked through the tough rawhide. His own horse was free now. Looping its bridle around his wrist, he caught the nearest animal, braced himself against a foreleg and cut its bonds as well. Soon a second horse was free, then a third.

He was working on the last hobbled horse when a monstrous lightning bolt split the heavens with a shattering boom. For a fragment of time the world was frozen in blue light. Almost instantaneously, the universe seemed to explode. Ahkeah felt the sound like the crack of a giant whip. The earth quivered under the shock of the blow, throwing him off his feet.

In the next instant all hell broke loose as the narrow

wash erupted into a melee of screaming horses and staggering, shouting Comanches.

Ahkeah was struggling to his feet when the hoof of a rearing horse caught him across the temple. Dazed, he reeled and went down again with the mustang's reins still looped around his wrist. There was little he could do except hang on as the panic-stricken animal screamed, wheeled and began to run, dragging him down the wash.

Chapter Ten

Miranda had been mounted and waiting in the shadow of the mesquite bush, armed with a club-size root, when the lightning bolt struck.

Blinded by the flash and almost deafened by the shattering boom, she had clung to the squealing, bucking bay, fighting to get the horse under control. Only when the world had stopped shaking and her eyes and ears had begun to clear did she become aware of the uproar coming from the direction of the Comanche camp—screaming horses, shouting men and, suddenly, sickeningly, the metallic pop and whine of rifle shots.

Without stopping to think, she wheeled the bay, kicked it to an explosion of speed and raced toward the commotion. She knew what Ahkeah had told her. She knew the risk she was taking. But this was no time to think of her own safety.

Another lightning bolt crashed across the sky. Its stark blue light outlined the edge of a wash in her path, so close that in seconds she would have ridden over the crumbling rim. Thunder boomed around her as she swung her mount one way, then another, searching for a slope that the horse could manage. Searching for Ahkeah.

Below her, in the wash, she could make out flashes of movement. Men and horses milled crazily in the darkness, colliding with snorts and shrieks, like players in a scene from hell. She saw one man go down under the hooves of a rearing horse. Was it Ahkeah? Fear, sick and heavy, pulsed through her body as she strained to see through the murk.

Only when another flash of lightning lit the heavens did she see a way down. Without a moment's hesitation she swung the bay toward the spot where the edge of the wash had crumbled away, leaving a fan of rocky earth. Bent low along the horse's neck, Miranda rocketed down into the chaos.

"Ahkeah!" she shouted, glancing frantically around. "Ahkeah!" He did not answer, of course. Even if he was still alive, she knew he would not be able to hear her above the din.

Something clutched at her leg. Turning, she stared down into the savage face of a stranger. In a paroxysm of terror she swung the thick mesquite root, which miraculously was still in her hand. The wood connected with solid flesh and the face disappeared. But she and the horse had been seen, and a cry went up. With bloodcurdling screams two more Comanches surged toward her. Hands grabbed her skirt, and in the next instant the big bay was whirling and rearing. One man seized its bridle. Miranda kneed the horse, shot over the top of him and went pounding up the wash with the two Indians in pursuit.

Ahead of her, she could make out a pale blur against the earth. Was it Ahkeah? She shouted his name and he rose, struggling to his knees as she rode toward him. He moved like an injured man, and his horse was nowhere in sight.

Realizing she would have to get him up behind her, she slowed the bay. Hands clutched at the stirrup as the Comanches caught up with her. Something closed around her ankle, yanking roughly to pull her off the horse. She swung the club, only to have it snatched out of her fingers. Screaming, she clung to the saddle as more hands caught her jacket and ripped it in two.

When lightning cracked across the sky again, she saw that Ahkeah was up and wading into the fray. Wrenching the mesquite club away from one startled Comanche, he swung it with terrible strength, cracking bone where it struck home.

"Come on!" Miranda shouted as the heavens split open and rain descended in full fury. Taking advantage of the confusion, he sprang up behind her. She swung the horse again to clear the way, praying they could get out of the wash before the Comanches recovered their guns and started shooting.

Through the driving rain she could see the fan of earth where she'd ridden down into the wash. Now it was slippery mud. The bay struggled upward. For an instant it sank back on its haunches. Then it regained its feet, lurched the rest of the way, and suddenly they were on top, racing headlong across the desert.

Miranda pushed the horse, leaning over its neck as they flew into the storm. Her heart pumped terror through her veins, blunting the edge of her reason. She wanted only to get away from that place—as far away as possible. Rain streamed down, soaking her hair and clothes. The wet chill intensified her panic. Only the strength of Ahkeah's arms holding her from behind kept her from giving way to full-blown hysteria.

Not until he reached around her, took the reins from her chilled hands and pulled the horse to a stop did she realize she'd been out of control. She sank back against him, her whole body quivering. The storm, she realized, had diminished to a misty, gray drizzle.

"We can slow down now, Miranda." His voice was rough against her ear. "Those devils are in no condition to follow us, and we need to rest the horse."

She nodded shakily, her breath escaping in a broken sigh. "Are you all right?"

"Just skinned and bruised. My horse dragged me down the wash before it got away." His muscles hardened against her. "You crazy little woman!" he rasped. "What did you think you were doing? I told you to leave if there was trouble!"

Miranda swallowed hard. "I know...but I couldn't just ride off. I couldn't leave you there to die, Ahkeah."

He muttered something in his own language. "You could have been killed—or worse, captured. Facing death is nothing new to me—I've done it more times than I can count, and I'm still here. But you—''

"Stop it!" she whispered. "I'm safe. We're both safe. There's nothing more to say."

She felt him relax against her. "We were lucky," he muttered.

"Yes…lucky." Miranda leaned back to let her head rest in the hollow of his throat. His arms circled her tightly, crossing just above her waist, hands placed carefully—too carefully—on her ribs. A strange wildness crept over her senses—a wildness born of danger and rain and the warm, smoky nearness of Ahkeah's body. She closed her eyes, yearning, suddenly, to feel his hands in other places, to feel things she had never experienced in her rule-bound, sterile life.

Could this proud savage feel her heart beating beneath his palm? Could he imagine what was going through her mind?

His breath was like warm silk against her skin, the rhythm of it deep and even. She felt it catch and stop as she found his crossed hands and lifted them gently upward to cup her aching breasts.

"Miranda, don't—" The words emerged as a groan, but he did not move his hands, and she did not try to take them away. Afraid, almost, to breathe, she sat transfixed, her heart fluttering like a caged bird, her body throbbing with a need she barely understood. She only knew she wanted more, wanted this man and everything he could give her.

Ahkeah held her as the rain streamed down around

them. The softness of her breasts burned into his palms through the thin wet fabric of her blouse. Her fingers trembled where they rested on the backs of his hands. His throat was so tight he could scarcely breathe. He had wanted this woman, he realized, from the first time he saw her. But his had been a safe desire, because Miranda Howell was so out of reach that there'd been no question of even touching her.

His desire was safe no longer. Miranda was here— warm and real, reaching out to him with a woman's need.

She leaned against him, her back slightly arched, her wet head cradled against his neck. Her nipples were taut little buds against his palm. The urge to stroke and caress them was a fever in his blood.

Tentatively, he bent and brushed her forehead with his lips. She moaned softly, pressing his hands tighter against her breasts. The scent of lilacs stole into his nostrils, sweet and erotic now, evoking no more memories of the past. Ahkeah knew he would never again smell those heady spring blossoms without remembering the feel of Miranda in his arms.

The bay snorted and shook its wet hide, startling them both back to the cold, dark present. Rain was dripping down on them and they were both soaked and chilled to the bone. Ahkeah had survived many such nights, but Miranda had not. She needed warmth and rest.

He felt her shudder as he forced his hands away from the sweet softness of her breasts. "We need to get you out of the rain," he said. "I know a place—

not much more than an overhang, but at least it's shelter."

"Is it far?" Her teeth chattered as she gazed out into the rainy darkness.

"Not far."

"How can you be sure?" she demanded testily. "We can't even see the stars!"

Without answering her question, he swung a leg over the bay's rump and slid down its haunch to the ground. The twinge in his wrenched shoulder reminded him of the lost mustang. He'd been lucky to get free of the tangled reins before the spooked animal dragged him through a clump of prickly pear or slammed his head against a boulder. As it was, the accident had left him dazed and vulnerable. Miranda's arrival had probably saved his life.

"Come on down," he said, reaching up to her. "We're going to walk for a while. You'll be warmer on foot than riding, and it will spare the horse."

She put her hands on his shoulders, avoiding his eyes as he caught her waist and eased her out of the saddle. Was she thinking about what she had done with his hands? Was she so ashamed that now she could not look at him?

Their bodies brushed lightly, triggering a rush of remembered sensation as he lowered her to the ground. She was so small and light. So cold. Ahkeah fought the urge to sweep her into his arms and storm the barrier that had sprung up between them. That would be foolish, he lectured himself. They had already taken things too far. And right now his main concern had to be getting Miranda out of the weather. The hidden cave in the escarpment didn't offer much in the way of comfort, but at least it would be dry. And with luck, the firewood and jerked mutton he'd stashed in its recesses, against just such an emergency, would be where he'd left it.

She turned away from him and stood rubbing the soreness from her lower back, the motion so sensual that Ahkeah forced himself to avert his eyes. He busied himself with checking the horse, fighting the memory of his hands cupping the soft swell of her breasts, the feel of her swollen nipples against his fingertips, and the fluttering beat of her woman's heart.

Should he apologize? Ahkeah pondered the question, but only for the space of a breath. He had done nothing she hadn't pressed him to do. Besides, it was clear enough that Miranda had no wish to talk about the matter. They would take the easy way out, then, and simply go on, pretending the moment had never happened.

Weary and sore, he caught up the dangling reins with one hand and stepped forward into the drizzling rain. Out of the corner of his eye he saw Miranda hesitate. Then she broke into a stride that brought her abreast of him. Leading the horse, they walked together in a truce of uneasy silence.

Miranda trudged through a rain puddle, too tired to step across. Water oozed into her boots, sloshing up between her toes with each step. Her feet were numb with cold, but she was long past caring. She had done a reckless thing, and Ahkeah's taciturn silence was enough to let her know how wrong she had been.

Even now, her breasts tingled at the memory of his touch and the wild, forbidden sweetness it had awakened in her body. Was she sorry for what had happened? Would she have been better off not knowing such feelings existed? Miranda had no answers. She only knew that she was cold, tired and confused—and that if he reached out to her again she would fly to his arms like a moth to a flame.

She glanced at Ahkeah's stern profile, dark against the mist of rain. He had scarcely spoken in the past hour. Was he angry? Did he hate her, as he hated all whites? Again, there were no answers, only questions.

Pain shot up her leg as she stubbed her toe against a rock. She bit back a whimper. She would die before she would complain to Ahkeah, who had walked with his people from Dinétah to the hell of Fort Sumner. She had read accounts of the Long Walk in Eastern newspapers. But these had been written by white reporters, who had almost certainly pieced their stories from secondhand information. What had that time been like for the Diné? Even now, chilled and exhausted as she was, Miranda could scarcely imagine the misery.

As if he had felt her eyes on him, Ahkeah cast her a sidelong glance. "It's not much farther," he said. "If you're too tired to go on I can help you back on the horse."

She shook her head. "I was just thinking about the

Long Walk and how difficult it was for your people. Surely it must have been a hundred times worse than this.''

Ahkeah's abrupt silence told her she had said the wrong thing. As he turned away from her with a low growl of disgust, Miranda realized her remark had sounded naive and crass. His wife had died on that hellish trek, as had hundreds of others. *Difficult* was just the sort of word a spoiled, protected white woman—the woman he perceived her to be—would use to describe that unspeakable time.

Suddenly Miranda could not keep silent.

''I know what you think of me!'' she declared, as if speaking to the rain and the wind and the desert. ''You think I'm nothing but a nuisance—a pampered, bored do-gooder playing games for her own amusement! But you know even less about me than I know about you!'' She took a deep breath and plunged ahead.

''During the war, while I was helping my uncle in the army hospital, I saw enough misery to last me for the rest of my life! I wrote letters for men whose eyes were burned away. I dressed festering wounds and held sixteen-year-old boys in my arms while my uncle sawed off their rotting legs! I watched them die, so young, so many of them…''

Her voice broke and trailed off into silence as she struggled to clear the horror from her mind. ''I chose to become a teacher because I hoped to prevent a little of the suffering in this world—the kind of suffering I saw in that hospital, the kind I see here at Fort

Sumner! I'm not the woman you think I am, Ahkeah! I know a thing or two about life, and I'm tired of your treating me like a backward child!''

The stillness that followed her outburst was broken only by the echo of retreating thunder. Ahkeah walked beside her, as coldly distant as the moon. Clearly, nothing she'd told him had made any difference.

But what had she expected? Miranda berated herself. After all, the war had only touched those parts of her she'd allowed it to touch. She'd lost no one she truly loved, nothing she truly valued. Every blessed night, after those grueling days at the hospital, she'd gone home to a hot meal, a warm bath and a soft, clean bed.

Ahkeah's war was different. It was inside him, ravaging every part of his life. He had lost everything except the pain and rage that was etched into every fiber of his character. And here she was, babbling like a schoolgirl, trying to convince him she had the wisdom to understand.

Why hadn't she stayed in the East where she belonged? Why had she traveled so far, only to find a father who didn't want her, a people who scorned her help, and this stubborn, infuriating man whose very silence challenged everything she'd believed herself to be?

She strode ahead, biting back the urge to turn and shout at him, to tell him he'd won, that she was giving up and going home, leaving him and his people free to wallow in their own misery. She wanted to scream at him that she'd had enough, that she didn't care—

But it wouldn't be true. She cared deeply and passionately. Standing in front of her class that very morning, looking into those somber little bronze faces, with their haunting eyes, she had burned with the need to help these children. Why couldn't Ahkeah accept that? Why couldn't he understand?

Why couldn't he at least look at her?

Tears of frustration welled in Miranda's eyes, blurring her vision in the darkness. She did not even see the washed-out badger hole before she stumbled into it. Her ankle twisted beneath her, throwing her off balance and causing one leg to buckle. With a little sob of pain and exhaustion, she toppled to one side, landing hard on the rain-soaked earth.

Her fists balled into the mud. "I'm all..." she started to say, then her voice trailed off as she felt Ahkeah's big, rough hands catching her elbows, lifting her up, supporting her from behind.

She turned in the circle of his arms. Then, suddenly, he was holding her, crushing her close, molding her to his lean, solid body.

Miranda gasped as she burst into flame against him. Her muddy hands clawed at his shirt, hungry, seeking, wild with the need to touch him, to feel him everywhere—his chest, his shoulders, the ebony knot of his hair... Catching the back of his head, she pulled him down to her and captured him in a long, devouring kiss. His mouth was hard and sweet and smoky, heaven against her own. She was ravenous for the taste of him, for the feel of his lips on hers, the smell of him, the wonderful textures of his beardless face, his rain-slicked hair, his sinewy male body.

Through the wetness of her skirt she felt him rise and harden against her. The ridge of pressure along her belly triggered a shock of heat that forked through her like summer lightning. She had seen such things happen to men in the hospital, and had learned to avert her eyes. But this was Ahkeah. She was in his arms. He wanted her. And, dear heaven, she wanted him. Here. Now. In the mud and rain, if need be, with the horse standing quiet guard over them.

Once more she reached down, lifted his hand upward and cupped it on her breast. She felt no misgivings, no shame. Nothing mattered except giving herself to this man, heart, soul and body.

"Miranda—" Ahkeah struggled to protest, for her sake, but her name emerged as a groan of desire. She was like living flame beneath his touch, searing his soul with need—this passionate little *bilagáana* who smelled of lilacs, thrust herself where she was not wanted, and fought him at every turn. This proud, courageous woman who had captivated him.

The wet blouse clung to her breast like skin, yielding softly to his hand. She arched upward. Her breath came in sharp gasps as he lifted her and bent his head, burying his face in her fragrant ivory sweetness until his lips found the taut nub of her nipple. She went molten against him as he nuzzled and sucked her through the gauzy fabric. Her hands clutched him wildly, kneading his chest and shoulders, her fingers working in and out like the claws of an eager little cat. It was easy to tell she'd never had a man before. She was so innocent, so vulnerable, and she was offering him all she had—the precious gift of her fresh, young love.

Swallowing the aching tightness in his throat, Ahkeah lowered her feet to the ground. "Miranda, I don't want to hurt you," he whispered.

"You could never hurt me." She clasped him fiercely, as if she could not bear to let him go. Ahkeah cradled her a moment longer, thinking how wrong she was. He could do more than hurt her. If what happened between them became known, it could destroy her.

"We need to get out of the weather," he said, forcing himself to release her. "There's a place in those rocks up ahead." He pointed to where the jagged, black silhouette of the escarpment rose against the cloud-mottled sky. "We'll get there faster if you ride." Catching her waist, he swung her up to the saddle. She scrambled into a place without a word, but the eyes that gazed down at him in the darkness were wide with questions.

How could he answer those questions? Even now his whole being ached for the feel of her in his arms, the unbridled joy of being wrapped in those silken legs as he buried himself to the hilt in her moist womanly warmth. The very danger of it made his head swim.

Turning away from her, Ahkeah picked up the reins and strode into the darkness. By rights, he should force her to leave, or walk away himself. But there was no place to send her, and no place for him to go. They were trapped together on this rainy night, the two of them wandering in a morass of desire, joy and impending tragedy.

The small cave cut only a few yards into the ledge, but its entrance was screened from view by the rocks that rose in front, making it an excellent hiding place. Even the horse was sheltered out of sight in the gully below, where a tiny spring fed a few precious clumps of green grass.

"How...did you find...this place?" Miranda's teeth chattered as she huddled on the sandy floor of the cave. Her gaze followed Ahkeah as he glided in and out of the shadows. How beautiful he was, his coppery skin gleaming where he passed through rays of moonlight. Oh, she knew it was foolish to want him. They were from two different worlds. But tonight only one thing mattered. He was a man, she was a woman, and she wanted him more than she had ever wanted anything in her rational, sensible life.

"I found this cave when I was tracking a bobcat." Ahkeah had emerged from beneath a low ledge, carrying something wrapped in a dusty Navajo blanket. "But my people have other hiding places, too. We leave them ready for anyone who needs them. Later I'll come back here and replace what we use."

He unrolled the blanket on the floor of the cave, and Miranda saw that it contained several mesquite roots, a few slivers of fatwood for kindling, a dozen strips of dried meat and a small box of matches. Here was fuel, food and the makings of a bed; and for anyone who needed it, there would be water from the spring below. A Navajo with reason to hide could disappear in such a place.

She watched Ahkeah as he crouched near the cave's entrance and arranged the wood into a small, neat pyramid. If only the two of them could disappear, just vanish together from the world of hate and prejudice that seemed to be all around them—the world that would ultimately tear them apart. If only she could spend the rest of her life with him, sharing the simple pleasures of a warm fire and a blanket on the sand...

But she was clasping at dreams now—dreams that would never come true. They had their duties, he to his child and his tribe, and she...

Her thoughts dissolved in a wave of tenderness as he lit the fire, and, sheltering the tiny flame with his hand, turned to look at her. Reflections of the kindled fire blazed in the midnight depths of his eyes, and she knew that, for her, tomorrow no longer mattered. For her there was only this secret place, this beautiful man, and this enfolding circle of light and warmth.

Chapter Eleven

Firelight danced on the sandstone walls of the cave, warming the darkness with soft gold. Ahkeah checked the entrance one more time to make certain the horse was safe below. The Comanches should be in no condition to ride, but long experience had taught him never to drop his guard.

Turning, he walked back toward Miranda, who huddled, shivering, on the floor of the cave. "You need to get out of those wet clothes," he said, lifting her by her elbows.

She nodded, too cold to speak. Her lips were tinged with blue, and the remnant of the jacket that the Comanches had ripped apart clung wetly to her shoulders. Her fingers shook as she fumbled with the ridiculously tiny shell buttons that secured the front of her rain-soaked blouse.

Gently he lifted her icy hands away and began working the buttons himself, pushing them awkwardly through their holes. Her eyes widened sharply as the blouse fell open and his knuckle brushed the ivory moon of bare skin that curved above the lace edging of her camisole. The brief contact recalled, achingly, the softness of her breast, cupped so perfectly in his palm.

Ahkeah reined in the urge to start once more where they had left off. He had fought that battle with himself as he knelt to make the fire, and his better side had won. Making love to Miranda would be sweet beyond imagining. But the thought of what she would have to face when it was over—no, the price would be too high. As soon as she was able to ride, he'd resolved, he would send her back to the fort untouched.

Now she stood before him, her skin glowing like polished opal in the firelight. A drop of water sparkled on her lower lip. He found himself longing to bend down and taste it, to taste her, every part of her.

His breath caught as her hand crept upward and, with trembling fingers, slipped beneath his tunic.

"Miranda—" he began, but her kiss blocked his words. Her lips were chilled, but their touch ignited currents of searing heat that flamed downward, igniting a bonfire in his loins. Ahkeah prayed for strength as he forced his arms to thrust her away from him.

"Miranda, we can't do this."

She stared up at him, her silver eyes so beautiful, so filled with distress that he had to swallow the tightness in his throat before he spoke again.

"Think about it. If we don't stop now, you'll regret this night for the rest of your life."

"Would *you* regret it?" she challenged him.

"For the harm done to you, yes," he said. "*Think,* Miranda. What if someone were to find out? What if I were to get you…" He hesitated, knowing that *bilagáana* women did not talk freely about such matters.

"With child?" She finished his sentence. Then her eager expression crumbled like a clay mask as her shoulders sagged in defeat. "Why do you always have to be right?" she asked in a small, thin voice. "For once why can't you be gloriously, wonderfully wrong?"

Turning away from him, she began buttoning up her blouse, her hands still clumsy with cold, her mouth set against any show of emotion. He watched her, longing to forget all their words and take her in his arms.

"You still need to get out of those clothes," he said, deliberately turning away and walking back toward the fire. "You can spread them on the rocks and wrap up in the blanket. But for safety's sake, you probably ought to take them off yourself."

Her fingers paused, then she sighed and began undoing the buttons again. "You're as wet as I am."

"I'm fine," Ahkeah muttered. In truth, he was not fine, but the worst thing he could do right now would be to undress and risk showing her the aroused state of his body. He wanted her so much that he could not even look at her without feeling a jolt of desire.

Staring out of the cave entrance, he struggled to ignore the sounds of her undressing—the pop of a button, the little feminine grunt as she worked the wet riding skirt down over her hips. Each minute was like being skewered with burning cactus thorns. Ahkeah forced himself to think about all the *bilagáana* he had known and how much he'd despised them. Even that did not keep him from wanting her.

"What time is it, do you suppose?" She had come up to stand beside him, and he saw that she was wrapped to the collarbone in the rough wool blanket, with only the lace straps of her camisole showing at the shoulders.

"Does it matter?" Ahkeah thrust his hands into his pockets and gazed out at the drizzling rain, avoiding her with his eyes.

"Not here, I suppose." She clutched the blanket, her teeth chattering again. "Your people don't use clocks, do they? They have the sun and the moon and the stars. Sometimes I forget that."

"You're still cold," he said. "You need to get closer to the fire."

"Tell me about the Long Walk."

The words, so softly spoken, struck Ahkeah with the force and pain of a bullet. Except for passing mentions, he never talked about that ordeal. Few of the Diné did. It was a dark time, best forgotten.

"You're tired," he said, choosing evasion. "Why not get some rest? I'll keep watch."

"Tell me, Ahkeah."

Her blanketed shoulder brushed his arm. He glanced down to find her gazing up at him, her eyes wide and sad. "Talking to you is like chasing a shadow," she said, "always changing, always slipping away before I can catch it."

"Why would you want to catch a shadow?" he asked, tasting bitterness. "What would you have if you could touch it with your hands and hold it in your arms? You'd have nothing, Miranda. The man I used to be is gone, and there's nothing left but the shadow. All of us—all the Diné—are shadows."

"Not the children!" She was at once passionate. "Not those eager little faces I see in my classroom! They're real and solid and bright, Ahkeah! And they need to look to the future, not to the past!"

Ahkeah groaned. He had no wish to argue with this stubborn woman about things that would never be reconciled. All he really wanted was to unroll that blanket on the sand, lie down with her in his arms and thrust himself into the sweet, warm honey of her body until they were both dizzy and sated with love-making.

Instead he wrapped his arms around her, blanket and all, and half carried her around to the inward side of the fire, where the glowing warmth was already diffusing into the dank air of the cave. "Firewood is scarcer than gold in these parts," he growled, settling himself against the slope of the wall. "We can't let the heat go to waste."

She sank into his warmth, cradled by his arms with her back against his chest. "Oh, Ahkeah," she whispered, "why does everything have to be so complicated?"

"Shh." He closed his eyes, drinking in the fragrance of her damp hair and skin. "Don't think about it,'' he muttered, his senses swimming. "Just rest and try to get warm."

"But I want to know you—everything about you—"

"Shh." His lips brushed the fine ridge above her temple. Through the blanket he could feel that she was still shivering, and he realized the dense wool was only serving to keep out the fire's heat.

And his own.

"Open the blanket, Miranda," he murmured, his voice thick with desire. He was losing the battle with his conscience, he knew, but the urge to touch her was like a cry inside him. She was so soft and beautiful, so needing. Even through the heavy wool he could feel the pounding of her heart. Her body tensing beneath the blanket as she hesitated. "Open it," he said. "Let the flame warm you."

She stirred against him. Then the blanket parted in front, exposing her damp underthings and the lushly curved body beneath. Her hands held the top edge, angling the corners upward like the unfolding wings of a bird. Ahkeah could see nothing of her. But his imagination ran wild, conjuring up delicious images of rain-dampened fabric clinging to her creamy skin, of swelling breasts and moist, forbidden folds. His body ached to possess her—this passionate, courageous white woman. This *bilagáana*. This enemy.

As the fire's heat caressed Miranda's chilled skin, she felt her senses uncurling like dark red poppy petals. She was exquisitely aware of Ahkeah's powerful arms cradling her from behind and the iron ridge of his manhood pressing against her lower back. Her blood simmered in the warm, intimate darkness of the cave. She knew that she should be afraid. She was not.

Still, her mind groped for a modicum of reason. They'd been talking, she remembered, arguing, something about the children. The safe course would be to continue the conversation. But now she found that the words—like her plans for a perfect life—had gone up in smoke, burned to ashes in the heat of her passion for this dark and splendid savage.

Ahkeah had spoken to her, wise words of caution and restraint. But Miranda knew, in her heart, that if he so much as touched her she would be his. Tomorrow... But there was no tomorrow. Here, in this warm, dark little world, there was only now.

He groaned as she pressed against him. "Miranda—" His voice rasped her ear like the caress of rough velvet. "Miranda, you can't—"

She let the blanket drop, turned around and moved into his arms.

He groaned, then caught her close, his strong hands molding her body to his. Her fingers plucked frantically at his tunic, baring his coppery chest to her touch, to her kisses. He tasted the way he smelled—clean and wild and smoky. Her mouth could not get enough of him.

Dizzy with need, she whimpered, incoherent little cries, as his mouth moved over her face, her throat. "Yes, oh, yes..." she whispered, as his hands found her breasts, peeling away the wet lace to cup her bare skin. His thumb fondled the sensitive tip of her nipple, triggering ripples of sensation that shimmered in the pulsing depths of her body.

She kissed his mouth, his throat, the smooth hollow where his collarbones came together. She wanted to kiss every beautiful part of him. Was this good little Miranda, who'd always done the proper thing? This wanton, so eager to plunge over the precipice into the sea of ruin and regret? "Yes," she whispered as he bent to nuzzle the cleft between her breasts. "Oh, yes...yes..."

The taste of her bare skin sparked pinwheels of sensation that rocketed through Ahkeah's body, setting off a conflagration that burned away the last of his resolve. His loins ached with the need to plunge inside her, to thrust hard and deep to his release. But that, he knew, would not be enough—not with this beautiful, giving woman who had so much to learn. He wanted to take his time, to drive her wild with the pleasure of loving, to watch her face as she shattered beneath him again and again. He wanted to make her soar like a falcon, all the way to the sky.

Releasing her, he tossed the blanket onto the smooth sand. Then, gathering her in his arms, he pulled her down beside him. She was still half-clothed, as he was. Ahkeah fumbled with the fastenings of her pink satin corset until she reached down and unhooked it with her more experienced fingers. As the garment parted and fell away, she reached up and caught his face between her hands.

"I love you, Ahkeah," she whispered, her voice

and eyes fierce with conviction. "Whatever happens, remember that—"

His kiss cut off the rest of her words. He knew what she wanted to hear, but he had no avowals or promises to give her in return. Miranda had captured his heart, but his whole life belonged to his people. Only this night could be theirs.

How lovely she was, lying there beneath him on the rough blanket, her lips wet and swollen, her tawny hair framing her face in a wild tumble. Keeping his eyes on her face, he allowed his hand to glide downward. Her lace-edged drawers parted at a touch, offering him the milky satin of her thighs. She gasped, then moaned as his fingers brushed the nest of curls at their joining. Her hips arched upward against his hand, begging for more. Ahkeah felt his heart swell and burst as he lowered his mouth to her breast and, with his fingertips, began stroking the delicate, moist folds of her womanhood.

Miranda exploded beneath his touch. She cried out, swept away by the power of her own response as he took her to the brink again, then again. His mouth suckled her breasts, pulling, licking, tugging. Creating sensations so exquisite she could hardly bear them.

Her hands fluttered over his smooth, muscular back, down along his ribs to the waistband of his trousers. Frantically she tugged at the drawstring, wanting what lay beneath, wanting all of him. "Take me, Ahkeah," she murmured, feverish with need. "Now...oh, please, my love..."

She felt a beat of hesitation in him; then, as if it

had not happened, he raised up on one arm and rid himself of the interfering trousers in a single motion. How beautiful he was, his body like burnished copper in the golden firelight. Dear heaven, how she wanted him. "Please," she whispered, wild with yearning. "Ahkeah—"

Her words ended in a gasp of wonder as he glided into her, his stroke so smooth—and her own body so ready—that she scarcely felt the twinge of pain that ended her maidenhood. She was aware of nothing except Ahkeah, filling her, loving her, touching her where only he belonged.

How natural it seemed to push upward, meeting his thrust, bringing him deeper, deeper…. She had been born for this, she thought, born for him.

The rhythm of loving took her, carried her on a journey that was like a flight into the heavens. She felt him rising with her, felt the swelling, the soaring until they burst like twin comets and spiraled back to earth in a glimmering shower of stars.

They lay spooned in the doubled blanket, watching the fire burn down to embers. Miranda curled her naked body into his, drifting in the warmth of his enfolding arms. They had made love until they were too spent to move. Now they lay in the afterglow, waiting for the rain to end, knowing that the secret world they'd created was too fragile to survive beyond this circle of darkness and firelight. Soon they would be forced to reenter the world they had left behind—a world of hardship and hatred, with no forgiveness for those who broke its rules.

The plaintive cry of a coyote echoed through the darkness, rising and falling on the desert wind. Miranda snuggled deeper into the blanket. She had grown accustomed to the animals on the ride from Santa Fe, and had come to enjoy their haunting nighttime calls. Thus, it surprised her to feel the shudder that passed through Ahkeah's body as the cry died away.

"What is it?" she whispered, alarmed.

"Nothing." His arms tightened around her. "Only memories."

"The coyote?"

Miranda felt the turmoil in his long silence, and she knew he was thinking about the Long Walk. "Tell me," she whispered. "I need to understand."

"You can't possibly understand." His body quivered with tension. "Not unless you were there. Not unless you walked with us every step of the way. People were driven like cattle over the frozen ground, some with no shoes, no coats. Anyone who fell behind—a child, a woman, it didn't matter—they were shot by the soldiers and left where they lay. We marched to the echo of gunfire up and down the line...." His voice trailed off. He swallowed hard.

"The coyotes and wolves fed on the Diné that fell along the way. At night, in our camps, we would hear their cries and know what was happening. You can't blame the animals. They were only following their nature. Still, to lie there in the dark and listen..."

Miranda twisted her body beneath the blanket and wrapped him in her arms as the coyote's lonesome wail drifted again through the rainy night. She clasped him close, knowing that no woman's love could erase what Ahkeah held in his heart. She had wanted to understand this man and his people. But their memories held pain beyond the power of her imagination. Even the horrors of the military hospital could not compare with what he was telling her now.

"My wife…" The words emerged slowly, forced one at a time from his throat. Miranda sensed the spilling of memories as she held him—all the dear and tender things he chose not to tell her. She could only imagine how beautiful Nizhoni's mother must have been and how deeply Ahkeah had loved her.

"Her child came—or started to come—on the third day of the march," he said, "more than a moon before its time. I did my best to carry her, but when the pains got worse we had to stop. I hid her behind a clump of sage—there was nothing bigger—and sent Nizhoni ahead with old Hedipa while I stayed to help. I knew the baby would not live. But at least I had hope that if the birth was fast and easy, she might be able to go on…."

A shudder passed through his lean body. Miranda tightened her arms around him, aware that she was glimpsing the raw core of a man's soul.

"The baby—it wouldn't come. I lay next to her most of the day, putting my hand over her mouth to smother her screams. By the time the soldiers found us, I knew she was dying."

"They shot her?" Miranda asked, aching for him.

"I would have forced them to shoot me, too," he continued in a hoarse whisper, "but I knew I had to live for Nizhoni and for my people. If they'd only let me bury her, to keep her body from the animals…"

Light from the dying embers cast a fiery glow over Ahkeah's haggard face, reflecting glints of flame in the midnight depths of his eyes. Miranda gazed up at him, her throat too constricted to speak.

"I turned my back on them and started scraping away the earth. But they jabbed me with their bayonets and forced me to go on with the others. They must have had orders not to kill me, or they would likely have done it then." His throat jerked as he swallowed. "Late that night I stole out of the camp and went back to her. The coyotes were already gathering, but I chased them away and dug the grave with my bare hands—I had no other tools. When it was done I piled rocks over her, hoping it would be enough…."

Again his voice trailed off. Miranda could feel the anguish in his body, the clenched muscles, the knotted sinews. She ached to gather him into her warmth and love away all the pain. But she knew better than to try. Ahkeah was speaking to her now from a place she could not reach.

"The soldiers caught me coming back—I was too tired to be careful. They tied me to a wagon wheel and whipped me as an example to the others."

"Oh—" Her arms tightened, but he only stiffened against her.

"The beating was nothing. After what had happened, taking my eyes or my hands would have been little more than nothing. But when two of them rode off with shovels and came back later, laughing at me where I lay tied to the wheel—"

"Oh, Ahkeah!" Tears flowed freely down Miranda's cheeks. Pathetic, inadequate tears, with no power to heal.

His hollow eyes stared into the dying fire. "I can only imagine they wanted to make an example of me, so no one else would try the same thing. That night, the coyotes...those hellish calls..."

Ahkeah bowed his head, unable to go on.

They left as soon as the rain stopped, riding double beneath the midnight sky. Miranda clung to Ahkeah's rigid back, her love made sharp by the painful weight of the silence between them. She had wanted to look into his Indian soul and know him for what he was. But the brief glimpse he had given her held so much pain that she could scarcely fathom what else might be hiding in the darkness of his spirit. How could she hope to know him? Ahkeah was far beyond her knowing.

She pressed her cheek against the back of his damp shirt, loving him with all her aching heart. She had once been naive enough to believe that the only barrier between them was the color of their skins. In her snobbish Anglo-Saxon way, she'd assumed that he was somehow beneath her station. She knew better now, and she felt years removed from the innocent young woman who'd stolen out of the fort for a forbidden ride with the most compelling man she'd ever known.

In the past twelve hours she had learned that race and station were matters of perception—matters that could, perhaps, be conquered by love. But Ahkeah's bitterness against whites ran deeper, infusing every fiber of his being. He had loved her with all the passion of his warrior's body. But Miranda knew he could never offer his heart to a white woman.

The storm had blown east, leaving only a chilly night wind in its wake. Stars glittered in the clean-swept sky, as beautiful and cold as diamonds above the desert, where moon shadows pooled like inky mirages.

Miranda peered past his shoulders, her eyes scanning the black horizon. Earlier they had decided to return to the fort by way of his camp. She had agreed readily to this plan, knowing that Nizhoni and the old woman would be worried. The place was not far, Ahkeah had told her, only a few miles out of the way.

In truth, the distance could not have been long enough for Miranda. She had spent the time pressed against his back, filling her senses with the scent of skin and hair, the hardness of bone and muscle, knowing that through the lonely nights to come, she would have only these memories to hold.

"There." He gestured to a pinpoint of light below the horizon, then suddenly went rigid against her.

"What is it?" Miranda asked, alarmed.

"Fire," he said. "They shouldn't be lighting a fire

at this time of night. Not with wood so scarce. Something's wrong.''

He kneed the bay to a gallop, the sudden jerk of motion almost throwing Miranda to the ground. She clutched at him, fighting to regain her seat as the horse shot forward.

''Could the fire be for you—to guide you home?'' she gasped, bouncing crazily. But there was no reply from Ahkeah. He was leaning forward in the saddle, pushing the horse full out as they raced through the night.

Chapter Twelve

The flames grew brighter as they neared the isolated Navajo camp. Miranda felt Ahkeah's dread in the tautness of his muscles and in the pounding of his heart where her hand lay against his chest. Was the fire a beacon, a signal for help? Or had the Comanches somehow recovered their horses and galloped through the night to burn and destroy the remnant of Ahkeah's family?

The last idea seemed far-fetched, but she strained forward with him, her heart pounding at a pace to match his own as they galloped up the last rise onto the small plateau where the camp lay.

She braced herself for the worst. But there were no dwellings ablaze, no mutilated bodies lying on the ground. Her searching eyes saw only the open campfire, small in the night, with several horses milling in the shadows beyond. One of them, she realized, was Ahkeah's spotted mustang. It had found its way home on its own.

Miranda had never seen a Navajo settlement. She

had read that they lived in small family groups, in six-sided log-and-earth structures known as hogans. But she saw no hogans here, only heaps of earth, like the dirt mounds she'd seen in prairie dog warrens. Only as she looked closer did she realize that, with no logs or bricks to work with, the Navajos had been forced to dig into the ground for shelter, roofing their dugouts with stiffened hides to keep out the weather.

As Ahkeah reined the bay to a halt, a frail, hunched figure emerged from a dugout and hobbled toward him, uttering shrill, birdlike cries of distress. Miranda's heart contracted as she recognized the old woman the soldiers called Crazy Sally.

"Wait here." Ahkeah flung himself out of the saddle and sprinted toward the old woman. The two of them met at the edge of the firelight—she clutching at his arm with her tiny crab-claw hands; he bending over her, questioning, agitated. As Miranda watched, hoping to learn more, he turned suddenly, rushed to the entrance of the nearby dugout and vanished from sight.

Miranda clung to the back of the horse, feeling as if she'd just been left alone on the moon. Ahkeah had told her to wait, but if something was wrong—if someone was sick or hurt—shouldn't she be helping? She was, after all, a trained nurse. Ahkeah knew that, but he hadn't even bothered to tell her what was happening.

As she peered into the darkness around her, she became aware that she was not alone. Curious eyes, she sensed, stared at her from the shadows, inspecting her pale, tangled hair and strange clothes. Dark shapes moved, half seen beyond the fire—not many of them, but very real.

Miranda fought the impulse to kick the horse and bolt into the night. These silent watchers probably hated whites as much as Ahkeah did. But if she wanted their respect, she could not show fear. She had come here under Ahkeah's protection, she reminded herself. Anyone who harmed her would surely answer to him.

Resolving to be bold, she slid off the horse, dropped the reins and strode confidently toward the fire. As she neared the light, the shadowy forms became people—men and women bent with age, dark-eyed children and their shy mothers—weak and helpless beings that Ahkeah appeared to have taken under his care. How could she have thought to be afraid of them?

Stepping close enough to feel the fire's welcome heat, she stood rubbing her chilled hands and wishing someone could tell her what was happening. She was weighing the wisdom of following Ahkeah into the dugout when she felt a gentle tug at her skirt.

Looking down, she saw a boy of about eight, wearing nothing but a ragged and stained blue shirt that looked as if it had once belonged to a cavalryman. When she took an involuntary step backward, the tugging became an urgent yank. Only then, as she allowed him to lead her away from the fire, did Miranda turn and see what her boots had nearly trampled.

There on the ground, a four-foot circle of buckskin,

perfectly shaped, had been placed within the ring of firelight. On its flat, smooth surface, an intricate design, perfect in every detail, had been laid out in patterns of what looked to be colored sand.

Transfixed, she backed off a little to watch the old Navajo who sat cross-legged on the earth, using his leathery fingers to dribble sand, cornmeal and charcoal in precise lines and shapes onto the unfinished parts of the design. It was a creation of exquisite beauty, with three tall, stylized figures—gods, perhaps—filling its center, bordered by rings of bird and animal shapes, suns, moons and abstract lines in shades of brown, black, red and yellow. Where the sand grains caught the glow of firelight, the painting seemed to pulse with a life force of its own. How could anyone think of these people as backward and uneducated when they were capable of such artistry? Miranda thought. What if her clumsy boots had destroyed one of those beautiful edges? She would never have forgiven herself!

The sand painting's purpose remained a mystery. Perhaps it was to be part of some celebration…. But no, the people around the fire seemed edgy and worried. No one was taking pleasure in the old man's masterpiece. Oh, where was Ahkeah? What was wrong down there in the dugout, where he had vanished so suddenly?

As she watched, the old man let the last of the sand trickle between his fingers. Then, with the design complete, he gathered up the bags and small bottles that held his precious materials and put them to one side. A deep hush had fallen over the watchers. Even the children were silent as they waited.

Suddenly a flicker of candlelight lit the entrance of the dugout. All eyes turned toward Ahkeah as he emerged from the earth and moved like a sleepwalker toward the fire.

Small in his arms, head lolling, limbs dangling helplessly, lay the semiconscious body of Nizhoni.

Ahkeah cradled her gently, this child of his heart, this precious little girl who was all life to him. He could feel her weightless body twitching against his chest, her heart jerking spasmodically like a tiny pocket watch gone berserk. Her eyes were half-open, their dark pupils rolling aimlessly, unable to focus.

The scorpion had been hiding in her bed, someone had told him. Its vicious tail had stung her on the leg just as she was snuggling down for sleep. Now only the Holy People knew whether his daughter would live or die. There were many scorpions in this foul place. Only one kind, small and yellow, had venom powerful enough to kill an adult. But for a child, any scorpion sting could be deadly.

His aunt, experienced in such matters, had done what she could with her herbs and potions. But when Nizhoni did not improve, the old woman had sent for the *hataali* to invoke the Holy People with his chanted prayers and the gift of his sacred painting.

Tenderly, now, Ahkeah knelt on the ground and laid his daughter's tormented body across the sand painting. A proper healing ceremony would take place within the walls of a hogan. But the Diné had no hogans here, only the open dome of the sky. Likewise, he knew, the Holy People did not favor this land or bless the ceremonies with their presence. But there was nothing else that could be done for his child. Ahkeah could only hope the Holy Ones would listen from afar, that they would hear the prayers of the old *hataali* and listen with compassion.

From the darkness beyond the fire, Ahkeah could feel Miranda watching him, her soft silver eyes clouded with worry. But he could not allow himself to think of her now, even with love. His heart and mind must be fixed on the ceremony—on the painting, on his daughter and on the prayers of the old man.

Miranda kept herself a few paces back from the Navajos who clustered around the sand painting. She understood that something of grave importance was taking place, and she had no wish to intrude.

Her gaze darted between the watchers to the center of the circle, where Ahkeah's beloved daughter had been placed across the sand painting. Dressed in her threadbare woolen shift, she lay on her back, her eyes half-closed, her head falling to one side like a worn-out rag doll's. Grains of colored sand from the painting clung to her damply matted hair, catching the firelight like tiny stars in a midnight sky. She whimpered softly as the wizened artist raised his face skyward and began to sing.

The old man's voice was surprisingly strong. It rose

and fell in a gripping chant that prickled the hair on the back of Miranda's neck. Its power heightened her senses, sharpening the brightness of the stars, the keenness of the wind on her face.

The boy who had pulled her away from the painting tugged at her skirt once more. His curving fingers pantomimed the shape and motion of a striking scorpion, then gestured toward Nizhoni. Miranda's throat contracted as she realized what he was trying to tell her.

She had read a little about scorpions in one of her uncle's medical books. Their venom was neurotoxic, acting on the nervous system, somewhat like a cobra's. That would explain Nizhoni's twitching limbs and her frightening inability to focus her eyes. But as far as Miranda knew, there was no cure. Whether Ahkeah's daughter lived or died would depend on the amount of venom injected, its potency and the fighting strength of Nizhoni's frail little body.

Now that the sand painting was finished, no one tended the fire. The embers deepened to the hue of glowing blood, then slowly faded as the old man's chant droned on and on, rising skyward like the smoke from the dying coals. He was offering a prayer, Miranda realized, and she silently added her own. She had not been raised in a religious home, but her work in the hospital had shown her what faith could accomplish. Miracles were very rare, but they did happen.

Night deepened into early dawn as the fire burned down to gray ash that crumbled and blew away in the wind. Now, above the eastern horizon, the sky showed a faint gray like the hue burnished pewter.

One by one, the watchers had wearied and gone to bed. Only Ahkeah remained to hear the old man's song. He had scarcely moved except to take a blanket from one of the women and place it carefully over Nizhoni's body. Not once had his eyes looked Miranda's way. She would have known if he had, because her own gaze had scarcely left him. But no, he had not even glanced at her. It was as if the boundaries of his world had shrunk to include only the sand-painted circle, the old medicine man and the stricken child.

As the sky paled, Miranda's searching eyes found Nizhoni where she lay. The little girl's eyes were closed, her limbs quiescent beneath the blanket. Her skin was waxen in the ghostly light, and her small beautiful face was fearfully still.

As abruptly as he had begun it hours before, the old man ended his song. In the startling silence, Ahkeah, his face in shadow, crouched low, worked his hands carefully beneath his daughter's body and lifted her in his arms. She sagged limply against his chest, her head falling to one side like a freshly killed sparrow's. Was she alive? From a distance, there was no way of knowing.

Miranda's lips parted, but no sound emerged from her aching throat. Heartsick, she watched as Ahkeah carried the little girl to the dugout and vanished from sight.

She knew better than to follow him. This tragedy

was, in part, her doing. If Ahkeah had not been with her in the night, he would have been at home, and everything might have come together differently. Nizhoni might have gone to bed at a different time, or perhaps Ahkeah would have checked her bed, found the scorpion and killed it. Even now, Nizhoni would be curled beneath her blankets, lost in healthy slumber.

The darkness had faded, leaving the western sky streaked with color like the watery surface of an abalone shell. Soon the sun would be up, flooding the desert with light.

Horses stirred and milled on the far side of the camp. Someone had removed the saddle from the bay and tethered the tall animal with the others—a small kindness from a stranger's hand. It was time she left this place, Miranda told herself, time she mounted and rode away before she caused any more trouble for these poor people. Her very presence was an affront to their beliefs and their way of life. But how could she go without speaking to Ahkeah? How could she ride away without knowing what had happened to Nizhoni?

The old man had fallen into a light doze where he sat cross-legged on the earth. Miranda watched as the first fingers of light crept across his ruined masterpiece, glistening on each scattered grain. The vitality she had sensed in the newly finished painting was gone, but even now it was beautiful, with parts of the design remaining here and there around the edges.

Stirring, the old man blinked himself awake, rose

to a crouch and gathered up the edges of the buckskin, forming a bag where the sand slid to its center. Walking to the edge of the camp, he began tossing handfuls of sand into the morning breeze—to the east, to the west, to the north, to the south. When the sand was nearly gone, he opened the buckskin and shook it clean. Then, rolling it beneath his arm, he gathered up his collection of bags and bottles, hobbled down the slope and disappeared like a phantom into the silvery dawn.

Alone in the silent morning, Miranda stared down at the circle of flattened earth, feeling as if she had just awakened from an exotic dream. Only now did she begin to realize how cold, dirty and hungry she was. Her muscles shrieked with the strain of too much riding and sitting. Her hair was a damp, dusty mass of tangles, and as for her clothes...

But what did such things matter when a child's precious young life hung in the balance? Impatient with herself, Miranda strode into the wind, following the route the old man had taken off the eastern edge of the plateau. Winding her way down the rough trail, she stopped on a level spot where she could gaze out over the desert while she wrestled with her emotions.

She had been so full of herself, so convinced that she could lead these people out of darkness to the proper way, the white man's way. What a fool she'd been! Ahkeah was right—she should have left well enough alone. Her meddling had brought on a terrible tragedy. If Nizhoni died, Miranda would never forgive herself.

Oh, why hadn't Ahkeah told her what was happening? Why couldn't she summon the courage to walk down into the dugout and face his grief, his anger, even his hatred? That, or saddle her horse and ride away from this place?

Behind her, muffled by distance, she could hear the sounds of the awakening camp. The wind was fresh with the scent of last night's rain, and the rising sun had painted the clouds with streaks of rose, flame and amber. A wren caroled a song from atop a blooming cactus. It was going to be a glorious spring day. But would Nizhoni awaken to see it?

Too drained for tears, Miranda closed her eyes. Her lips moved in the broken fragments of a prayer. "Please…she's so young, so little. And Ahkeah loves her so much…."

"Miranda."

The sound of her name, spoken softly by Ahkeah, sent a quiver of response through her body. Afraid to turn around and see his face, she stared intently out at the desert.

"It's all right, Miranda." The words were gentle, like soft rain. "Nizhoni's asleep. The poison is fading. She's going to live."

Now the tears surged, stinging Miranda's eyes as she struggled to hold them back. His hands touched her shoulders, turning her. Then, suddenly, she was in his arms.

He held her tightly, his body trembling against hers, telling her without words how frightened he had been. Her own arms encircled his rib cage, binding him close as her senses drank in the miracle of his nearness—the sinewy strength of bone and muscle, the smoky aroma of his skin and the sound of his heart hammering against her ear. Love for this man glowed, throbbed, ached inside her, made all the more precious by the knowledge that their time together was about to end.

She sighed, forcing herself to speak. "I have to go back to the fort. They'll be sending out search parties at first light."

"I know," he whispered, his chin brushing her temple. "Wait here. I'll get the horses."

"No." Her arms tightened around him, holding on a moment longer. "I can find my way alone now that it's light."

He shook his head. "Even by day, it's too dangerous for a woman alone. The Comanches could still be out there, and who knows what else."

"But you need to stay with Nizhoni."

"Nizhoni will likely sleep all morning, and if she does wake up, my cousin will be there to take care of her." He eased her away, his expression stern. "No more arguing, Miranda. You're not riding off alone."

She sighed in agreement, suddenly afraid for him. "But you mustn't come with me all the way. As soon as we reach the main road to the fort, I'll leave you and ride in by myself. If you and I are seen together…" She let the words trail off, her meaning clear.

"I'll get the horses. The sooner we start back, the safer it will be." His arms tightened around her, lingering for the space of a breath. Then he let her go and, turning, strode back up to the camp.

The distance to Hweéldi, the fort, could be walked in half a morning—about two hours. By horse the time was much shorter. Today, for Ahkeah, the minutes flew as he clung to his time with Miranda, knowing that soon he would have to let her go.

He rode in silence, barely responding to her half-hearted attempts at conversation. The enormity of what they had done weighed on them both, and they knew that, no matter what happened now, their lives would be forever changed.

The long, sleepless hours were beginning to tell on him. His thoughts wandered, drifting again and again to the memory of last night—the rainy darkness, the tiny, crackling fire, and Miranda lying with him on the blanket, her eager body molding to his, sheathing him in the heaven of her moist, silken warmth. He remembered her little cries as they'd soared together, burst and shattered, the wonder in her eyes when it was finished and she lay in his arms, gazing up at him, a contented little smile playing about her lovely mouth.

The gift of this, her first time, had warmed the coldest, loneliest parts of him, reawakening his spirit to life and love. Ahkeah spoke the *bilagáana* tongue as if he had been born to it, but now, with their parting at hand, he could find no words to tell this woman what was in his heart.

And that, he reminded himself, was just as well.

The knowledge of his true feelings would only make matters worse for her. As it was, his best hope was that Miranda would be wise enough to go back to her own world and forget last night had ever happened.

The sun, fully risen now, blazed across the glittering desert, its heat searing away all traces of last night's rain. High above, against the turquoise sky, two great, dark birds circled on the rising air. Ahkeah's spirit brightened as he watched them, thinking they might be a mating pair of golden eagles. But no—they turned, showing him the high angle of their wings, and he realized they were only vultures, watching the desert for signs of death.

Ahead he could see the hump of rocks where the rough trail joined the arrow-straight road to the fort. Ahkeah remembered it now as the place where he had first seen Miranda—standing beside the buckboard in a swirl of falling snow, her skirts whipping as she bent to wrap her fine wool cloak around the pitiful shoulders of old Hedipa.

Soon he would remember it as the place where they had said farewell.

Glancing at her now, he could see her straining forward in the saddle, her expression taut and apprehensive. For the space of a heartbeat he thought she was only staring at the road. Then, following her gaze, he saw the distant body of mounted cavalry that had left the road and was galloping swiftly toward them.

Miranda swung her horse in Ahkeah's direction.

"Get out of sight!" she hissed. "Hurry, before they see you!"

Ahkeah did not alter his path. "It's too late," he said quietly. "They've seen us both."

Urging the bay to a canter, Miranda rode forward to meet the six blue-clad riders. Ahkeah hesitated only an instant before he kneed the mustang and galloped after her. Everything now depended on their behaving as if they had nothing to hide.

As Miranda narrowed the distance, the lead rider hailed her, shouting something across the desert. Ahkeah's stomach tightened as he recognized the voice of Sergeant Jethro McCree.

By the time Ahkeah caught up with Miranda, she had nearly reached the soldiers. McCree's mouth stretched in a toothy grin as he reined his mount to a halt.

"Well, now, ain't this a sight?" he chortled. "The major's priss-proud daughter with a filthy, murderin' Injun! Wait till the boys at the fort get a load of—"

"Shut up, McCree!" Ahkeah growled before Miranda had a chance to speak. "Miss Howell's horse ran away. I found her in the desert, and she spent the night at our camp." True, all of it, he thought. But something told him the story wouldn't satisfy a man like the sergeant.

"What you got to say about that?" McCree leered at Miranda, his little pig eyes taking in her disheveled hair, torn jacket and damply clinging blouse. "Judgin' from the look o' things, I'd say you and this uppity redskin's had yourselves a nice little roll in the bushes.''

"That's enough!" Miranda snapped furiously. "I wouldn't be alive this morning if it hadn't been for this man and his people! Ahkeah's only here because he wanted to see me safely back to the fort!"

McCree picked a morsel of breakfast from between his front teeth. "''Scuse me, Miss Miranda Howell," he drawled, "but if that's all there is to your story, I'm General Robert E. Lee's white horse!" His eyes narrowed as he glanced back toward the mounted detail. "Surround them!" he barked.

Miranda jerked the bay's reins, causing it to rear as the soldiers closed in with their mounts. Ahkeah pressed close on her flank in an effort to protect her, but it was no use. He was outnumbered six to one and had no weapon except his small knife. In seconds they were both prisoners.

"This is an outrage!" Miranda stormed at the sergeant. "When I tell my father, he'll have you drawn and quartered!"

McCree grinned, savoring his power. "Now, that just might have to wait," he said. "Seems Iron Bill took sick in the night. He's down in bed this mornin', doin' right poorly. Medic can't say as he'll make it through the day."

Miranda's face turned ashen. "Take me to my father," she demanded. "Now!"

"My pleasure," McCree said with a mocking tilt of his grease-stained hat. "Johnson! Calloway! Escort the lady back to the fort, pronto! The rest of us…"

His eyes narrowed to slits as he glanced toward Ahkeah. "The rest of us will stay and teach her friend here what happens to Injuns that get too friendly with our white women!"

Hearing his words, Miranda began to struggle, but the two husky soldiers had a firm grip on her arms and were already forcing the bay toward the road. Ahkeah kneed the mustang in a frantic effort to break loose, but his captors were ready for him. They closed in, tightening the circle, eyes narrowed, pistols drawn....

"No!" Miranda screamed, her voice becoming faint with distance as they dragged her away. *"No!"*

Ahkeah heard McCree's triumphant snort of laughter. Then someone dragged him from his horse, and the blows began to fall.

Chapter Thirteen

By the time her military escort reached the fort, Miranda was biting back anguished sobs. Too exhausted to struggle, she rode between the grim soldiers, her back ramrod straight, her chest convulsing in hard little gasps as she imagined what McCree's men might be doing to Ahkeah. Given so much as a moment's freedom, she would have wheeled and galloped back down the road to find whatever was left of him. Not that it would do any good. It was already too late to help him.

As they passed between the low adobe buildings, every pair of eyes turned to stare, taking in her disheveled hair, her torn, dusty clothes. Miranda kept her head high, her gaze fixed straight ahead. In the face of those who tried to shame her, she knew, Ahkeah would want her to remain proud.

A pillowy figure in ruffled heliotrope emerged from the mess hall. Violet's parasol bobbed like a bright pink poppy as she hurried across the parade ground.

By the time she reached Miranda and the soldiers she was flushed and out of breath.

"Oh, my dear!" she gasped, clutching a lace handkerchief to her bosom. "Just look at you! Where on earth have you been?" Without waiting for an answer, she glared up at the soldiers who still flanked Miranda, holding her prisoner. "What do you two think you're doing? Miss Howell doesn't need your protection inside the fort! Let the poor girl off her horse before she faints!"

Exchanging nervous glances, the two soldiers moved apart. One of them kept a firm grip on the bay's bridle as Miranda slid wearily to the ground. Her knees wobbled, refusing to hold her. She stumbled and might have fallen if Violet hadn't opened her arms and caught her. "There, now," she soothed as the soldiers departed, leading the bay toward the stable. "Don't tremble so, child. After a bath and a good hot meal, you'll be as good as new!"

Miranda heard what Violet was saying, but the woman's voice seemed to be coming from far away—almost as if she, and this place, were no longer a part of Miranda's own world.

"Miranda, you *are* all right, aren't you?" Violet's eyes narrowed sharply. "Did anyone hurt you out there—any of those filthy savages—?"

With effort, Miranda pulled away and forced herself to speak. "I'm fine," she said. "Just take me to my father, please."

Violet smiled. "Your father's resting comfortably,

in his own bed, dear. I looked in on him not more than twenty minutes ago. Meanwhile—''

''Tell me what happened to him,'' Miranda said.

''Truly, there's not much to tell. The major was at the stables yesterday afternoon, about to mount and ride out with the search party to look for you, when he suddenly doubled over in terrible pain and passed out on the ground. The medic gave him some of the tonic he had to help him rest, and he's been drifting in and out of sleep ever since—though he seems sensible enough when he's awake.'' Violet twirled her parasol. ''We've no real doctor on the post, you know. But your father's a tough man. It's far too soon, I'd say, to give up on him.''

''Thank you,'' Miranda said, meaning it. She willed herself to walk without reeling as she crossed the parade ground. It helped having Violet by her side, even though the woman would have been outraged if she'd known how Miranda had spent the night.

High on its iron pole, the Stars and Stripes flapped smartly in the morning breeze. At one time the flag's beauty would have stirred Miranda's spirit. Now the sight seemed strangely alien, as if she were seeing it through Ahkeah's eyes. Under that banner, his people had been crushed, beaten, starved and torn from their homeland. No wonder the Diné were bitter. No wonder they wanted nothing to do with so-called civilized ways.

Her heart cried out for Ahkeah as she trudged across the parade ground, trying to look as if nothing had happened. Where was he now? What had McCree and his men done to him? She could not rest until she knew.

The desert wind dried the tears on her face as she passed the building that held her little classroom. Through the open screen door she caught a brief glimpse of children seated on benches. Miranda's jaw went slack as she realized someone else was teaching her class.

"It's that little Navajo whore!" Violet huffed, answering her unspoken question. "When she saw that you weren't here this morning, she marched into the kitchen, bold as brass, and told the cook you'd ordered her to make sandwiches. By the time the children showed up, she was ready and waiting for them. The very idea! You'd expect a slut like that one to know her place and not come around here in broad daylight, while decent people are going about their business!"

A faint smile, the first of the day, tugged at Miranda's lips. "Why, Violet," she said gently. "I do believe Juana does know her place. And it's right there in my classroom."

Violet's breath made a little sucking sound. She began to walk faster, her pink parasol bobbing furiously.

"I declare, Miranda, I don't know what gets into you sometimes! But never mind. There's something I haven't told you—a surprise!"

"A surprise?" Miranda felt a nervous prickle

creeping up the back of her neck. "What kind of surprise?"

"You'll see." Violet gave her a tight-lipped smile. "You'll see quite soon."

"I just want to go to my father," Miranda said, hurrying toward the door of the major's quarters. "When I've seen to his comfort and let him know I'm safe, there'll be plenty of time for surprises."

She mounted the porch, strode toward the door, then hesitated with her hand on the knob. Dear heaven, what awaited her inside? Her father had always appeared so large and ferocious. The thought of Iron Bill Howell lying pale and helpless in his bed, more dead than alive, was almost beyond imagining.

But the last thing he'd want, Miranda knew, would be for her to show emotion. She was a soldier's daughter. She would be strong, as he wished her to be. And she would care for him cheerfully, even though her heart was already aching for all they had missed of each other's lives.

She remembered the army hospital, and how she had always paused before entering the wards to compose her features and freeze her emotions, enabling her to get through one more day of nursing the wounded. Now she forced herself to do the same, preparing herself, detaching herself from all feeling.

With Violet pressing close behind her, she turned the knob, flung the door resolutely open and strode into the small parlor—only to stop as if she had just run headlong into a cement wall.

An elegantly slim figure had risen out of the rocking chair and was walking slowly toward her.

"Miranda!" The cultured, masculine voice seemed to come from a distant planet. "Thank heaven you're safe! Are you all right, my dearest?"

She swallowed painfully, forcing herself to speak. "Yes," she whispered, her voice shaking. "Yes...I'm quite all right, Phillip."

Ahkeah lay facedown, twenty paces beyond the rocks that marked the spot where the trail joined the road. Blood trickled from a gash above his eyebrow, crimson against white where it soaked into the alkali dust. He groaned softly as he drifted in and out of consciousness.

McCree and his cohorts had used their fists, their boots and their pistol grips to beat him to a bloody pulp. In his moments of clarity, Ahkeah couldn't help wondering why he hadn't been shot or castrated. Most likely there were laws against such heinous acts, and McCree hadn't wanted to risk the possibility that one of the men would turn on him and talk. But beating up an Indian was another matter. Even if he died, no one would be punished for that.

Twisting his head to the side, he willed one swollen eye to open. Through the narrow slit he could see black specs spiraling against the bright azure sky. For a moment he tried to blink them away, thinking they were a trick of his vision. Then he realized they were vultures, circling lower and lower toward him.

"Damn!" Ahkeah swore a white man's oath. The

foul birds thought he was dead, or dying, and were moving in for a meal. But he was far from dead. He was a warrior, strong enough to stand, to walk, to find his way back to his people. But first he needed to get out of the hot sun to the patch of shelter behind the rocks—and to do that he would have to crawl.

Gritting his teeth, Ahkeah inched himself forward. Fiery daggers of pain stabbed through his body. McCree's thugs must have broken some ribs. What else had they broken? It was hard to tell when every joint, bone and muscle was screaming in agony.

Bracing against the pain, he moved a little, then a little more. He was making progress, but he was growing light-headed and his vision was beginning to blur. He seemed to see the black specks moving, flapping down around him—three, then five, then hundreds as the darkness spun in his head and he tumbled headlong into it.

"Look here, sir. Lord, who could've done such a thing to the poor devil?" The voice was young, almost boyish. Ahkeah heard it through a thick, dark fog.

"Looks like he's been in one helluva fight, that's for sure." The second voice carried the ring of authority. "See if he's alive, Simpson."

Ahkeah heard the snort of a horse. His tortured nerves felt the vibration of footsteps coming toward him. He willed himself to open his eyes, to move, to speak, but his body refused to obey.

"He's breathing, sir! He's alive!" the young voice exclaimed.

"Well, more's the pity," the older man said with a weary sigh. "Here, I'll help you get the poor beggar across the back of your horse. Then you can cut across that far field, dump him off and meet the rest of us back at the fort."

"Dump him off, sir?"

"At the Indian hospital. Not much in the way of treatment there, but at least they'll give him a bed and a clean place to die. There's nothing more we can do."

Miranda stood at her father's bedside, her legs boneless beneath the skirt of her muddied riding habit. She struggled for composure as Iron Bill, awake now, gazed up at her with watery gray eyes.

"Thank God you're safe," he croaked in a voice she had never heard before. "What happened to you?"

"My horse ran away." She repeated the same half truth she'd told Phillip. "The Navajos found me and saved me—" She hesitated, wondering if she dared press him further, then plunged ahead in desperation. "Ahkeah was bringing me back this morning when we met a party of men under Sergeant McCree. They—they thought he'd harmed me, and they took him—I couldn't stop them. But you, Father, you're their commanding officer—please…"

She was shaking, losing her precious control. As

her father gazed vacantly up at her she felt Phillip's restraining hand on her arm.

"That's enough, Miranda. You're overwrought, and you're upsetting your father. Whoever this…this *Okeya* is, I'm sure his problems can wait until the major is feeling stronger." He was tugging her elbow, pulling her away from the bed, and she saw that her father's eyes had closed in sleep.

"He appeared to be in considerable pain when I arrived last night," Phillip said. "He asked me for a dose of the medicine he keeps in the cupboard, and I gave him all he wanted. I gave him more just before you arrived, but there's only one bottle left. I hope you're able to get more, because it seems to give him a good deal of comfort."

"The medicine's nothing but laudanum and molasses. It helps the pain, but I fear he's become addicted, and you've given him too much. He'll sleep for hours now, and wake up wanting more."

"Oh." Phillip's blandly handsome face fell. "But sleep's a good thing, isn't it? Surely so much rest will help him recover."

Miranda sighed. "He's not going to recover. My father is dying, Phillip. I'm no doctor, but I'd guess it's a tumor of the stomach or something similar. From what I've seen of it he has a few weeks—two or three months at most. Meanwhile he'll be in a great deal of pain. And, yes, he'll need more of the medicine." Where would she track down Hagopian? she wondered. How often did the old man visit the fort? Perhaps Violet would know.

"We need to talk, Miranda." Phillip was pulling her arm more insistently now—though gently still. Her fiancé was a gentleman to the very bone.

Oh, why had he come here—and now, of all times, when she had not given him a thought in the past twenty-four hours? What was she going to tell him about last night? The truth? That she had given herself, heart, soul and body, to another man? A Navajo?

They had gotten as far as the bedroom doorway. Phillip drew her out into the parlor and closed the door softly behind him.

"Can't this wait?" she asked, still frantic for Ahkeah. "There's something I need to do—"

"Sit down, Miranda," Phillip said quietly. "I've come all this way to be with you, and you've scarcely looked at me. What's happened to you?"

Seeing there was no way out, she sank onto the edge of a straight-backed chair and clasped her hands in her lap. As he studied her from the seat he had taken in the rocker, she became acutely aware of her tangled hair, her torn and dirty clothes—and her face. Did a woman's face change when she'd been with the man she loved for the first time? Would Phillip guess what had happened?

His gaze was all innocence and hurt, the look of a child who'd been punished without knowing why. No, Miranda concluded, a more experienced man might notice the deeper change in her, but dear Phillip would not look beyond her outward appearance. Unless she chose to tell him, her secret would be safe.

"You've changed," he said softly.

Miranda clenched her hands tighter, forcing herself to meet his eyes. "Yes," she said, "I suppose I have."

He eased back into the chair in a failed attempt to look relaxed. "Your father and I had a long conversation about you last night."

"Oh?"

"He said you'd set up a school to help the Indians."

"I've tried. But the only real way to help these people is to send them home where they belong!" The passion in her voice startled her. She sounded almost like Ahkeah.

He sighed heavily. "Why, Miranda? Why waste your time on a cause that has nothing to do with your own happiness?"

"If you knew me better, Phillip, you wouldn't be asking that question."

"Sometimes I don't think I know you at all," he said. "But that doesn't mean I don't love you. You've already overstayed your time here. Our wedding day is only six weeks away and there's a great deal of planning to be done. I want you to come home with me. We can leave tomorrow, or the day after if you like."

"Have you forgotten about my father?" she asked. "Even if I were to give up the school, how could I leave him at a time like this?"

Phillip nodded gravely. "Somehow I knew you'd say that. That's why I conversed with your father at some length last night before he went to sleep."

She stared at him, sensing an impending trap.

"Your father gave his permission for us to be married here, tomorrow," Phillip said. "As post commander, he can perform the ceremony himself."

"You had this conversation while I was missing?" Miranda was on her feet, pacing, agitated. "What if I hadn't come back? What if they'd found my body out there in the desert?"

"Surely you know I thought about that." Phillip did not move from the chair. "I was sick with worry, Miranda. If I'd had a prayer of finding you, I'd have spent the whole night searching. As it was, I could only promise myself that if you returned safely, I'd never let you out of my sight again."

"I can't marry you, Phillip."

He stared at her as if she had just fired a pistol into his chest.

"I'm sorry." She let the words spill out, afraid that if she stopped, her courage would fail her. "You deserve so much better, but there's no kind way to say this. I've changed—in more ways than you can imagine. This perfect, beautiful life you've offered me— it's just not possible. Not for me. Not anymore."

"Is there someone else?" he asked quietly.

She groped for the right thing to say. No? That would be an outright lie. But confessing her love for Ahkeah would only hurt everyone involved, including Ahkeah himself.

"The reason doesn't matter," she said. "Oh, Phillip, you're a good man. A wonderful man. I'm so sorry."

"Miranda, you're not yourself right now," Phillip said, rising from the chair. "I was wrong to speak of this so soon after your ordeal." His clean, aristocratic face paled slightly. "But you need to know this much. If anything happened out there—if you were attacked, if you were, uh, harmed…it won't make any difference to me. I'll understand that it wasn't your fault, and I'll still be willing—no, honored—to make you my wife this very day."

His speech all but undid her. She turned away and walked toward the window, her eyes brimming with tears of exasperation. Oh, why did Phillip have to make things so difficult? Why couldn't he be outraged? Why couldn't he shout at her and call her vile names? That would make everything so much easier!

"I think what I really want is to be alone," she said, staring out through the dusty glass, to where the wind was blowing a tumbleweed across the parade ground. Strange, how familiar this desolate place had begun to feel, as if she'd been born to the harshness of the desert and had finally come home.

"I can give you as much time alone as you need," Phillip said. "What's a few more days when we have a whole lifetime ahead of us?"

"No." She turned around to face him, knowing she had no choice except to be cruel. "What I'm saying is that maybe I was meant to be alone—to not marry at all."

He gazed at her in shocked silence, looking as if she had slapped him. Dear Phillip, so earnest, so kind, so deserving of a woman who truly loved him.

"One day I may be sorry for this decision," she said. "But it's the only one I can rightly make. In this place, I've come to discover how little I know of my own heart. How can I be a wife to any man when I'm so much a stranger to myself?"

"You're talking nonsense, Miranda." He was becoming irritated. "We need to get you away from this miserable place. We can take your father with us by wagon if need be. Once you're back where you belong, you'll come to your senses. This whole time here will seem like nothing but a bad dream."

She shook her head. "It's no use, Phillip. One day, when you find the woman you were meant to love for the rest of your life, you'll thank me. But for now…" She strained toward the door. "Please excuse me, there's something I must do, something that can't wait!"

"We haven't finished our discussion," Phillip said with a scowl.

"I fear there's nothing more to discuss." She opened the door and felt the desert wind catch her tangled hair. Somewhere in the bright morning Ahkeah lay where McCree's men had left him—hurt, bleeding, perhaps even dead. She had to learn what had happened. She had to find him.

"Miranda," Phillip said, "I'm warning you. If you leave now, I won't be here when you come back."

She stepped out onto the porch and closed the door behind her. Only then did she give way to her emotions and break into a tearing run.

* * *

By the time she reached her classroom, Miranda was gasping. But she had arrived in time. School had just ended and the children were bursting free, scattering across the parade ground like birds released from a cage. She took a moment on the front step to catch her breath and steady her trembling legs. Then she crossed the threshold and stepped into the classroom.

Juana was cleaning the blackboard with an oiled rag. She turned, startled, as Miranda spoke her name.

"I teacher today," she said, her hopeful eyes belying her brazen grin. "Damn good job. Kids learn like hell."

"So I see." Miranda gave her a reassuring smile and saw the girl's face soften. "Thank you, Juana. I'm proud of you and very grateful."

Juana turned away to hide her pleasure and began scrubbing furiously at the blackboard. Then, abruptly, she swung back around.

"You look like hell," she said. "Where you go, miss?"

"That doesn't matter," Miranda said. "I'm here now because I need your help."

"Need my help?" The girl's eyes lit expectantly. Miranda moved closer, lowering her voice.

"It's—Ahkeah. Sergeant McCree and his men— they took him prisoner, said they were going to punish him. I need you to help me find out where he is. Do you understand?"

The girl hesitated, and Miranda felt her heart lurch.

She remembered the night she'd seen the drunken McCree crossing the parade ground with the two Navajo girls. One of them had been Juana.

"Please," she whispered. "They may have hurt him badly, even killed him. You know people, Juana. You can ask, find out."

Juana's lips tightened. Slowly she nodded. "I ask. You wait here, miss." She was gone before Miranda could reply.

Restless to the point of frenzy, Miranda began straightening the room, sweeping the floor, rearranging the benches, scrawling tomorrow's lesson on the blackboard that Juana had cleaned.

Time crawled past—ten minutes, twenty, an hour— and still Juana had not returned. Glancing out through the dusty windowpane, Miranda saw Phillip riding toward the road with a packhorse and the rough-looking man he had hired as a guide. Dear Phillip. He had come such a great distance for so little. Now she could only wish him a safe return home and a happy life. He was a fine man. She had liked him, respected him, cared for him. But as for love...

She sank onto a bench, reeling as the flood of memories swept over her. Ahkeah, glaring angrily down at her from the back of his mustang, the snowstorm swirling around him as he whipped off his woolen poncho and draped it over the shoulders of a half-mad old woman. Ahkeah, holding Miranda in his arms, his body loving her, his spirit still beyond her reach. Where was that proud spirit now? And where was Juana? What in heaven's name was taking her so long?

By the time the girl reappeared, the morning had ripened into early afternoon, and Miranda had begun to worry about her father waking up alone. She watched, her heart in her throat, as Juana meandered across the parade ground from the direction of the stables, taking her time. Was the news bad? But how could it be anything else? Miranda asked herself. She had no choice except to prepare for the worst.

Her hands twisted her skirt as she waited in an agony of dread, fighting the urge to rush outside, seize the girl by the shoulders and shake the story out of her. But no, this was a dangerous time. And Juana was a smart girl—too smart to draw attention to herself by running. Patience. Discretion. These were the bywords now.

An eternity seemed to pass before Juana opened the door and stepped into the classroom. The expression on her round Navajo face betrayed nothing. Only her sharp black eyes were troubled.

"What is it?" Miranda asked softly. "Is Ahkeah alive?"

She nodded gravely. "He hurt. Bad. Damn bad."

"How bad? Did you see him? Who did you talk to?" The questions poured out of Miranda like water from a bursting dam. Only when Juana's face took on a look of helpless exasperation did she realize she had outstripped the girl's limited grasp of English.

"Please," Miranda said, speaking slowly. "Just tell me what happened."

"Mac-ree, he bastard," she said. "Mac-ree, soldiers beat Ahkeah like hell. Bad, miss. Much blood."

"But he's alive?" Miranda seized the strong brown hands in her own.

"More soldiers come. Find Ahkeah. Put on horse."

"Then what? Where is he now?" she asked, her heart pounding.

"Bad place."

"Bad place?" Miranda stared at her.

"Ghost place. Diné die there. All die there."

Chapter Fourteen

Ahkeah lay on a narrow canvas army cot, alone in the pitch-black night. In the darkness of the Navajo hospital, he could feel the terror of all the men, women and children who had died in this place—died of smallpox, measles, cholera and consumption; died of snakebite, childbirth and, all too rarely, old age. Their ghosts moaned and whispered in the darkness, tearing at his heart.

The young medic on duty had sponged his wounds, bound his shattered rib cage and gone away at dusk, locking the door and leaving his sole patient to live or die as fate decreed. Now Ahkeah lay rigid on the hated bed, nerves steeled against the twin specters of pain and despair. The ghosts called to him in their silent voices, beckoning with invisible hands, begging him to slip away and join them.

Was he, too, going to die in this place? No, he vowed. His daughter needed him. His people needed him. And he was a warrior, too strong to give in to the power of things he could not see or touch.

A cool night breeze swept in through the high, barred window, carrying with it the sharp, alkaline scent of the river. The hoot of a desert owl—a ghost creature—echoed through the night. Ahkeah closed his ears to the sound, filling his mind, instead, with good images—the deep sandstone canyons of Dinétah, glowing with the colors of a western sunset…the music of his daughter's laughter…the feel of Miranda's body, hot and sweet and silken, in his arms.

It was last night's memory of Miranda that pulled him back from the edge of gloom. He closed his eyes and let himself drift back into the healing bliss of her warmth, her strength, her softness. He remembered the sheer joy of filling her, thrusting deep as she shuddered around him, whimpering with need, her arms and legs clasping him, holding him deep inside her. He remembered their wild skyward spiral, the bursting of a thousand stars before they floated back to earth, shimmering with contentment.

He could not allow himself to see her again, that much he knew. It was too dangerous for them both. She belonged in her world, he in his. But he would always be grateful for that night of loving her. And to the end of his life, he would never, ever forget what Miranda had given him.

She had given him back his life.

The moon emerged from its blanket of clouds. Its light shone through the window, casting a barred pattern on the floor. Had the *bilagáana* put in the bars to keep their Diné patients from escaping or to protect their sad little store of medical supplies? Tonight the answer made no difference, Ahkeah thought. He was too weak and sore to escape, let alone steal anything.

His broken ribs screamed as he shifted his weight on the cot. His arms and legs were only bruised, but his face was a mass of purpled, swollen flesh and his groin throbbed where the soldiers had kicked him again and again. He had fought like a wounded bear, but four strong, armed men had been too many even for him. In the end he had been unable to protect himself. Fueled by the whiskey McCree had brought along, they had pounded him until they wearied of their sport. Then they had mounted their horses and galloped away, leaving him to die.

What would he do if he saw them again? Would he be strong enough to keep himself from killing them?

Ahkeah's thoughts were shattered by a small but unmistakable sound in the darkness—the click of a key turning in its lock.

He was instantly alert, his danger sense shrieking in silent alarm. Was it McCree or one of his men, coming back here to finish him off? Forgetting pain, he groped for a weapon—a bottle, a tool, anything he could use—

"Ahkeah?"

At the sound of Miranda's voice his heart began to beat normally again. He knew she shouldn't have come, and he would tell her so. But he could not stop his pulse from leaping as she closed the door behind her and moved toward him, groping in the darkness.

"I'm here," he said, guiding her with his voice. "There's no one else. We're alone."

She found the cot and sank to her knees beside him. Her hands reached out in the moonlight, fingers as gentle as the brush of falling petals.

"Oh..." She felt his face, the blackened, swollen eyes, the broken nose, the puffed lower lip. "Dear heaven, what have they done to you?" she whispered.

"Nothing that won't mend," he muttered, grateful for the concealing darkness. "What about you? Are you all right, Miranda?"

"Yes." She fumbled for one of his hands and, lifting it, kissed the bruised knuckles. Her lips were soft and moist, and he felt the salty sting of her tears on his broken skin. "It's all my fault," she said. "It was because of me they did this to you."

He stroked her hair, his fingers tangling in the loose, tawny silk. "McCree's been itching for an excuse to take me down," he said. "If not for this, it would have been for something else. You're not to blame." He paused, suddenly afraid for her. "Did anyone see you leave the fort? Your father—?"

"My father took his medicine and went to sleep. I brought his keys to open the door."

"You shouldn't be here, Miranda. If anyone sees you—"

"No one saw me. I know it's dangerous, but I had to come. I had to make sure you were alive." She slipped her arms around him, then drew back as he flinched from the pain in his ribs.

"You're the one who's in danger," she said,

clutching his hand. "McCree knows you're here. Juana heard him talking with one of the men who found you. He was drinking, laughing—said maybe he ought to ride out to the hospital and finish what he started."

"What for?" Ahkeah's teeth ground as he forced his swollen lips into a bitter smile. "It's only talk. Killing me would spoil McCree's fun."

"Stop it!" Miranda glared at him, fiercely beautiful, searing him with the intensity of her love. "What if you're wrong? Listen to me, Ahkeah, you'd be helpless in this place! You have to get out of here!"

Ahkeah weighed her words and swiftly realized she was right. To remain locked in the hospital, helpless and alone, could be an invitation to death.

"Can you get me a horse?" he asked her.

"I brought one. It's just outside. But how can you think of riding? The pain—"

"I'll manage it." He grimaced as he worked an elbow beneath him and tried to sit up. The pain was excruciating. Riding, he knew, would be even worse. But there was little choice. He was too weak to get far on foot.

"I brought some of my father's medicine," she said, reaching into a pocket of the old army coat she wore. "It should dull the pain enough to—"

"No. No medicine." He spoke through clenched teeth. "I've—seen what Hagopian's medicine can do, and I—" The words ended in a groan as he heaved himself to a sitting position, then used the strength of his legs to push himself fully erect. The dark room seemed to spin around him. He fought back waves of nausea.

Miranda had dropped the medicine bottle back into her pocket. She reached out as if to support him, then pulled her hand back as if suddenly fearful of hurting him. "Take my shoulder," she said, turning to one side so that he could reach her from behind.

Ahkeah's bruised and beaten body had stiffened in the hours of lying down. He clasped her shoulder, leaning on her as he had never leaned on anyone in his proud, defiant life. He owed her more than she would ever know, this small, brave *bilagáana* who had reawakened his body and spirit. But he knew he could not allow himself to see her again.

With the agony of his broken ribs, he could not even hold her in his arms to say goodbye.

Step by teeth-clenching step, they made their way out the door and around to the side of the hospital. The horse was there, saddled and bridled, where she had left it. Dizzy with pain, Ahkeah let go of Miranda and leaned against the animal's flank. One hand touched the army brand that had been seared onto the crest of its haunch. He would have to watch out for patrols, he reminded himself. The last thing he needed tonight was to be caught with a stolen horse.

"Hurry!" Her whisper was urgent. He followed her gaze across the broken field and saw the bobbing flicker of a torch, moving closer through the darkness. There was no time to lose.

Steeling himself, he clasped the saddle horn and lifted one foot into the stirrup. Pain ripped through his body as he heaved himself upward, straining broken ribs and bruised flesh to drag himself into the saddle.

"Hurry! They're coming!" Miranda's hair caught the night wind and unfurled like a banner as she spun to face him. "They mustn't see you—in your condition, you'll never be able to outride them!"

Ahkeah straightened in the saddle. Through a jagged haze of pain he looked down at Miranda, so wildly beautiful there in the moonlight. He would remember her just this way, he thought, filling his eyes with the sight of her. And on lonely nights he would have the memory of their loving to warm his heart.

One pale hand reached up to him. He caught and held it for an instant. The silver eyes that gazed up at him glittered with unshed tears.

"Be careful," he warned, wishing he could stay and protect her. "There's an empty irrigation ditch just beyond the hospital. It's deep. You can hide in it and follow it back as far as the river."

She nodded in understanding. "Don't worry about me. I'll be fine. Now, go. Go, my love."

Their fingers clung for an instant, then separated as he nudged the horse to a careful walk. Another moment, and he was lost in the darkness.

Miranda stood gazing after him as he melted into the night. Her lips moved in a silent prayer for his safety. Ahkeah was well ahead of the approaching torches, but he could not travel fast, and there was little cover on the open plain. Once McCree and his cronies realized he had gone...

Thinking fast, she flew to the open door of the hospital and used her father's key to refasten the lock. With luck, they would assume Ahkeah was inside. By the time they broke in and learned differently, he would be safely away.

Glancing back over her shoulder, she saw that there were three torches, not just one. They were moving rapidly in her direction, the flames bobbing and weaving—a sign that the men who carried them were mounted, riding fast, and probably drunk.

It was time to see to her own safety. She was on foot, and the fort lay nearly a mile away across the open, fallow fields. Ahkeah had said there was an empty irrigation ditch—but where? A cloud had drifted across the moon, and where he had pointed she could see nothing but darkness.

Acting on blind faith, she plunged ahead, stumbling across the rough ground, praying she would not be seen. Anything could happen to a lone woman out here in the middle of the night, and her fate could always be blamed on the Navajos.

By the time she reached the ditch, the moon was emerging from its cloudy veil. She dropped gratefully over the high bank, feeling a sudden jab of pain as she came down hard on one ankle. The dry ditch was deeper than she'd expected. So much the better, Miranda told herself. Keeping low, she should be able to follow it all the way to the river. From there, she should have no trouble slipping across the bridge and back to her father's quarters.

But she could not leave yet. Not until she was sure Ahkeah had made a clean escape.

Heart slamming, she peered over the bank. She could see the riders clearly now. The one in the lead, without a torch, was McCree. The others were known to be his friends, men of the same crude stripe, with dirty habits and boorish manners. Such men would thrive here at Fort Sumner, with a whole nation of people to bully and exploit. No wonder Ahkeah despised whites so much.

As they rode up to the hospital, McCree drained the last of his whiskey bottle and flung it away with a curse. The bottle flew through the air and struck a rock just short of Miranda's hiding place. She flinched, crouching lower as a shard of glass grazed her cheek. Too late she realized she should have gained some distance while she had the chance. The four men were too close now, their presence far too dangerous for her to risk movement.

McCree swung off his horse and swaggered up to the small, square adobe building. Drawing his pistol, he tried the door.

"Locked." He muttered a string of foul curses. Miranda thanked heaven as she realized he'd neglected to bring along a key. The more time they spent trying to get into the hospital, the more time Ahkeah would have to get away.

"Listen to me, you stinkin' Navajo bastard!" he shouted into the wind. "I know you're in there! And

I know you can hear me! Say your prayers to your filthy heathen gods, Injun, because you're goin' to die, and it won't be pretty!''

The door was made of rusty iron plating, left over, perhaps, from an abandoned piece of mining equipment. McCree aimed his pistol at the lock. Then, as if realizing the danger of ricochet, he cursed and thrust the weapon back into its holster. His boot kicked at the door, the blows reverberating through the metal. ''You awake in there, Injun?'' he shouted. ''You'd better be! I want you to be so scared you'll piss your damned pants! I want to hear you scream!''

Miranda watched in horror as he untied a large tin container from behind the saddle and unscrewed the cap. The sharp odor of kerosene swam in the air as he splashed it against the walls. The adobe bricks were nothing more than dried mud and straw. They soaked up the volatile liquid like sponges.

Only when the kerosene was spent did McCree step back, mount and bark an order at his cronies. Whooping with drunken glee, they spurred their horses and galloped around the small, crude building, swinging their torches against the saturated adobe. The walls roared into flame, blazing with a heat so fierce that it singed the hair on the horses. The animals reeled backward, shrieking in terror as the men shielded their faces with their arms.

''We got the bastard!'' McCree shouted above the uproar. ''Let's get out of here 'fore somebody sees the fire from the fort! Come on!''

The four riders wheeled away and galloped back

toward the river, whooping and laughing as they vanished into the night.

Miranda crouched in the ditch, trembling as the shouts and hoofbeats faded. The only sound in the darkness now was the crackle of the burning walls. Now and again, from inside the hospital, she could hear the sound of shattering glass as bottles exploded in the inferno. The thought that Ahkeah might have been inside made her physically ill. Her skin felt clammy, her stomach nauseous. Her eyes burned and watered from the acrid smoke.

What if she hadn't come tonight—or what if she'd arrived too late? How could she have gone on living, knowing what had happened?

Steeling herself, she rose to her feet. She had to get out of here, she reminded herself. By now the sentries at the fort would have seen the blazing hospital. Soldiers would be mounting up or running across the fields on foot. She could not afford to be here when they arrived.

And, unjust as it might seem, she could not tell anyone what she had witnessed tonight. Revealing her own presence would only put Ahkeah—and herself—in more danger. For now, the only safe course lay in letting McCree and his friends believe they had gotten away with arson and murder. In truth, they had little to fear. The Navajos would likely be blamed for the blaze and forced to rebuild the ruined hospital.

For a moment longer, she paused, staring at the flames. Ahkeah would be seeing the fire, too, as he made his way through the night. The memory of it would serve as a lesson, reminding them both of the terrible things that could happen when two people crossed lines drawn to keep them apart.

Her throat and lungs were raw from the stinging smoke. She fought back tears as she thought of Ah-keah's brutalized face and body, knowing that, for his own sake, she could never go near him again.

"Goodbye, my love," she whispered into the night wind. "Live. Be well. Be safe."

Miranda stood in the doorway of her classroom, watching the Navajo children scatter happily across the parade ground. It was late May. The sun was bright and hot, the sky a cloudless, blazing blue. Soon the summer heat would sear the desert with the breath of a furnace. Would the Navajos be here long enough to see the land wither again? Rumors had been flying since last month, when the Navajo agent, Theodore Dodd, and the tribe's most respected headmen, Man-uelito and Barboncito, had returned from their long railway journey to Washington, D.C. President Andrew Johnson himself had promised them relief. But how, and when? Washington was so far away, and promises were so easily broken.

Whatever was happening, Miranda knew she would be among the last to hear about it. Her father had been relieved of his command and replaced by a junior officer. Now Iron Bill Howell lay dying in his bed, soothed by the laudanum that dulled the edge of his pain. He remained at the fort because he was too ill to be moved. Her own presence, Miranda suspected, was tolerated only because she served as his nurse. Each day she breathed silent thanks that Theodore Dodd had allowed her to continue her little school. Without it, she would have sunk into despair.

Through the rising heat waves she could see the fluttering figure of Violet Marsden crossing the parade ground, keeping to the far side. Miranda stifled the urge to call out to her former friend and ask if she'd heard any news. It would avail her nothing, she knew. Violet had not spoken to her in weeks.

With a sigh she turned back inside her classroom, where her four advanced pupils were waiting for their extra lesson to begin. Juana and her three young friends were making great strides in their learning of English. Miranda had even succeeded in weeding out most of the swearwords they'd picked up from the soldiers. The girls' appearance and demeanor had changed as well over the past few weeks. Now they came to class with their faces washed, their hair neatly braided and their blouses discreetly buttoned. Their bright young eyes glowed with the excitement of new possibilities.

Smiling now, Miranda passed out the readers she had cajoled Uncle Andrew into sending her. When Juana had shown up at school with her friends, Miranda had eyed the girls skeptically. But when she'd discovered their eagerness to learn, a grand scheme had sprouted in her mind.

Hers was only one small classroom, far from adequate for the task of teaching these people to live in the modern world. But if she could create teachers among the Navajos, she could multiply the scope of her efforts. Ideally, these native teachers would know English and the basics of reading, writing, arithmetic and geography, as well as hygiene, money management, gardening and other simple skills. But they would also be sensitive to the traditions and beliefs of their people. These four young girls, so bruised and sullied by the white man's world, would be her first teachers—but if her plan succeeded, there would be more. Many more.

"Really, now!" Violet had huffed on hearing Miranda's plans. "Those little Indian whores of yours are only good for one thing! How can you propose to turn them into proper teachers? If you fail, you'll have wasted your time. And even if you succeed, you'll only have them luring others into wickedness. Those girls will never be anything but what they are— worthless little sluts!"

"Worthless sluts?" Miranda had flared. "The girls were starving, Violet! They did the only thing they could to feed themselves and their families. But their lives aren't over. If they can be made to see their own worth—if others can be made to see—"

"I've heard enough!" Violet had snapped. "You've chosen your friends, Miranda. Birds of a feather, as I always say…" Letting the implication hang, Violet had turned and walked away. The two of them had not spoken since.

"Miss!" Juana was raising her hand as she'd been taught to do, but she was wriggling like a puppy, bursting with something to say—something she'd been holding back all morning while the younger children were in class.

"Yes, Juana, what is it?"

"I hear something soldiers say!"

"I *heard* something," Miranda corrected. "And a lady doesn't pass on gossip."

"No gossip!" Juana hissed impatiently. "News, miss! Big news! I tell?"

"All right, Juana. Tell us." Miranda was as hungry for news as anyone on the post. She could only hope Juana had heard something truthful for a change.

Juana beamed with self-importance. "You know president, miss?"

"You mean the president of the United States?"

"Yes, miss. President. He send man to come here. Number one big man. Damn big."

"No swearing," Miranda cautioned.

"Sorry, miss." The girl plunged ahead. "Big man, he come here soon. Come to tell Diné where we go."

"Oh!" Miranda clasped her hands together, interlacing her fingers until her knuckles hurt. This was big news, wonderful and frightening at the same time. The Navajos had been waiting months for the quagmire of bureaucracy to move. At last someone in authority would be making a decision, and they would be leaving this terrible place.

But where would they go? That was the question to be decided by the "Big Man" who was coming.

"Did you happen to hear who the man was?" she asked.

Juana's forehead creased in concentration. "Soldier man. Number one soldier man."

"A general, you mean?"

"General!" The girl nodded, still thinking. "General Sure Man."

"Sure Man?" Miranda frowned, then her eyes widened as she realized what she was hearing. "Sherman! General William Tecumseh Sherman! He's coming here? When?"

"Don't know." Juana's lack of concern was not surprising, given the Navajo view of time. Things happened when they were ready to happen. Miranda was slowly learning to accept that idea.

"But you're certain it was General Sherman the soldiers were talking about?"

The girl nodded gravely. "Yes, miss. Sure Man."

Miranda had met Sherman briefly when he had visited the military hospital after the war. The general had taken her hand and greeted her so gently that it was hard to believe this was the man who had stormed like a juggernaut through Georgia and broken the back of the Confederacy. With the Navajos he would be a tough negotiator, that much was certain. But Sherman was also known to be unstable and erratic. Would he be fair? Would he be wise? So many lives would depend on his decision.

"Does Ahkeah know?" she asked, feeling the familiar ache as she spoke his name. The morning after the fire, when the horse she'd lent him had galloped, riderless, into the fort, she had been frantic. She had fretted for days, until Juana assured her that he had indeed reached home safely, and that both he and Nizhoni were recovering from their ordeals.

Still, he had not appeared at the fort. After watching the ration lines for weeks, Miranda had learned that his friends, with the help of Theodore Dodd, had arranged to deliver supplies to his camp.

Since then Juana had brought her occasional news of Ahkeah, but Miranda had not seen him. Would not. Must not.

"I tell Ahkeah tomorrow, maybe. Next day, maybe. When I see," Juana replied in answer to her question.

"Thank you, Juana." Miranda burned to carry the news to him herself—to watch the emotions flicker across his lean, dark face as he learned that his people's future was about to be resolved. Perhaps, if time and circumstance allowed, she might even hold him close one last time, feel his strength and warmth all around her. The longing deepened, as it had every day since their parting.

The discovery that she was not with child had left her more disappointed than relieved. The thought of holding a tiny, beautiful black-eyed baby in her arms, Ahkeah's and hers—

But this was no time to dream of things that could not be, she admonished herself. She had meaningful work to do here and now, and it was time to give it her full attention.

"Open your books to page 20, girls," she said, picking up her reader. "Let's begin our lesson."

Chapter Fifteen

After the four girls had left, Miranda lingered in the classroom, tidying up for the next day of class. Her mind raced as she swept the floor, straightened the benches and cleaned the blackboard. Juana's news had carried the ring of truth. How else would the girl have heard of General Sherman? All the same, there were so many questions to be answered. How soon was Sherman coming? How much authority had he been given? What and who would influence the final decision?

And what of her own fate? Miranda wondered. If the Navajos were removed, say, to Oklahoma, would she be allowed to follow them and continue her teaching?

Theodore Dodd would have answers for many of her questions. Unfortunately, the hardworking agent had gone to Santa Fe, perhaps to await Sherman's arrival. And there was no one else she could turn to for the information she needed.

Miranda's thoughts scattered as her eyes caught a

flash of bright color through the open window. Hagopian's wagon. He must have driven in while she was teaching her class. For Miranda, it was never a pleasure to see the man. His manner toward her was so unctuous that it made her squirm. Once he had even kissed her hand while his piggish eyes peered directly at her bosom. After that she had kept a careful distance from the self-proclaimed doctor. But she continued to deal with him out of necessity. His wagon was the only source of the ''tonic'' that kept her father from the grip of excruciating pain.

The supply of bottles in the kitchen cabinet was getting low, she reminded herself, checking her pocket for money. Best to get more now, while she could. There was no telling when the greasy old charlatan in the checkered coat would come around again.

Stepping outside, she closed the door and strode across the dusty parade ground. The very sight of the wagon, with gaudily painted nymphs and satyrs cavorting along its wooden sides, made her flesh crawl. She hated everything it stood for, most of all her father's dependence on the laudanum that only Hagopian could provide.

She remembered crouching in the rocks beside Ahkeah, watching as the old man sold liquor to the Comanches. She remembered what Ahkeah had told her about how Hagopian was in the pay of the land speculators and others who wanted the Navajos exterminated from the face of the earth. What was he doing here today? Was this simply a business call, or was he here to gather information that he could sell to others?

How much would Hagopian know about Sherman's visit? she wondered. What would he and his fellow scavengers do when the Navajos were gone?

She approached the wagon, hoping to make a quick purchase and be on her way. But as she drew nearer she saw no sign of Hagopian or anyone else. Only the two mules stood dozing in their traces, switching flies with their long tails.

Frowning, Miranda circled the wagon. Maybe the old man was elsewhere on the post, or someone might have even taken pity on him and invited him to lunch. No matter. She knew where he stored the tonic and how much it cost. If she could get into the wagon, she would just take a few bottles and leave the money in their place. Hagopian would know she had been here.

The padlock was open, hanging from its hasp. Miranda's hand reached for the door handle, touched it, then froze as she heard voices coming from inside the wagon.

"So the Comanches will do the job for fifty new repeatin' rifles?" The speaker, Miranda realized, was Jethro McCree.

"Yes, but they won't agree to their part until you deliver," Hagopian answered. "Can you get the guns in time?"

"We can get 'em," McCree said. "Shouldn't take more'n a day or so. What about the Navajo clothes for them to wear?"

"That part will be easy. No one will know those Comanches aren't Navajos. Can you imagine the uproar when they attack the column and kill General Sherman? Why, my good friend, the whole country will be up in arms!"

"Then we'll have an excuse to wipe out them Navajos to the last snot-nosed papoose!" McCree gloated. "An' we can git that bastard Sherman in the bargain. Let's have a drink on it!"

Miranda stood outside the door, paralyzed with shock. They were planning to attack General Sherman on his way to the fort—with renegade Comanches disguised as Navajos! They—

Her thoughts broke off as she suddenly realized her own danger. If McCree and Hagopian were to open the door and see her now, she would be as good as dead.

Swiftly and stealthily she edged around the side of the wagon, then forced herself to walk calmly away, back toward her classroom. *Tell someone!* The alarms screamed in her head. But who? Her father was helpless. And she had no way of knowing who else at the fort was involved in the mad scheme to murder Sherman. Anyone might talk. Anyone might turn on her— even Violet.

Agent Dodd could surely be trusted—but he was in Santa Fe. Worse, in any planned attack, Dodd's life could be in as much danger as Sherman's.

There was only one person she could count on, Miranda realized. She had to find Ahkeah now, before it was too late.

*   *   *

The sun had dropped behind the western rim of the desert, leaving in its torrid wake the coolness of evening shadow. Birds and insects filled the twilight with an airy symphony of squeaks and chirps and twitters. Mosquitoes rose in whining clouds from the mud flats along the Pecos. Bats darted among them, cutting zig-zag paths in the darkness. A full moon rose above the jagged horizon, a pearl on blue velvet, pale and cold.

Dressed in her riding clothes, Miranda stood beside her father's bed, gazing down at him where he lay in his laudanum-induced slumber. Iron Bill's flesh had melted from his bones, leaving little more than skin stretched over his skull. His eyes were closed, his breathing shallow and ragged.

He would not wake up until morning. He never did. All the same, she had asked the army medic—an earnest young man who seemed to adore her—to check on him before he retired. She had told him she was spending the evening with the family of one of her students. It was a flimsy story that put her at risk, but she could not bear to leave her father unattended on a night when she might be riding into danger.

Her gaze lingered, now, on his sleeping face. She had done her best to make him comfortable, but even on his most lucid days Iron Bill was grumpy and harsh with her. He had not spoken so much as a word of gratitude or endearment. She knew him no better now than she had on that first night when he had ridden out to meet her escort on the road.

Bending, she kissed his waxen forehead—something he would never have permitted had he been awake. Then, gulping back the ache in her throat, she turned away, slipped outside and closed the door softly behind her.

Within twenty minutes she was mounted on the horse she had taken from the stable, flying across the open fields in a parallel course to the road.

Darkness flowed around her like cool water, alive with small sounds and the prickling sensation of danger. Her mind churned with questions.

She had hoped to learn more during the interminably long afternoon, while she waited for nightfall, but there had been no one she felt she could safely ask about Sherman's arrival. Even the young lieutenant who had replaced Iron Bill as interim commander was not above suspicion. A word in the wrong ear, and she could be placed under watch. Faced with the risk, she had simply waited, agonizing over what could go wrong tonight. What if she were caught taking one of the horses? What if she failed to find Ahkeah's camp or arrived to find him gone?

Ahead now, she could make out the blocky outline of the rebuilt Navajo hospital. From there she could cut back to the road and, under cover of night, ride flat out until she came to the rocky outcrop that marked the trail leading to Ahkeah's camp. After that she would have to rely on instinct and memory. If she lost her way, she could spend the entire night wandering in the desert.

She reached the hospital and swung left along the

rutted wagon trail that led toward the main road. Her lips moved in a silent prayer.

"Please let me find him. Please…"

Ahkeah crouched beside the dying cook fire, too restless to sleep. His eyes gazed up at the glittering stars that spilled across the clear night sky. Around him, the light of the full moon cast inky pools of shadow along the ground.

The day had been hot, promising another summer of searing drought. Would his people be forced to spend it here, breathing alkali dust and living on promises and government handouts? Would they be marched all the way to Oklahoma in the deadly heat, or maybe crammed into boxcars like so many cattle and hauled to an alien land? Would they live out their lives among enemies and strangers, never to see their sacred mountains again?

Unable to bear the bitterness, he turned his thoughts inward, to the memory of Miranda in his arms, her body soft and giving; the smell of rain around them, the smoky darkness of the cave…

Wherever he went, Ahkeah would carry the memory of that night—of *her*—in his heart. It would sweeten his lonely nights and warm him when the world was cold.

Miranda's students had brought him occasional word of her. It gave him an ironic sense of pride to know that she had not given up on her little school, and that she was taking on wayward girls and turning them into teachers. He knew, as well, that her father was near death. Soon Big Hat would be gone, and so, perhaps, would the Diné. Then Miranda would have no choice except to return East, to that other world where he could never follow. She would be lost to him—as she was lost already except in his heart.

The sound of hoofbeats broke into his thoughts—a single rider, Ahkeah quickly surmised, and still distant. His first impulse, born of long wariness, was to smother the fire. His fingers had scooped up a handful of earth before he checked himself, struck by a new possibility.

The lone rider was making no effort to be stealthy. Perhaps it was someone who needed help, someone lost or injured. It was not the custom of the Diné to turn away a person in need.

Making up his mind, he tossed a few precious chips of kindling onto the coals. They ignited in seconds, their blaze making a small beacon in the darkness. He heard the hoofbeats pause, then change direction, coming closer.

Still cautious, Ahkeah slipped into the shadows and waited, his hand on his knife. He saw the flash of a pale horse in the moonlight. An instant later his heart seemed to stop as he recognized Miranda. She was leaning forward in the saddle, her hair loose and blowing, her eyes wide in the darkness as she glanced around the silent camp.

Stepping into plain sight, Ahkeah raised a finger to his lips to signal silence. She stared at him, her mouth forming his name without a sound. Then she was out of the saddle, flying across the circle of firelight into his open arms.

Ahkeah caught her close, feeling the rapid flutter of her heart against his chest, feeling her warmth, her tenderness, her passion, and sensing—inexplicably—that his own spirit, ignited by hers, had returned to life.

For a long moment Miranda allowed herself to cling to him—loving him, sinking into his strength, drowning in the solid, sinewy feel of his body and the smoky fragrance of his skin. She buried her face against his chest, overcome by the feeling that, after a long and perilous journey, she had come home where she belonged.

Exactly where she belonged.

She pressed closer, wanting nothing more than to stop time and spend the rest of eternity in his arms. He was her love, her only love. But she had come here on an urgent errand, and there was no more time to lose.

Sensing her need to talk, Ahkeah led her away from the sleeping camp, down to the rim of the plateau where they had once stood and watched the sunrise. She willed herself to keep still until he settled her beside him on a flat boulder. "Now," he said, "what is it?"

She told him everything, watching the emotions flicker across his face—hope, elation, dismay and outrage. It was a subtly different face from the one she remembered. The terrible beating had altered his flawlessly chiseled features. His broken nose had healed with a downward twist, and a jagged scar ran like a lightning bolt down the left side of his face from temple to jaw. He looked older and even more ferocious than before.

"This general, is he a good man?" His question broke into her thoughts.

Miranda spoke slowly, weighing her reply. "He's a hard man. But I would judge him to be fair and honest. You could do far worse." She watched Ahkeah's face for a moment as he considered her words. "Sherman is a hero in the North," she continued, "but there are people who hate him because of the war, people who'd take pleasure in seeing him dead."

"And if he dies—or even if he doesn't—my people will be blamed for the attack and probably massacred." Anger strained the cords in his neck and roughened his voice. His face was a warrior's face now, a mask of cold fury in the moonlight. "When?" he demanded.

Miranda shook her head, desperately wishing she had more answers. "That's what I don't know. Hagopian said something about McCree's needing to get fifty new rifles for the Comanches, and McCree said he could get them in the next day or so. After that, the time of the attack would depend on Sherman's arrival."

Ahkeah's breath eased out in a ragged sigh. Miranda felt some of the tension leave his body as he reached behind her and, catching her waist, pulled her close against his side. "I will tell Barboncito and Manuelito before first light. But we need to know more—everything. And with Little Gopher in Santa Fe, there's no one at the fort we can trust.''

Miranda closed her eyes, resting her head against his shoulder. She wanted nothing more than to stay right here, close beside this man, loving him, bearing and raising his children, sharing whatever life he chose.

But no—she felt Ahkeah's silence in the night, and she knew what he didn't have the heart to ask of her. Only she could do what was needed. Only she was in a position to help his people. There was no other choice, and they both knew it.

''I will go back and find out what you need to know,'' she said quietly. ''As soon as I'm able, I'll bring word back to you.''

''It could be dangerous,'' he murmured, his lips brushing her tangled hair. ''There'll be no one you can trust. Be careful, my love.''

''I will.'' She slid her arms around his waist, grateful that he had not argued against her decision. The fate of eight thousand Navajos hung on what she could learn. This was no time to consider her own safety. Not even for the man who loved her.

Turning, he gathered her close. His mouth found hers in the darkness, hungry and seeking. With a need that blazed from the depths of her soul, she responded, wanting him, all of him, under any conditions, now and forever.

The decision was made, Miranda realized; and with it came the peace of knowing she had heard the voice of her heart.

"I'm coming back to you," she whispered between frantic kisses. "And when this trouble is over I'll follow you anywhere! To Oklahoma, to Dinétah…wherever fortune takes us. Just let me be with you, Ahkeah, that's all I want…all I need."

Easing her a little away from him, he gazed down into her face with troubled black eyes. "Do you know what you're saying, Miranda?" he asked softly. "Do you have any idea what that would mean? The poverty? The danger? The rejection by your own people?"

"Yes." Her heart broke into a thundering gallop as she realized he had not refused her outright. "I've seen the poverty. I've shared the danger. And I've already tasted rejection at the fort. I can bear it all. I can bear anything except the thought of life without you!"

He continued to look at her. She read dismay in his eyes, then frustration, then wonder. Only when she felt she could not stand it another instant did his resolve crumble. A moan escaped his throat as he caught her close, crushing her to him as if he never wanted to let her go.

For a long moment they simply stood and held each other, the dark night wind whispering around them, stirring their clothes, their hair. Miranda felt his body rise and harden against her. Eyes closed, she pressed herself into his masculine strength, savoring every breath, every second of this time in his arms. But even with effort she discovered she could not keep still. The liquid heat that shimmered in her loins compelled her to move, to strain against him, quivering with need, demanding more…demanding everything.

Without a word, he lifted her in his arms and strode down the slope, away from the camp. She wrapped her arms around his neck, holding him tightly, feeling the wild drumming of his heart against her ear. Would this be their last time together? But no—she would not even allow herself to think of the future. In this world of danger there was only here and now, only this night that would seal their promise forever.

Carrying her with ease, he made his way into the gully, moving through pools of moonlight to a shaded hollow overhung by mesquite, where the spring floods had covered the ground with a carpet of velvet-smooth sand. Here he lowered her feet to the ground and captured her mouth in a long, deep kiss. There was no need for words between them. For as long as they both lived, she would be his woman.

Miranda's fingers pulled open his shirt to reveal his broad, bare chest. She tasted the smoky sweetness of his golden skin, her hands groping beneath the weathered fabric to feel the sinewy muscles, the lumps and scars that marked a warrior's body. How she wanted this man. How she loved him.

Gently he lowered her to the sand. For the space of a long breath she gazed up at him in the moonlight, her fingers tracing the contours of his face. Then, with a little cry of love, she pulled him down to her, burying that dear, battered face in the hollow between her breasts.

He nuzzled her hungrily through the thin muslin,

and after a moment's fumbling, she felt the touch of his lips on her bare skin. A shiver of pleasure coursed through her body. The slickness between her thighs told her that even now she was ready for him, aching for him. She whispered her need into the night, pulling him close as she opened to him like a flower.

When he entered her it was as before—the feeling so natural, so perfect that the sweetness of it brought a rush of tears to her eyes. She arched to meet his thrust, letting him fill her. Her hands cupped his firm buttocks, drawing him deep into her warm, pulsing center. Her lips formed his name. She heard the cry of a night bird as he carried her with him, higher and higher. Her body sang, every cell and nerve and fiber alive with the joy of loving him. ''Ahkeah…'' she whispered. ''My love…my love…'' Then there was only breathless silence as the two of them soared and shattered, then spiraled slowly downward to lie on the bare earth once more, trembling in each other's arms.

Ahkeah gazed up through the lacy canopy of the mesquite bush, his eyes tracing the patterns of the stars that shone in the midnight sky. His arms cradled Miranda. She lay quietly, her face pressed against his chest, her legs tangled with his own. They had said little, but both of them knew their time together was growing short.

A veritable army of questions battered at the gates of his mind. How could any white woman endure the life he had to offer—the hardship, the backbreaking work, the isolation from all that was dear and famil-

iar? And what about his own people? How would
they accept her? How would they accept *him*, with a
bilagáana as his wife?

So many questions, and no answers. The answers
would have to come later, Ahkeah reminded himself.
Tonight the wonder was enough—wonder and joy
that this tender, courageous beauty had offered him
her life. It was a stunning gift.

She stirred beside him, straining upward to kiss the
corner of his mouth. His heart contracted as he drew
her closer. "It's time," he said softly.

"I know." She drew back and sat up, filling her
eyes with the sight of him as she brushed the sand
from her hair. "I should at least be able to find out
when Sherman is expected to arrive. The rest of it—
when and where the attack will take place and where
McCree plans to get the guns—that will be harder,
but I'll do what I can."

"Just be careful." His hand captured hers, fingers
gripping fiercely as he rose to his feet and pulled her
up beside him. "I don't want you hurt."

"I know." She lifted his hand and brushed a kiss
across his knuckles. "But we have to stop this terrible
thing from happening, no matter what the cost."

He gathered her close once more, knowing he was
sending her into terrible danger and that he could not
protect her. "I'll ride to Barboncito's camp, then to
Manuelito's, and warn them both," he said. "By mid-
morning I should be back here, waiting for word from
you. If you can't come, send Juana."

She shook her head adamantly. "Juana is too close

to McCree. He could hurt her, force her to give him information. I can't involve her or anyone else.''

''Then don't take any chances.''

''I may have to.''

''I know,'' he whispered, clasping her to him. ''I know.''

He watched her mount, keeping his eyes on her pale figure until it vanished into the darkness. All his hopes and prayers went with her. She was infinitely precious to him. But the lives of his people depended on what she could learn about the plot to murder Sherman. She was risking her life for them all—and he had no choice except to let her.

Ahkeah waited until the last echo of hoofbeats had died away. Then, striding back down along the gully, he found his horse in the makeshift corral where he kept it hidden from Comanche raiders. Slipping the rawhide bridle over its head, he led it up to the clustered dugouts. He took a moment to duck inside one of them and inform his sleepy cousin he was leaving. Then he mounted and rode silently away, swinging north in the direction of Barboncito's camp.

As he raced his horse across the barren alkali flats, the howl of a coyote echoed on the dark desert wind, chilling his blood like the cry of a ghost.

Chapter Sixteen

Miranda reached the main road and slowed her tired mount to a walk. This was no time to hurry, she reminded herself. A galloping horse could be heard from a long way off.

For a moment she gazed down the road, weighing the wisdom of returning the way she'd left against that of riding straight in past the provost marshall's office. Slipping into the stable undetected would be best. But what if the young medic had made it known that she'd left for the evening? What if someone else had come looking for her? Any number of people could know she had been away from the fort, including Jethro McCree.

It would be wiser to return openly, she decided. The sentries might question the lateness of the hour, but she should be able to come up with a ready excuse—perhaps that she'd been tending a sick child or that she'd lost her way in the darkness.

As she rode down the straight, tree-lined road, Miranda struggled to focus her thoughts. She had spent much of the long ride across the desert remembering the past hour in Ahkeah's arms. Now it was time to abandon her dreams, collect her wits and make her plans.

Learning the time of Sherman's arrival was at least possible, she reasoned. The trick would be to do so without alerting McCree and his cronies. Perhaps she could visit the fort's young commander and play the innocent. Yes—she could say that she'd met Sherman in the East and would like to plan a party for the general. The idea was such a good one that Miranda berated herself for not having thought of it sooner. It might have given her one more piece of information to carry to Ahkeah.

The rest—whatever she could discover about the planned attack—would be far more dangerous. She would need to balance what she could learn against the risk of not getting word to Ahkeah. Her every move would have to be calculated, and even then, so fearfully much would depend on luck and timing.

Through the darkness, she could see the glow of the lantern that hung outside the provost marshall's office. Fear constricted her throat as the sentry stepped out of the small adobe building to challenge her.

"Halt! Who goes there?"

Miranda felt her heart stop, then start again as she recognized the man—a grizzled corporal who had no known association with McCree. Before she could form a reply he recognized her and stepped out into the light.

"Evenin', Miz Howell—or should I say, mornin'? What's a lady like you doin' out at this hour?" He grinned up at her, implying no threat.

"I could say I was just riding." Miranda laughed. "But the truth is, I was visiting my students in the camps and got lost on the way back. You can't imagine how glad I am to see you, Corporal!"

"Right glad you made it back safe and sound, miss," he said kindly. "But you shouldn't be out here by yourself in the dark. No tellin' what might happen to a young lady in a place like this."

"Thank you for the warning. I'll keep it in mind." Miranda nudged the horse forward. "Now, if you'll excuse me, I'm truly anxious to get home, check on my father and go to bed."

"You sure you'll be all right?" He squinted up at her. "Private Tomkins is just inside. I could ask him to ride in with you and take your horse to the stable."

"Thank you, no," she said, wanting only to get clear of such an exposed place. "I should be perfectly safe from here on, and I can see to the horse myself."

"You're sure, now?"

"Quite sure." Miranda flashed him a smile and a farewell wave as she nudged the horse to a trot. "Thank you for your trouble, Corporal!"

She was out of hearing before the man could answer, her heart pounding, her body chilled and sweating beneath her clothes. It was all right, she reassured herself. *She* was all right. All she had to do was return the horse to the stable and walk back to her father's quarters. There she could rest for a few hours and mull over the remainder of her plan.

She slowed the horse to a walk as she neared the parade ground, turning right to skirt the back of the officers' quarters. The stable lay beyond the barracks, placed so that the prevailing winds would blow away the smell of manure. There was a corral, but the horses would be shut up inside for the night, the doors at both ends of the long wooden structure locked against marauders.

Dismounting, she used her father's key to open the heavy iron padlock, and swung the door open just far enough to admit herself and the horse. Inside, the stable was dark and musty, smelling of horseflesh, manure and stale tobacco. Horses nickered and stirred in the darkness.

Long fingers of moonlight shone through gaps in the roof, which no one had mended in too many seasons. Miranda led her horse down the row of stalls, her eyes straining in the meager light.

Her heart lurched as a wild dove exploded from its perch on a rafter. Its fluttering wings beat a wild tattoo as it veered off the inner slope of the roof, searching for an escape before it vanished, squawking, into the night.

Taking deep gulps of air, Miranda willed her galloping pulse to slow. "Don't be a silly goose," she lectured herself, speaking aloud. "It was nothing. Just a bird."

Ahead she could see the empty stall where her horse belonged. Relieved, she hurried forward, pulling the animal behind her. She had made it! She was safe!

Only then did she see it—looming large and hideous out of the shadows at the far end of the building. It was Hagopian's wagon, standing just inside the closed double doors. The back end of the wagon was open, the mules hitched and waiting in their traces as—

Miranda saw no more as something struck the side of her head and she tumbled into blackness.

Hastiin Dághaá, known to outsiders as Barboncito, was not an imposing figure of a man. He stood half a head shorter than Ahkeah, his body as slender as a weasel's. His features, marked by the drooping mustache that had given him his nickname, looked more Mexican than Diné. But among all the people, no headman was more respected for wisdom, courage and eloquence.

"Stay and talk," he said, motioning Ahkeah toward a flat boulder. "My son, Ti-co-ba-sha, is already on his way to Manuelito's camp with your news. There is no need for you to leave so soon."

"It was generous of you to send your son," Ahkeah said politely. "Even so, I mustn't stay long. The sooner the plan to attack Sherman can be stopped, the better it will be for us all."

"It was your *bilagáana* who told you of this plot?" The graying headman's expression did not so much as flicker, though Ahkeah was stunned by his choice of words. There were few secrets among the Diné.

"She heard it at the fort, by accident," he managed to answer. "Now she's gone back to learn more. It will be dangerous for her."

"Yes." Barboncito nodded slowly. "The son of my wife's sister attends her school. She's a good woman, your *bilagáana*. Not like most of them."

Ahkeah swallowed a surge of emotion. Barboncito's simple acknowledgment of Miranda was a gift beyond all expectation.

"How can I help you stop this evil?" the headman asked. "Do you need warriors? Weapons?"

"Not until I know more," Ahkeah replied. "It may be that we can end it quietly, without a fight—find the guns, perhaps, or manage a way to get word to Little Gopher."

"That would be best. But keep yourself safe. You have been the bravest of our warriors. But when General Sherman comes it is your voice we will need."

"You should be the one to speak for the Diné," Ahkeah said quickly. "You or Manuelito."

"That may be. But whoever speaks will need your tongue to make his words understood by the *biligáana*. I, for one, would trust no one but you to speak for me."

"Then I will do my best to return." Ahkeah glanced toward the eastern horizon, where darkness was just beginning to fade. Concern for Miranda's safety had been gnawing at him from the moment she'd left him. By now it had deepened to become slow torture. He had asked too much, expecting her to risk her life gathering secrets. This was his fight, not hers, he berated himself, and it was up to him to end it before she paid the price.

He could not risk precious time waiting for her return. For Miranda's sake and for the sake of his people, he had to act swiftly.

"Forgive me, my friend, I can't stay." He strode toward his horse, glancing back just long enough to see Barboncito raise his hand in understanding and farewell.

"Our lives are in your hands," the headman said. "May the Holy People ride with you."

Ahkeah returned the sign of blessing. An instant later he was mounted and flying across the desert.

Miranda stirred and moaned. Her head throbbed dully and her mouth was as dry as cotton. Through a haze of pain she realized she was lying on her side, on a hard surface that jerked and swayed in sickening motion.

Her eyes shot open, seeing only darkness at first. Then, as her pupils widened and focused, she recognized the inside of Dr. Hagopian's painted lair. She remembered the stable, the sudden blow. Someone had knocked her out. Now she was inside the medicine wagon, and the wagon was moving.

Seized by sudden panic, she struggled to sit up. Only then did she realize that her limbs were bound with ropes as thick as her middle finger. Her hands were tied behind her back, her ankles lashed tightly together. The coarse hemp bit into her flesh, rasping her skin as she twisted helplessly.

Exhausted, she collapsed back onto her side. Every bounce of the wagon jarred her head, shooting hot nails of pain through her skull. Only when she raised up to ease the punishment did she realize that the hard surface beneath her was not the bed of the wagon. No, she was too high for that. There was something beneath her. Something solid and heavy that shifted with each sway of the wagon.

Gasping with effort, she writhed onto her chest. Light flickered through small cracks in the roof, the thin beams shifting and moving, worsening the dizziness she felt. Miranda gulped back nausea as she focused on what was beneath her. Her heart lurched as she realized she was lying across several long wooden crates. Gun crates! McCree had loaded the rifles into the wagon and flung her in on top of them.

"So you're awake are you, Miss Priss?" Jethro McCree opened the small door behind the wagon seat, almost blinding her with light. "Thought I heard somethin' movin' around back there."

As Miranda's eyes adjusted to the glare, she glimpsed Hagopian's ample rear on the driver's seat beside him. Raising up as far as her position would allow, she glared at the sergeant through the tangled curtain of her hair.

"Running guns to the Indians is a federal crime, Sergeant," she snapped. "So, I believe, is kidnapping."

"Kidnappin'?" McCree hooted with laughter. "Hell, you ain't kidnapped, lady! You're just extra baggage we brung along for the ride! When we saw them fancy little footprints outside the wagon this afternoon, we figured takin' you with us might be a good idea.''

"So you were waiting for me in the stable?"

McCree snickered. "I ain't as dumb as you might think, Miss High and Mighty. First I noticed the horse was gone. Then when I saw the medic stoppin' by the major's quarters, I reckoned you'd skedaddled off to tell your Navajo pals what you thought you'd heard, an' that sooner or later you'd come sneakin' back. I was dead on target.''

"So you really are taking these guns to the Comanches?" Miranda knew it was too late to play the innocent. McCree and Hagopian had guessed her every move.

"That's right." McCree grinned like an ape. "An' we're takin' 'em somethin' else, too. Call it a bonus. A little extra for their trouble." His eyes narrowed wickedly.

Miranda felt her stomach lurch. *Not the Comanches. Dear heaven, anything but the Comanches.*

"What's the matter, Sergeant?" she challenged him, hiding her terror. "Don't you have the guts to kill me yourself?"

"Murderin' white women ain't my style." McCree picked his teeth with his fingernail. "'Sides, if them Comanches got any smarts, they'll keep you alive and sell you to the Mexican slavers after they've had their fun. If they don't cut you up too bad, you could fetch a right handsome price. 'Course, I never did credit Comanches with havin' much business sense…"

Laughing uproariously, he closed the door, plunging Miranda into darkness again. Sick with terror, she lay on the rifle crates, teeth clenched against the jarring pain. Reason screamed that she was trapped. But she knew she could not surrender to fear. To do so would be to die, and she had no intention of dying. She was Iron Bill Howell's daughter and she was not giving up. Heaven willing, she would survive to see Ahkeah again, to hold him in her arms and live out the full measure of their love. But first, whatever the cost, she had to stop this evil plot against his people.

The only question was how to do it, when her limbs were bound and her head was spinning so crazily she could scarcely think. There had to be a way, she told herself. There was always a way. *Always…*

By the time Ahkeah reached his own camp, his mind had weighed and rejected several plans. His first impulse had been to gallop straight to the fort and find Miranda. But that, he'd swiftly realized, was out of the question. His presence there would be nothing but a danger to her and to himself.

He could borrow a fresh horse, then, and strike out on the long road to Santa Fe in the hope of meeting Sherman's party and warning them off. Again, Ahkeah had abandoned the idea. Any Navajo caught outside the boundaries of Bosque Redondo could be— and likely would be—shot on sight. Even if he survived, it was possible he would have to ride all the way to Santa Fe. Such a journey would take him far from his people and from Miranda at a time when they needed him most.

He had already given up on waiting to hear from her, which left him with one choice—perhaps the most dangerous choice of all.

He had followed the movements of the Comanche raiders for four long years. He knew their trails, their habits and their secret meeting places. If he could find and disable them now, the ambush on Sherman would be far less likely to happen.

Barboncito had offered him braves and weapons. But a war party would only call attention to itself, and even in large numbers the Navajos were no match for Comanche rifles. Ahkeah knew his best chance lay in going in alone, relying on nothing but his own stealth and cunning.

Stopping by his own camp, Ahkeah paused long enough to water his horse and to speak quietly with his cousin. Keeping his plans to himself, he asked her to keep Miranda there if she arrived before his return, and to see her safely to the fort if he was not back before sundown. Naahooyéí was a stout, friendly woman, and she spoke a few words of English. Ahkeah knew he could trust her to put Miranda at ease.

Nizhoni had awakened. She came tumbling up out of the dugout like a sleepy little fox cub, tripping over the ragged hem of her oversize shirt as she plunged toward him.

"You are leaving, my father?" Her eager little hands reached toward him, the fingers long and graceful. He scooped her into his arms, cradling her close, filling his senses with her sweet morning smell as she flung her arms around his neck.

"Leaving, yes, little mischief. But not for long. I'll be back soon." Ahkeah glanced past his daughter, his eyes meeting Naahooyéí's gaze. He had not told his cousin what was afoot or what he planned to do, but she clearly sensed the danger. Even now, the understanding hung between them that if he did not return she would take Nizhoni and raise the little girl as her own.

For a moment longer he held his daughter close, knowing that if he gave his life today it would be for her. Then, with an ache in his throat, he lowered her to the ground and watched as she scampered back into the dugout to dress.

Now, he thought. He had to leave now while he could still bear the pain of going.

Naahooyéí had turned away to busy herself with making the fire. She did not raise her eyes as Ahkeah swung onto his horse and galloped out of the camp.

He had already calculated where the Comanches might be. An hour's ride into the desert there was a hidden arroyo where the renegades often met to drink and trade. Hagopian knew the place—Ahkeah had seen his wagon there more than once. With luck the renegades would be there now, waiting for McCree and the old man to deliver the contraband rifles. With even more luck, they'd be drinking and gambling to pass the time, or sleeping off last night's drunken brawl. Even with that he knew the odds would be stacked against him.

How could he defeat so many alone? Stealing or scattering their ponies would be easiest—all Diné warriors were accomplished horse thieves. If that proved too difficult there were other ways—riskier and bloodier, but still possible. First he would have to find the enemy. Only then could he weigh his chances and make a plan.

In the east the day was dawning in a glorious blaze of mauve, flame and azure. For the space of one long breath Ahkeah allowed himself to bask in its beauty, remembering Miranda and the morning they had watched another sunrise, wrapped in each other's arms. He remembered the sunlight, the rosy gold on her skin, the sprinkle of tiny freckles across her nose and all the reflected colors of the sky glowing in her deep silver eyes.

Miranda would be safely within the fort now, maybe just waking up to the day. He imagined her tawny hair spilling across the white pillowcase and the throaty little sounds she made as she emerged from sleep. He knew beyond all doubt that he wanted to spend every morning of his life with her. He wanted to awaken to the sight of her sleeping in his arms, to cradle her close beneath the blankets and watch the colors of dawn spilling through the open doorway of their hogan….

But this was no time for dreams, Ahkeah reminded himself as he scanned the horizon for danger. This was to be a day of war.

A war he had chosen to fight alone.

* * *

The medicine wagon lumbered across the rugged desert terrain, its wheels lurching over rocks, crashing through holes and sinking into patches of soft ground. Unable to brace with her hands, Miranda was at the mercy of every bone-crushing bump. Her body was a mass of bruises from being tossed back and forth like a rag doll. Her wrists and ankles were bloodied from straining at the heavy ropes, all for nothing. The knots refused to give so much as a finger's breadth.

Fighting panic, she forced her frenzied mind to think. At the speed it was careening over the desert, the medicine wagon had to be taking a good deal of punishment. Surely Hagopian would not risk so much damage to his property unless—

The obvious conclusion struck her like a mule kick. Hagopian and McCree were in a hurry because they were late. The time for their plan was running out.

Had her own late arrival delayed them? That was possible, since the wagon had appeared ready to go when she'd seen it in the darkness of the stable. Clearly, they hadn't wanted to risk leaving her behind to implicate them in the attack. Now they were trying to make up for lost time.

They had to get the guns to the renegade Comanches before it was too late to ambush Sherman.

The wagon's left front wheel crunched into a deep hole and stopped dead. Through the thin wooden walls Miranda could hear Hagopian cursing and lashing the mules with his whip. She could hear McCree's foul response as he jumped down to brace his shoulder against the wheel to push. For a heart-stopping moment Miranda dared to hope the wagon might be stuck right there. But in a moment it heaved out of the hole, pausing only long enough for McCree to clamber aboard before it rumbled forward again.

Inside, the jarring motion had flung open cabinets and cupboards, spilling their contents helter-skelter. Pots and pans, utensils, tinned food, packets of tobacco and bottles of medicine littered the wagon. The bitter smell of laudanum struck Miranda's nostrils, and she saw that some of the bottles had broken, spilling their contents onto the gun crates. Would the broken glass be sharp enough to cut through her ropes? She twisted closer, but soon discovered, to her dismay, that she could not put enough pressure on the shifting glass to do any harm to the sturdy hemp. But it was too soon to give up. A knife, perhaps, or a razor, if she could manage to brace the handle between the crates...

She searched frantically, twisting this way and that to peer into the dim spaces around her. She found no knife of any kind—nothing, in fact, that had any possibilities except—

Miranda's heart crawled into her throat as she saw them—the matches that had tumbled from a shelf to scatter inside a large open basket of rags. Perhaps...but no, the very idea sickened her with terror. If she lit a match to burn through her ropes, she would almost certainly set the wagon on fire. There had to be some other way. Any other way.

Shaking now, she sank back against a heavy trunk

and stared at the basket where the matches had fallen. The rags, she suddenly realized, were the old clothes Hagopian had brought along to disguise the Comanches as Navajo warriors. Dressed in those clothes, the renegades would swoop down on the small party of travelers, killing Sherman and ending once and for all the hope that the Navajos would leave Fort Sumner and survive as a nation.

Incensed by the murder of the man who was, to many, a national hero, the enraged citizens of New Mexico would mount up and ride against eight thousand defenseless Navajos, massacring them all—men, women and children—in one terrible bloodbath.

That was how the Navajo world—Ahkeah's world—would end, unless one woman possessed the courage to change things here and now.

Crawling on elbows and knees in the pitching wagon, Miranda reached the basket and used her chin to move it out of the corner, toward the small front door. How soon would McCree and Hagopian notice the smoke and come rushing around to save their precious rifles? Not before the clothes were ruined—at least she could be sure of that.

Would they rescue her from the blazing wagon? Not likely, Miranda realized, her heart sinking. Her best chance would be to press against the back doors, then tumble out onto the ground as soon as they were opened. Even then, McCree and Hagopian would probably kill her. But what was one life worth when thousands more were at stake?

She had to do this. There was no other way.

Fighting for balance, she managed to pick three matches out of the basket with her mouth. Two of them she dropped onto the top of a gun crate, where she anchored them with her knee in case she needed more than one. Then, spotting a shovel with a rusty blade nearby, she gripped the remaining match between her teeth and leaned close.

I love you, Ahkeah, she whispered silently. Then she touched the tiny glob of phosphorus to the rusty metal and, with a jerk of her head, struck the match against the rough surface.

The matched sputtered, then flamed up in her face, its heat singeing her eyelashes. It was all she could do to keep from dropping it as she moved toward the basket, bent low and dropped the burning twig onto an oily-looking rag.

For the space of a heartbeat nothing happened. Then small tongues of fire began to lick at the edge of the fabric, tasting, growing, devouring.

Within seconds the entire basket was ablaze.

Chapter Seventeen

The wagon was beginning to fill with smoke. Miranda shrank against the rear doors, gulping air through the narrow crack as the flames licked upward. Any second now they would burn through the roof. Then surely the two men would stop, leap out of the wagon and fling open the back to rescue their precious guns.

Even then she would probably die, she reasoned. They would shoot her on the spot or turn her over to the Comanches. But at least she would be out of this blazing, choking inferno.

An eternity seemed to pass before she heard McCree curse loudly and violently. "What the bloody, stinkin'— Smoke! The whole damned roof's smokin'! That hell bitch's gone and set the place on fire! Stop the wagon—we got to get them rifles outa the back afore they burn!"

The reeling wagon shuddered to a halt. Miranda felt the shifting weight as both men clambered down from the wagon seat. Closing her smoke-scorched eyes, she murmured a silent prayer of gratitude. Soon she would be out in the blessed air to face whatever came next. Clinging to the door, she added another prayer—a prayer for courage.

Seconds crawled past. Then, suddenly, she heard McCree shouting from behind the wagon, inches from her ear.

"Hagopian! You damned old fart, where you runnin' off to? You got the blasted key, an' I need you to help me drag the guns out! Get your ass back here!"

"Not on your life!" the old man called out from farther away. "Got a keg of black powder under the bed! Took it in trade a few weeks back. When the fire gets down there, the whole wagon's gonna blow to kingdom come!"

McCree swore roundly, calling the old man every vile epithet in his army vocabulary. "We got at least a minute!" he shrieked. "You come back here, or so help me, I'll shoot you down like a blasted coyote!"

"Don't be a—fool, McCree!" Hagopian was panting, his hoarse voice fading as he fled. "If you've got any—sense, you'll—"

The report of McCree's pistol was so loud and so close that it seemed to shatter Miranda's ears. She felt rather than heard her own scream as the startled mules, already spooked by the smell of smoke, exploded into panic-stricken flight.

The wagon shot forward, its wheels rumbling, its top swaying wildly, trailing smoke. Inside, the potbellied stove snapped its pipe and rolled backward, pinning Miranda against the bolted door. Helpless now, she clung to the sooty weight, watching the fire burn lower and counting the breaths that remained of her life.

Ahkeah saw the smoke as he was nearing the top of a rock-strewn ridge. Comanches, up to no good, was his first thought.

Cautiously, he slid from his horse, dropped to the ground and bellied his way to the ridge top. Peering between two boulders, he blinked, then stared outright as he recognized Hagopian's wagon, thundering across the flat, driverless and shooting flames. The two mules were running blind, stampeding from the terror behind them, unable to get away.

From his high vantage point, he could see the shallow wash just ahead of them, the sharp drop below its edge as high as a man's waist. It was too late to stop the animals or head them off. They plunged over the rim, dragging the burning wagon after them.

The mules screamed as the wagon crashed down behind them and came to rest on the bed of the wash, its front axle shattered, its charred roof split open. Ahkeah saw the animals thrashing in the dust. Even if it meant exposing himself, he knew he could not ride away and leave them to suffer. It would take no more than a minute or two to cut them loose, or to slit their poor throats if they were too badly hurt to survive.

Mounting, he scanned the flat. In the far distance he saw two dark figures, little more than dots. One appeared to be flat on the ground, the other standing, moving. Hagopian and McCree, most likely. Either they'd been thrown off the wagon seat or they had jumped. Never mind, they were no threat. He could deal with them after he saw to the mules.

As he galloped down the long slope, he tried to piece together the implications of what had happened. The wagon destroyed, the two men on foot—did it mean the plot against Sherman had failed, or had they already delivered the guns and disguises to the Comanches?

Tying his horse at a safe distance, Ahkeah hiked down into the wash. The wagon lay half on its front end, still burning. The mules, lathered and coated with alkali dust, were struggling to stand. Neither of the animals appeared badly hurt. They rolled their eyes and laid back their ears, wheezing with fear as Ahkeah's sharp knife sliced through the leathers that held them to the shattered wagon tongue. Once free, they scrambled to their feet, shook their dusty hides and fled, braying and bucking, up the wash.

Up close, he could see that the top of the wagon enclosure was little more than charred embers. The impact had shattered the overhead supports in front, causing the weaker parts to collapse forward on impact. This had lessened the fire toward the back, but the sides were still burning, the flames licking their way down the walls, where Hagopian, or someone before him, had glued layers of old newspaper to seal out the wind. Beyond that, billows of acrid smoke obscured the depths of the wagon, making it difficult to see any farther inside.

How had the fire started? Ahkeah could imagine the chain of events—McCree and Hagopian delivering the promised goods to the Comanches, then something going wrong. Maybe there'd been an argument. Or simple perversity had goaded one of the renegades into shooting a flaming arrow at the departing wagon. As the blaze was discovered, McCree and Hagopian had bailed off the wagon seat, Hagopian injuring himself. Then the mules had spooked and run off. Was that how it had happened? Or could the fire have somehow started *inside* the wagon?

He was wasting time here, Ahkeah reminded himself, turning away. Hagopian and McCree were no longer a danger, but if the Comanches already had the guns, they had to be stopped, or at least diverted long enough to—

A low, whimpering sound stopped him in his tracks.

He froze, straining his ears. Was it an animal he'd heard, or only the sound of a burned timber giving way?

"Is anybody there?" he demanded, his voice ringing in the smoldering silence.

Nothing. Then, as he was about to turn away again, he heard a cough.

"Ahkeah..." The voice was weak but unmistakable. Suddenly he was tearing into the side of the wagon, burning his hands, kicking and ripping away the weakened wood. He saw her then, at the back of the wagon, singed and bloodied, her body all but buried by debris.

"Run, Ahkeah!" she whispered, her voice hoarse in her smoke-burned throat.

"Keep still." He was fighting his way toward her, his progress nightmarishly slow.

"No…listen to me. There's black powder in here—it's going to blow—you have to get away!"

"Not without you." He redoubled his effort to reach her. "If we go, Miranda, we go together."

"Please, Ahkeah…"

He had her then, his arms working beneath her body as the flames crackled around them. Praying her back wasn't broken, he lifted her free.

She hung limp in his arms, too weak, even, to hold on to him. Her skirt was smoldering, her skin and hair blackened with smoke. "Hurry!" she whispered.

Ahkeah ran then, leaping free of the burning wagon, plunging up the bed of the wash to where the sharp curve of the bank offered some shelter. Behind them, the wagon exploded in a monstrous fireball, the sound echoing across the barren hills, all the way to the banks of the Pecos.

Major William Davenport Howell lay in peace at last, beneath the rocky earth of Bosque Redondo. He had passed away quietly, in his laudanum weighted sleep, the day after Miranda's return to the fort. There had been no words of farewell between father and daughter, no gesture of love, only his silent passing in the night, with no one at his bedside.

Miranda arranged the tiny bouquet of wildflowers on her father's grave, tucking the stems into the earth in the vain hope that they might not wilt at once in the blazing heat. Slowly she rose, feeling with every movement the soreness of her bruised body. Miraculously, she had suffered no broken bones. Even the burns on her face and hands were slight and not likely to leave scars. She had been lucky. More than lucky.

Favoring her right leg, she made her way out of the dusty little cemetery and back toward her father's quarters. She had set aside the rest of the morning for sorting out his possessions. The task would not take long. Iron Bill had been a true Spartan, keeping little that was not for immediate use. She had already decided to box up his personal effects and send them to his unmarried sister in Albany. She herself would not be able to take them where she was going.

Dry-eyed still, she crossed the parlor and entered her father's bedroom. Even now, except for the lingering scent of stale tobacco, little of his presence remained. The bed was already stripped, the sheets, pillow and blanket returned to the supply officer. There would be nothing to dispose of except his clothes and the contents of his dresser drawers.

She had come here to know her father. But he had died a stranger. Even the small intimacies of nursing him had been no more than she had done for a hundred sick and wounded soldiers in the hospital. Her father had not loved her. He had not wanted her. He had not even thanked her.

On leaden feet she moved to the wardrobe and took

out his gold-braided dress uniform. It was little worn, and so large that its size would have drowned Iron Bill in the last weeks of his life. Folded neatly, the uniform went into the trunk on top of the carefully polished boots that still held the shape of his feet, and the dress sword in its long leather sheath. How dashing he must have looked in his younger days. No wonder her mother had fallen in love with him.

And no wonder she had finally gone East and left Iron Bill to his soldiering.

On the floor of the wardrobe, Miranda discovered, stacked and pushed into a back corner, were two wooden boxes of the size that might hold cigars or cheroots. The smaller one, which she opened first, contained his medals, six of them, carefully polished and pinned to a threadbare cushion of dark blue velveteen. She touched each one of them, knowing how her father must have treasured them. Perhaps she ought to keep just one, to show her future children that their grandfather had been a brave man. But that would not do, she reminded herself, since he had won most of them fighting Indians. With a sigh she closed the lid and slipped the little box between the folds of his uniform.

Then she reached for the second box, unfastened its metal clasp and raised the lid.

She sank onto the edge of the mattress, her knees failing her as she recognized what was inside.

For a moment she stared into the box, a lump rising in her throat. Then, slowly, she turned the box over.

Everything she had ever sent to her father tumbled out, to scatter on the blue-and-white ticking.

He had saved them all—the letters; the childishly scrawled drawings; the weathered tintype of her at the age of ten, posing with a long-forgotten puppy; a single pale curl, snipped and tied with a pink ribbon.

The letters were worn from handling, their creases almost transparent from countless unfoldings and re-foldings. The envelopes and the little portrait were crushed and stained, as if they had been hastily stuffed into pockets and carried there for weeks on end, through heat, storm and battle.

The icy weight inside Miranda's chest stirred and began to crumble. So sweet was the ache of it that she could scarcely bear the pain.

She remembered how he had ridden out to meet her the night she had arrived here, the concern on his face masked by his gruff manner. She remembered the long trips he had made to the East during her growing up years, for no apparent reason except to see her.

He had loved her. Her father had loved her.

She felt the tears come then—bitter, scalding tears that would not stop. She buried her face in her hands as great, gulping sobs shook her body.

"Miranda."

The spoken sound and the light touch on her shoulder filled her with warmth and peace. Ahkeah lifted her gently and gathered her in his arms, cradling her close, filling her world with love.

She felt him stir, glancing down at the scattered

papers on the bed. His arms tightened around her, and she knew he understood.

"Why was my father so cold with me?" she whispered. "Why didn't he ever tell me the truth, when it would have meant so much?"

"Maybe he didn't know how," Ahkeah said gently, "or maybe he didn't want you to mourn him when he was gone. Your father was a good man and he cared for you. That's all you need to remember."

Miranda buried her face against his chest, feeling cherished and protected. Ahkeah, too, was a man of few words, she reminded herself. It would never be like him to spout declarations of love or bring her poems and flowers. But the love that burned in his gaze and in his touch would be strong enough to nourish her for the rest of her life.

He held her in warm silence, giving her time to collect herself before he spoke again. "Do you feel well enough to come to the council meeting? Barboncito will be giving his final speech. Then Sherman will decide where we are to go." He paused, sensing her hesitation. "It's all right," he added, his lips brushing her forehead. "Everyone wants you there, Na-ne-tgin."

Miranda's eyes misted again at his use of her new Navajo name, which came from their word for teacher. "Then nothing could keep me away! I can finish this packing later."

She hurried to the basin to splash her tearstained face with cool water. The two of them had not been able to steal much time together in the past few days.

She had been caught up in the shock of her father's death and the preparations for his burial. Ahkeah had been deeply involved in the negotiations with General Sherman. That he wanted her with him now, at this critical time, meant more to her than he could know.

She glanced up at the glass above the washstand, then turned swiftly away. It would be weeks before her burns healed; months, perhaps, before her singed hair regained its softness and shine. Until then, Ahkeah's eyes would be her only mirror. When those eyes met hers, she would see the love in their depths and know that she was beautiful.

They opened the door on a world that had changed drastically since Sherman's arrival. With the Navajos preparing to leave any day, the military presence at the fort was down to a small garrison. Violet and her husband had departed for Santa Fe two days earlier. They had not even stopped in to say goodbye. But then, Miranda no longer found such treatment surprising. She had become invisible to Fort Sumner's white population. Only Theodore Dodd, an outsider in his own right, remained her steadfast friend.

The meeting with Sherman had been set up in the open area behind the rebuilt Navajo hospital. Miranda and Ahkeah walked side by side down the road in the bright sunlight, no longer concerned about the likes of Jethro McCree. A patrol had found the sergeant's body, shot and scalped, near the box canyon where the Comanche band had camped. It was easy enough to guess what had happened. Furious at the loss of the promised guns, the renegades had taken their re-

venge and left the remains for the vultures and coyotes. McCree's few surviving friends had scattered
like the cowards they were. Without their leader they
were no longer a threat to anyone.

The almost palpable tension in the air pulled Miranda's thoughts back to the present. She could feel
it in Ahkeah's silence as he strode beside her. She
could see it in the faces of the people who were hurrying back to the negotiations after the short rest pe-
riod. She knew that Sherman had been appalled by
the conditions under which the Navajos were living,
and that he intended to move them out within days.
But where? That was the question that tore at eight
thousand hearts.

Rumor had it that the general favored relocating
the Navajos to Oklahoma, where the government
could keep close watch on them. Other tribes, such
as the Cherokee, had been successfully resettled there.
With such a ready solution at hand, why send the
Navajos back to Dinétah, with all the risk that decision entailed? Why send them back to the country
where they had caused nothing but trouble?

On the open land behind the hospital, Navajo families thronged, clustered on the bare ground to witness
this crucial moment in their history. Only those who
were closest to the speakers would be able to hear
what was said, but that seemed to make no difference.
They spread like a human flood across the unplanted
fields, oblivious to the hot sun and to the flies and
mosquitoes that swarmed in the dry summer air.

Ahkeah's cousin Naahooyéí, seated with her two

sons and Nizhoni, moved over to make room for Miranda. Some of the people nearby smiled or spoke soft words of greeting. Miranda's courageous role in stopping the plot against Sherman was known by all the Navajos. They welcomed her now as Ahkeah's woman.

Squeezing in beside Naahooyéí, she settled back to watch as Ahkeah took his place among the Navajo leaders. The sight of him there touched her heart with pride. How handsome he was with his golden skin and regal bearing. How deeply she loved him.

She felt a nudge at her side. Nizhoni wriggled onto her lap, to settle there like a contented kitten. Heart overflowing, Miranda wrapped her arms around the little girl and held her close.

Ahkeah's black eyes flickered toward them as General Sherman took his seat next to Theodore Dodd. Then, at once, everyone's attention turned to the slight, graying man who had stepped forward from his place among the Navajo headmen.

Barboncito had been ceremonially blessed to prepare his mind and spirit for this day. His lips moved in swift, silent prayer before he turned toward Sherman and began to speak.

Ahkeah stood off to one side, translating in a low voice for Sherman, Dodd and the other whites who were there. Miranda could barely hear him, but she knew he would match the headman's words and meanings as closely as possible, with no added embellishments of his own. This was Barboncito's time, and Ahkeah would have no wish to draw attention to himself. Yet she found she could not take her eyes off him. She leaned forward, straining to catch every word he spoke.

Barboncito's simple speech, as translated by Ahkeah, painted an eloquent picture of misery and hopelessness that would move even the callused heart of a man like General Sherman. "...When we first came here, there were mesquite roots to burn for firewood. Now there aren't any for twenty-five miles around. During the winter many die from cold and sickness, and from working too hard carrying firewood such a long way on their backs.... If we are taken back to our land, we will call you our father and mother. If you would only tie a goat there, we would all live off it. We all feel the same. I am speaking for all Navajos and for their children who aren't born yet. All that you hear me say is the truth. I hope you will do all you can to help us. I am speaking to you, General Sherman, as if you were a holy spirit. This hope goes in at my feet and out of my mouth. I wish you would tell me when you are going to return us to our own country."

Barboncito exhaled as he finished speaking, drained of energy and emotion—the same emotion that echoed in Ahkeah's voice as he translated. Silence hung over the assembled Navajos as Sherman hesitated, then rose to his feet.

For a long moment he gazed across the crowd—a spare, restless man with sharp features, a grizzled beard and thinning brownish hair that fluttered in the desert wind; a hero to some, a monster to others. No one could predict what he would say or do.

Clearing his throat, he turned to Barboncito and unfolded the map he had taken out of his coat. "This is your homeland," he said. "If you returned, you would have less land to settle on than before. The boundaries would be here, where these lines are drawn. Do you understand?"

Ahkeah translated swiftly, and Barboncito nodded in understanding, his features alight with restrained joy. No one in the field of watchers spoke. Hardly anyone breathed. Miranda's eyes were riveted on Ahkeah's face, seeing the hope that flickered behind his stoic expression.

"Please..." Her lips moved in silent prayer. "Please..."

Abruptly, Sherman refolded the map and thrust it back into his coat. "I don't think it's a good idea," he growled. "If you go back, all your old enemies will be waiting. Soon you'll be fighting them again, just as you were before. Why would you want to take such a risk, when there's more than enough land in Oklahoma—decent soil, plenty of wood and water? Your people would do fine there. What's it going to take to make you listen to reason?"

Ahkeah translated in a flat voice, his features rigid. Miranda's hand crept to her throat as Barboncito's face went pale and the other headmen stared at Sherman in dismay. She could sense the struggle raging behind Ahkeah's mask of impassivity, and for a moment she thought he would break protocol and speak for himself. Then Barboncito, recovering a little from his shock, stepped forward and addressed the general again.

"I hope to God you will not ask me to go anywhere except to my own country," he said, with Ahkeah's English echoing his passion. "If we go back, we will follow whatever orders you give us. We will not go right or left, but straight back to our own land!"

Again, no one breathed. Sherman rubbed his whiskered jaw, pondering long and hard. At last he glanced from Ahkeah to Barboncito. "I still think you're being foolish," he said, thrusting his hands into his pockets. "But if that's where you want to go...we'll draw up the treaty in the next few days. Once you've signed the agreement to stay inside your boundaries, with no more fighting or raiding, you'll be free to start back."

For an instant Miranda could scarcely believe her ears. Then she saw the tears glimmering on Ahkeah's cheeks as he translated, and she knew it was true.

They—the Diné, all of them—were going home.

Epilogue

June 18, 1868

"Wake up. It's time." Ahkeah's voice was a quiet whisper in Miranda's ear. She opened her eyes and pulled him down to her for a morning embrace. Not that either of them had gotten much sleep the night before. No one could have slept at a time like this.

Hurriedly Miranda dressed and twisted up her hair. The dugout was dark, Nizhoni still curled in her blankets. The little girl had slept alone since old Hedipa's death eleven days earlier. Ahkeah's aunt had lived to hear the news about Sherman's decision, but now only her spirit would return to Dinétah. Perhaps it was already there, soaring above the rocky towers and deep, shadowed canyons she had loved so much.

Ahkeah had flung aside the skin that covered the entrance to the dugout. Silvery fingers of dawn crept into the darkness, touching the carefully bundled belongings—food, blankets, clothing and the few small treasures that were too precious to leave behind.

While Ahkeah readied the horse, Miranda bent to wake Nizhoni. They would eat on the trail, a simple breakfast of corn cakes and mutton that Naahooyéí had prepared for them the night before.

Still drowsy, Nizhoni snuggled deeper into her nest of blankets. Miranda scooped her up and gathered her close. "It's time to leave," she said in English. "You don't want to stay here while the rest of us go away to Dinétah, do you?"

Nizhoni had caught only the word *Dinétah,* but that was enough. Her black eyes shot open. She scrambled to dress as Miranda rolled up her bedding. This would be a morning like no other, the first of many they would spend on the long road home.

Miranda had married Ahkeah a week ago in a simplified Navajo ceremony. Ahkeah's people had already accepted her as one of them, but Miranda had no illusions that she would ever be fully Diné. Their life together, she knew, would be a long series of compromises, of spirited debates, of differences that could only be overcome by their unconditional love for one another.

But then, wasn't that true of most marriages?

Nizhoni was ready now, her little flower face shining with excitement in the early morning light. Miranda gathered up the last of their belongings, stuffing them into the bundle she would carry on her back. Then she took the small hand in hers, and the two of them came up into the morning, where Ahkeah was waiting with the horse, its pack saddle already loaded.

Are you ready? his eyes asked her.

She took his hand and held it tightly for the space of a breath, loving him more than life.

Around them the camp was stirring. Some people were already moving out, funneling toward the trail that led to the main road out of Bosque Redondo. A few had horses. Some even had small flocks of sheep. They would be marching together, all the Diné, as one body.

Something moved against Miranda's leg. She looked down and saw Nizhoni gazing up at her father, fearful, perhaps, that in the confusion she might be left behind. Ahkeah laughed openly, freely, as she had never heard him laugh before. Bending, he picked up his little daughter and swung her high, onto his shoulders.

For an instant his eyes met Miranda's. She saw the love there, the trust, the wonder that they were making this journey together as a family.

Blinking away tears, she caught the horse's halter rope and moved forward beside her husband and daughter, in the direction of the road. Behind them the sun rose, streaking the eastern sky with the glorious colors of a new day.

* * * * *

Historical Note

For the eight thousand Navajos who left Fort Sumner, the long walk home to Dinétah took more than a month. When they saw the first of their four sacred mountains, some cried, others sang for joy.

Even in their native land, life was not easy for the Diné. Their fields were ruined, their stock largely gone. An entire year passed before the government delivered the sheep and goats the treaty had promised. Rather than butcher the livestock that was so vital to their future, many Navajos continued to live on government rations or forage off the land.

Little by little, they began to prosper. But even then they were beset with conflicts on all sides. Most insidious, perhaps, was the assault on their language and customs. In an effort to wipe out their culture, the government forced thousands of children to leave their homes and attend distant boarding schools. New political and economic systems were forced on their leaders.

Through all this, the Diné fought to preserve their

language and beliefs. Today there are over two hundred thousand Navajos living on a reservation the size of West Virginia. Although they continue to struggle with modern social and economic problems, they remain a powerful and resilient nation, fierce in their independence and rich in their traditional way of life.

The above information and the earlier excerpts from Barboncito's speech were adapted from the book, *DINÉTAH, an Early History of the Navajo People,* by Lawrence D. Sundberg, Sunstone Press, Santa Fe, New Mexico, 1995.

Pick up these Harlequin Historicals and partake in a thrilling and emotional love story set in the Wild, Wild West!

On sale May 2002

NAVAJO SUNRISE
by Elizabeth Lane
(New Mexico, 1868)
Will forbidden love bloom between an officer's daughter and a proud warrior?

CHASE WHEELER'S WOMAN
by Charlene Sands
(Texas, 1881)
An independent young lady becomes smitten with her handsome Native American chaperone!

On sale June 2002

THE COURTSHIP
by Lynna Banning
(Oregon, post–Civil War)
Can a lonely spinster pave a new life with the dashing town banker?

THE PERFECT WIFE
by Mary Burton
(Montana, 1876)
A rugged rancher gets more than he bargained for when he weds an innocent Southern belle!

 Harlequin Historicals®

You are cordially invited to join the festivities as national bestselling authors

Cathy Maxwell

Ruth Langan
Carolyn Davidson

bring you

Wild West **Brides**

You won't want to miss this captivating collection with three feisty heroines who conquer the West and the heart-stoppingly handsome men who love them.

Available June 2002!

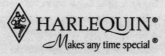

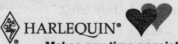

My Lady's Pleasure

The intoxicating new Regency from

JULIA JUSTISS

bestselling author of
My Lady's Trust

New to the passion galloping in her veins, Lady Valeria Arnold was shocked by the wanton impulses that drew her to Teagan Fitzwilliams. The dashing rake was nothing more than a wastrel with the devil's own luck at cards—surely not the kind of man that a woman could trust her heart to. Or was all that about to change...?

"Justiss is a promising new talent..."
—*Publishers Weekly*

MY LADY'S PLEASURE
Available in bookstores June 2002

Harlequin Historicals®
Historical Romantic Adventure!

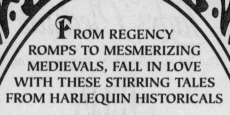